Darkness Below

BARBARA COTTRELL

ISBNs:
979-8-9865938-0-7   Darkness Below   Trade Paperback
979-8-9865938-1-4   Darkness Below   E-book

DEDICATION

To Lance, for giving me the courage to jump.
And to Dr. Peter Weber, for giving
the Scarecrow a new brain.

You dig these tunnels, you *intrude* upon the earth, and you
create all these points of potential failure. You introduce weakness. And with weakness, things break.
—Chuck Wendig, *The Book of Accidents*

Now I know what a ghost is. Unfinished business, that's what.
—Salman Rushdie, *The Satanic Verses*

Chapter One

Stephanie Lansdale stood on the ledge of the clock tower. It was over. The creature raged inside her, gnawing at her brain. Shredding what was left of her sanity. The chomping sound was so loud she could no longer think.

She looked down at Miskatonic University. The campus glowed in the darkness. Ribbons of light crisscrossed the commons. Even the grim brick buildings seemed less threatening from above. Everything looked calm. No one knew what was coming. No one sensed the nightmare that lurked just beneath their feet.

She wanted to warn them but . . .

A blast of heat tore through her body. Stephanie howled into the warm summer night. She saw them all the time now. Men trapped deep in the earth, reaching out to her for release. Torturing her with their need.

The wind picked up. It whipped around her body, pushing her closer to the edge. She raised her eyes to the cold, distant moon.

"No more," she whispered. "Please. No more."

With those words, Stephanie Lansdale took her last step.

Deep. Down. Dark.
????-??-1945

Am I dead? It's hard to tell. Beyond this tiny puddle of light, the world no longer exists. Everything is silent, except for the groan of the earth shifting above me. And the scurrying of rats.

Rats?

I'm doing it again.
I told myself I wouldn't lie anymore.

This is supposed to be a confession.

No more lies!

The sounds I hear are the men, the ones who survived the cave-in.

They're trapped.

So am I.

You see, the thing that fills this space with so much light . . .

Light can be dark. Unclean.

I know that now.

It's too late, but I know that now.

Chapter Two

"Is it true this place was once an insane asylum?"

Still is, Ellen Logan thought as she followed a group of new students onto campus. Even though she was running late, she joined them. She loved hiking up the steep hill that led to Miskatonic University, of reliving the moment she first laid eyes on the campus. A shiver shot through her as she slipped into its shadow. The school was a relic, a medieval fortress that loomed defiantly over the modern world.

She looked back at Arkham. The city spread like a carpet beneath her feet. The Miskatonic River wound through it, splitting it in two. Ellen peered at the sparkling water.

Old Arkham, New Arkham.

Us and them.

"This place wasn't just any insane asylum," the guide insisted. "It was Arkham Asylum, run by Dr. Nathaniel West."

"Arkham Asylum? *The* Arkham Asylum?" one of the students blurted.

"The one in the Batman video games?" another person asked.

The guide pretended not to hear.

"There were always rumors about the place," he continued, "about what kind of psychiatry Dr. West practiced. Most of the patients at Arkham Asylum were wards of the state. Poor. Abandoned. No one cared about them. He felt free to put them to, um, good use."

He paused to point at a building. "See that tower? That's where Dr. West performed his medical research. He did horrible things. Performed all kinds of experiments. Without anesthesia. At the time the place was so remote that he could carry out his work undisturbed. If patients died under his care, the staff disposed of them. Tossed them out like they were garbage."

The man's nose crinkled in disgust. "A disgruntled worker finally tipped off the authorities. When the police stormed the asylum, West was in the middle of drilling a hole in a patient's skull. They arrested him, but before he was prosecuted, a mob stormed the jail. His body? Never found."

The guide led them deeper into the campus. "The place was abandoned for almost a decade. In 1850 a mysterious benefactor bought the land and founded Miskatonic University. The school opened its doors five years later. It's been here ever since."

One of the students turned away from the group. "Hey, what's going on over there?"

Ellen followed his gaze. The clocktower was roped off with police tape. People in dark windbreakers scoured the perimeter.

"Oh, that? It's probably some fraternity prank," the guide said, dismissing the activity with the wave of a hand. "We get a lot of them this time of year."

The bald-faced lie shocked Ellen. No campus prank, no matter how outrageous, was severe enough to warrant so much attention.

The guide steered the freshmen away from the clock tower. "Our next stop is the student health center. Trust me, you'll want to know where it is."

Ellen stared at what was obviously a crime scene. She wasn't the only one. Everywhere she looked students milled around in pods. No one stepped forward to find out what was going on. That was one of the strange things about Miskatonic. The school was dedicated to investigating the supernatural, to protecting people from the dark places of the world. But when the time came to put those ideas into action, very few students rose to the challenge. Most people hung back and let others take risks. In that way Miskatonic was like the normal world.

She headed toward the yellow tape. A young police officer stepped forward to intercept her. "Hey, Miss! You can't—"

A flash of movement caught Ellen's eye. A ghostly figure swayed on the clock tower. At first she thought the woman was drunk. Or suicidal. Then she saw the smoke rising off her body. Light blazed inside her, so deep and intense that . . .

Ellen gasped as the woman jumped off the edge. She closed her eyes, but it was too late. The woman's descent burned across her eyelids.

"Miss," the police officer called out. When she didn't respond, he grabbed her arm. "Miss, are you okay?"

Ellen opened her eyes, trying not to look at the blood on the concrete. "Yeah," she lied.

The policeman squinted at her. "You're psychic, aren't you?"

"Yeah," she said again, in a quieter voice.

Ellen waited for the sneer, the inevitable blast of skepticism. When she first arrived at Miskatonic she thought people would be more accepting of her abilities. They weren't. If anything, people at Miskatonic were more resistant. Claims of extrasensory power got in the way of establishing the university as a legitimate center of research.

The officer moved closer. "She was a junior," he told her. "You'd expect this sort of thing from a freshman, but a junior? She was more than halfway there. They're usually okay once they've passed the halfway point."

A technician in a Forensics windbreaker looked up from his work. "Officer, your assignment is to stand guard, not flap your gums!" he called out.

Ellen and the campus cop exchanged a knowing look. Even at the best of times the relationship between the university police and the Arkham police was tense. The two forces constantly battled over jurisdiction.

"Nothing but storm troopers," the officer muttered as the technician returned to his work.

"Don't let them get to you," Ellen consoled him as she glanced at his nametag. "Thank you for your time, Officer Collins."

Collins's face split into a wide smile. "Any time, miss."

Ellen wanted to stay. Officer Collins was friendly. Friendly *and* cute. But she couldn't linger any longer.

Today she had a date with a legend.

Everyone had to take "Weird Art Through the Ages." It was required for graduation. The only choice students had was who their professor was. Most chose to get the course out of the way during their freshman and sophomore years, with whatever teacher was available. Ellen held out until her junior year when Andrew Carter taught the class.

Andrew Carter was a local legend: the grandson of Randolph Carter, the occult explorer celebrated in the "fiction" of H. P. Lovecraft. He was one of the few links to the glory days of Miskatonic University. How much Andrew took after his grandfather (and how much Lovecraft made up) was the subject of endless debate. Some claimed he inherited Randolph Carter's ability to travel across space and time. Other people fervently believed that Andrew Carter *was* Randolph Carter. That the old man had discovered a technique to jump from one body to another.

By the time Ellen arrived at the auditorium all the seats were taken. Students spilled into the aisles. As she searched for an open patch of floor, she wondered whether she made the right choice. *Could Andrew Carter really be that good? Could anyone live up to such high expectations?*

Her foot snagged on one of the students camped on the stairs. "Watch it, Riding Hood!" a man snarled.

Ellen's cheeks flared as laughter erupted around her. She ignored the outburst and kept moving. She was used to the sarcastic remarks. Ellen didn't look like the typical Miskatonic student. She had no tattoos, no body piercings, no unnatural hair color. With her long blond hair, fair skin, and unmarked body, she looked like a victim, someone to sacrifice on an altar. Not the person who performed the dark ritual.

The only hint she belonged were her eyes. They were gray green, the color of a stormy sea, and had an intense, otherworldly glow. When Ellen was in grade school, the kids attacked her because they thought she was a witch. Now, at Miskatonic, she felt out of place because she looked too normal. On any other day she would have laughed at the irony, but she was too tired to see much humor in it. A terrible dream kept her up the night before—of men trapped deep underground, their bodies wedged in the earth. Their grubby hands reached for her, tugging her hair, grabbing onto anything to free them from their tomb.

An excited buzz rose from the front of the class.

A man crossed the stage in long, confident strides. When he reached the podium, his image appeared on the giant screen above him.

Ellen had seen pictures of Andrew Carter. The photos didn't do him justice. Tall and handsome, with short dark hair and chilling blue eyes, he looked like a vampire from a paranormal romance novel. He was in his midthirties, an age when the demands of Miskatonic usually began to take their toll. Andrew Carter was the exception. He bore only the slightest signs of age—wrinkles at the corners of his eyes, a whisper of gray at the temples. These small flaws failed to detract from his looks. If anything, they gave his chiseled face an added dignity.

"While I appreciate your interest in art, I regret to inform you the class is full," he informed the crowd in a rich baritone voice.

The girl sitting next to Ellen sighed.

"Students officially enrolled in the class were mailed tickets over the summer. May I see them please?"

The room burst into a flurry of activity as people rummaged for their slips of paper. Ellen flashed her ticket to the woman beside her. The woman glared and yielded her spot. Most of the exchanges were peaceful, but there were isolated scuffles in the back. Some people even tried to rip the tickets away from their rightful owners.

Carter stood at the podium, surveying the scene. His lips curled with pleasure as he watched people fight to stay in his class. *Bastard*, Ellen thought, *he's enjoying this*.

His eyes darted to Ellen, almost as if he sensed the thought. An electric sensation shot through her—a potent mix of attraction and fear. Ellen wondered if he was psychic, too. She dropped her gaze and distracted herself with poetry. "One, two! One, two! And through and through, the vorpal blade went snicker-snack!" she whispered.

"For those of you who don't already know, I'm Andrew Carter," he announced once the class settled. "And I am here to take you on a journey."

The lights dimmed, and a slide appeared on the big screen. Carter quickly flipped through a series of portraits.

"DaVinci, Michelangelo, Rembrandt, Van Gogh. Masters of art. They devoted their lives to exploring the human condition. To capturing the glory of nature. They're not important. We're not interested in them." His eyes swept the room. "We are interested in *him*."

Another portrait filled the screen. A murmur rose as students struggled to identify the strange, apple-faced man. Ellen smiled.

"Hieronymus Bosch was, by the standards of his time, a strange man. By the standards of any time he was strange. Very strange."

He cycled through some of Bosch's major works: *Garden of Earthly Delights, Temptation of St. Anthony, Bird-Headed Monster*. A strange parade of images marched by. Pigs dressed as nuns. Men with no torsos and insect legs. People condemned to endless varieties of damnation.

"Hieronymus Bosch was a man who lived more than five hundred years ago. Whose surreal work is as modern and shocking as Salvador Dali's. We know almost nothing about him. He left behind no letters or diaries. He appears only as a glimpse in municipal records. And yet he gave us this."

Carter hit a button, exposing one of Ellen's favorite works, *Noah's Ark on Mount Ararat*. In the painting, the floodwaters had receded and Noah's creatures had been unloaded. All around him were the drowned corpses of the damned.

A sudden chill swept through her. Ellen knew the murky figures in the painting were lost souls. But if she looked at the painting at just the right angle, one of the underwater figures strongly resembled the dread god Cthulhu—one of H. P. Lovecraft's most famous "creations." A godlike monster ready to rise out of the ocean and destroy humanity.

Ellen shifted in her chair.

"H. P. Lovecraft was not the first person to know about the terrible creatures that lurk on the edge of our world. Hieronymus

Bosch knew. Henry Fuseli knew. Richard Pickman knew. They kept these secrets hidden, locked in a world of fantasy. To do otherwise would put the artists at risk. Of ridicule. Persecution. Even death. My job, over the next ten weeks, is to teach you how to unravel the hidden messages in art, to teach you the ways we communicate. So, let's begin at the beginning, shall we? Four thousand years ago. In Australia."

The nightmare world of Bosch dissolved into a rock wall dotted with ghostly faces. Carter devoted the rest of his lecture to the Wandjina, the Aboriginal cloud and rain spirits who were so powerful they did not require speech. He took the class through time and place, comparing the Wandjina with other elemental creatures.

Andrew Carter lived up to his reputation. He made the connections seem effortless, the hidden language easy to spot. As he lectured Ellen felt like he was talking just to her. His eyes reached out to her, touching her in the darkness.

The moment the lights went up people mobbed the stage, competing for Andrew Carter's attention. It was only then that she realized she wasn't the only one who felt singled out. Special.

The whole thing was an illusion. Andrew Carter was just an incredibly charismatic person. *Charismatic and cold. Now there's a lethal combination.* She snorted and headed for the door.

Ellen paused long enough to soak in the warm summer day. Then she was off to work.

Chapter Three

Mote It Be was one of the many New Age bookstores that clung to Miskatonic like barnacles to a ship. The university didn't endorse these stores, but they didn't discourage them either. The shops provided a smokescreen, a way for the public to indulge their curiosity of Miskatonic without bothering the university.

Ellen worked part time at Mote It Be. She kept it stocked with incense, crystals, and books. She was also the store's resident psychic. She didn't mind the job, except for the dress code. The owner insisted she wear long, sweeping dresses, a mixture of velvet and lace that screamed fairy-tale princess. Or earth goddess. She supposed that was the connection Norm wanted people to make.

Ellen hated it. The getup made her feel ridiculous.

"Excuse me." A small hand tugged on her dress. She turned and saw a young girl with a backpack. Her face was solemn. Intent. A man in a suit and tie hovered behind her.

"What can I do for you?" Ellen asked.

The girl pointed at the owner. "That man said you could help me."

Ellen looked at Norm. He didn't normally let her work with children, but he gave her a nod of approval.

"I'd certainly like to try."

"I've, I've been having these . . ."

"Don't say anything else," advised the man behind her.

"But. But I—" the girl spluttered. She looked at her companion in a way that made Ellen's heart ache. Ellen was twenty years old, but she was close enough to remember the powerlessness of childhood.

"Your . . ." Ellen glanced at the man.

"Uncle," he offered.

"Your uncle is right. It's better if I know nothing about you. Except your name. I'm Ellen."

She extended her hand. The little girl hesitated. Then she carefully shook Ellen's hand.

"I'm Lindsey."

"Nice to meet you, Lindsey."

Ellen didn't bother to ask the uncle his name. Hostility rose off him like heat from a freshly tarred road.

She stood and waved the girl to a back room. "Why don't we go somewhere where we can talk?"

The uncle pulled Ellen aside as soon as Lindsey was out of earshot. "Look. I don't believe in all this. And I don't want to be here."

"I can tell," Ellen quipped.

"But she thinks you can help her, and if it makes her feel better . . ." He fixed her with a hard look. "I don't want you to sell her anything. Understand?"

Ellen bristled at the accusation, but she held back her anger. *You're working at a New Age store full of potions and spells,* she reminded herself. *Can you blame him for being suspicious?* "I just want to help her," she insisted.

The last thing she wanted was to take them to the "consulting" room, but it was the only private place in the store. Behind a thickly beaded curtain and packed with the usual occult clichés—Ouija boards, crystal balls, candles, and maps of energy centers in the body—the consultation area was everything the man feared. As she led them inside, she felt his suspicion rise even more.

The tarot cards on the table only made things worse. They were from an adult deck. Ellen swept them aside before Lindsey noticed them.

"Don't you need all of that?" the girl asked.

"Some people need them. I don't," she replied. She arranged the chairs in a semicircle and motioned them to sit. "So, Lindsey, how much do you know about what I do?"

"Mary says you get pictures in your head. Pictures that people send you. She told me you can talk to the living and the dead."

Ellen glanced at the uncle. "Mary?"

"Her older sister," he offered in a voice that made it clear that Mary was in trouble.

"Is it true? That you speak to the dead?" the girl demanded.

"Sometimes."

"Aren't you afraid of them?"

"They're just people. Maybe a little sadder, but they're still just people," she reassured the girl.

Lindsey bit her lip, clutching her backpack like a shield.

Ellen leaned forward. "What is it? Why are you here?"

"I think I'm having someone else's dream. A dead person's dream."

"Lindsey," the uncle warned her.

Ellen ignored him. "What makes you think you're having a dead person's dream?"

"I don't know. It's just kind of . . . they're not me. The things I see. And they're faded. The color's gone."

"Do you usually dream in color?"

"Uh-huh."

Ellen held out her hands. The girl looked at them anxiously.

"This is the way I see, Lindsey."

"Is it going to hurt?"

"No, but my hands might be cold."

Lindsey latched on to Ellen's hands.

The world plunged into darkness. Lindsey's hands were still there, but they jutted out of a dirt wall. Ellen looked around, at a deep, dark, damp world.

Underground, she thought as her eyes adjusted to the gloom. *I'm underground.*

Somewhere in the distance a light flickered, its glow strong enough to illuminate the walls.

Men. Everywhere she looked she saw men. Ellen's eyes swept the walls, over the bodies trapped in the earth. Most of them were dead, but some, some . . . Some of them reached for her, their fingers rasping against the fabric of her shirt.

Ellen jerked as a wave of shock shot through her.

Nightmare. This is the nightmare I had last night.

The earth lurched under her feet. She heard a sharp crack, followed by the roar of thunder.

"Earthquake," someone yelled.

Ellen blinked. The world was suddenly, painfully bright.

She was back at Mote It Be, holding hands with a frightened girl.

"What?"

"Earthquake," Lindsey's uncle repeated.

It took a moment for Ellen to feel the shaking, to realize the real world had bled into her vision.

"Under the table," she ordered them.

"Did we do this?" the girl gasped as they huddled together.

"No, honey," Ellen reassured her.

After a few seconds the tremor passed. As soon as the potions stopped jingling on the shelf, Lindsey's uncle pulled the girl toward the door.

"Come on," he barked. "We're leaving. Now."

"No!" The girl broke free and grabbed Ellen's hand. "What did you see? Tell me what you saw!"

The owner of Mote It Be stuck his head in the door. "We need to go outside. There may be aftershocks."

Lindsey refused to let Ellen go. She clutched her with damp hands as they headed outside.

The town square was already full of people. Some were confused, others frightened, another group was glad for an excuse, any excuse, to get out of work.

Ellen guided the girl to a bench outside the store. The uncle plopped down between them. The girl bowed her head, as if the decision was already made.

"You're not going to tell me the truth, are you?" she whispered.

Ellen leaned over to talk to the girl. "You're having dreams about men trapped underground," she replied. "They're stuck in the walls, trying to get out."

Her uncle stiffened. "How do you know that? How could you possibly know that?" he demanded.

"I think you're right, Lindsey. I think you're having a dead person's dream."

"How do you know?" the girl whispered.

Because we're having the same dream, she thought. *Someone's trying to communicate with us.*

"I'm scared," Lindsey whispered.

"Okay. That's enough," the uncle protested.

"Listen to me, Lindsey. Strange things happen in dreams. People drift in and out. Some are alive. Some dead. But you're in control. You're always in control. If you don't like what's happening, you can change it."

"What do you mean?"

"What's the most ridiculous thing you can think of?"

The girl scowled, thinking hard. "A hippo on roller skates."

Ellen smiled. She liked the image. *Maybe I'll use it*, she thought.

"Okay, a hippo on roller skates. When you're in the middle of the nightmare and something is chasing you, when you're running and you feel like your heart is about to burst, I want you to stop. I want you to stop and turn around. And what are you going to see?"

The girl giggled, the sound popping out of her like a soap bubble. "A hippo on roller skates."

"Not just a hippo on roller skates. A hippo waving its hooves, rearing its head, and trying hard not to fall on its big, fat hippo butt."

The girl's giggle blossomed into full-blown laughter. Several people nearby turned and smiled.

"That's it?" Lindsey asked once her laughter faded.

"That's it."

"I don't need any potions or spells or anything?"

"You already have the most important weapon you need." Ellen tapped the girl on the forehead. Then she offered her hand. "It was nice to meet you, Lindsey."

The girl threw her arms around Ellen. The gesture took her by surprise. Ellen tried to avoid physical contact whenever she could. Physical contact told her things about people she didn't want to know. But Lindsey was pure, full of goodness. The girl's energy seeped into Ellen like spring water.

"Thank you," Lindsey's words were warm against Ellen's dress.

"I'm glad I could help."

The uncle shattered the quiet scene. "How much do I owe you?"

Ellen scowled at him for breaking the mood. "Nothing," she insisted as she pulled away. "It's nice to get questions other than 'Is my girlfriend cheating on me?' or 'Does he love me?'"

Lindsey's uncle stared at her like she was an alien. Most people assumed that psychics exploited their powers, draining the gullible every chance they got. That they would offer their services for free? *Like a hippo on roller skates.* Ellen walked away before the man could say anything else.

"You know, the idea of a store is that people buy things, Logan," her boss grumbled when she joined him. He stood in front of Mote It Be, arms crossed, as if he expected looters to show up at any moment.

"Yeah, I know. You should probably fire me." She fell silent, watching some of the shopkeepers close their doors. "I lied to her, Norm. I told her that everything was okay. That she could change things if she wanted."

"Change what?" Norm asked.

Ellen didn't hear him. She looked at the people huddled in anxious groups. "Something strange is going on," she whispered.

"Something strange is always going around here," Norm insisted. "Look, Logan, your shift's almost over. Why don't you leave early? I'll probably close for the day. I don't think we'll be getting any more business."

"You don't have any potions or spells to prevent earthquakes?"

Norm shot her a sour look. "They're too expensive," he replied. "Now go on. Get out of here before I make you go inside and take inventory."

Deep. Down. Dark.
????-??-1945

Everyone thought it was my father. That he was the magician. My mother was the one who had the power. Of course the word magician never crossed her lips. But it was hard to ignore the people who called on her. Asking advice. Leaving offerings in exchange for the mysterious parcels my mother handed them. I grew up in the shadow of spectral things. Lying awake at night, I saw what responded to her whispered invocations.

She yearned for a daughter to teach the craft. She had to settle on me, her only son. My father was a religious man. Devout member of the synagogue. Faithful student of the Torah. Their marriage had been arranged. When he found out what she was, shortly after I was born, he broke off all contact with her. Walled her up in her own personal ghetto. Along with me, the tainted fruit of her womb.

I hated him for that. He was no better than the Nazis.

In her desperation she turned to me.

She told me everything. Shared all her secrets.

I gobbled it up. I needed to feel like I had some control.

You see, 1937 was a very dark year in Europe.

My mother seethed. She hungered. She yearned for a way to stop what was happening.

One day, when I returned from school, she was waiting for me.

"I've found it," she told me. "The answer."

"An extremely rare earthquake. Four on the Richter scale, centered in . . ."

Ellen yanked out her earbuds. The radio station kept repeating the same information. The damage to Miskatonic University appeared to be minimal. Fallen bookshelves in the library, some broken glass in the labs. Officials closed the school to inspect some of the older buildings. They found nothing serious. A few hours later staff and students were allowed to return.

Ellen smiled. That's what she liked about Miskatonic. *People just keep going*, she thought. *An earthquake? No damage? Get back to class!*

Still, she felt uneasy. Her session with Lindsey, the earthquake—it wasn't a coincidence. Ellen was sure of that. She kept going over the nightmare they shared. Tracing its contours. Comparing it to hers.

A sharp pain hit her between her shoulder blades. It was followed by another. And another.

It took Ellen a moment to realize someone was throwing things at her. She spun in the direction of the blow. "Son of a—"

A few feet away, Joey Richards lurked behind a tree. He was a casual acquaintance, the boyfriend of her old classmate Stephanie Lansdale. He frantically waved her over.

Ellen marched up to him and knocked the rocks out of his hand. "What the hell are you doing?"

Joey embraced her, holding her so tightly she struggled to breathe. "I'm so glad to see you, Ellen. So glad, so glad."

Ellen could feel people staring at them. She didn't care. What bothered her was his smell. Joey reeked. *No, it's worse than that,* she thought. *He smells unclean.*

Ellen pushed him away. "Jesus, Joey, what have you been rolling in?"

He tried to focus on her, but his eyes kept darting back and forth. "Stephanie. It got to Stephanie. She's dead."

"*W-what?* What are you talking about?" Ellen spluttered.

His eyes settled on a spot just above her shoulder. Ellen didn't want to turn around. She knew where he was looking.

The clock tower. The blazing woman.

"Oh no. Oh no, no."

"I don't have much time. They're coming. Take this," he pressed a cold piece of metal into her hand. "It's a key to one of the lockers at the bookstore. If something happens to me, everything you need to know is in my backpack. Do you understand?"

"Stephanie? Oh my God, Stephanie," Ellen gasped.

"*Do you understand?*"

She jumped at his raised voice. "Yes."

He gave her a long, lingering look. "I know you thought I was wrong for Stephanie, but you were always very kind to me. I want to thank you for that."

"Joey, wait a sec. I—" She tried to grab him, but he wriggled out of her grip and ran across the courtyard. Even though it was full of students, they parted for him.

"Are you all right?" a man asked.

"I'm fine. He—" The words caught in her throat as she faced the good Samaritan.

Andrew Carter stood in front of her.

He wasn't alone. A group of students flanked him. One of them, an elegant Goth, sneered at Ellen's long velvet dress. "Gee, I wonder where you work," she snorted.

The group tittered. Carter silenced them with a sharp look.

"Are you all right?" he asked again.

Up close Andrew Carter was much taller than she expected. Tall and imposing. Ellen struggled to maintain her composure.

"I'm fine. He made a mistake. He thought I was someone else."

Carter stared at the hand that clutched Joey's key. A thin bead of sweat trickled down Ellen's back. She wondered how much he had seen. How much they'd all seen.

"Bumping into a crazy man in the middle of Miskatonic. That's not so unusual, is it?" she joked in an attempt to distract him.

She didn't need to. His attention was already drifting. He and his entourage walked away.

Ellen waited until they were out of sight before she slipped the key in her pocket.

Chapter Four

Ellen didn't want to believe Stephanie Lansdale was dead. She convinced herself Joey was being his usual self, pulling one of Delta Delta Tau's stupid fraternity pranks. But that evening, as she cleaned up after dinner, her friend's face appeared on the news.

"Tragedy at Miskatonic" splashed across the screen. A local reporter recounted the details of her friend's suicide. A jumble of quick images followed: a picture of Stephanie from her freshman year, the roped-off clock tower, a university spokesman insisting that her death, though tragic, was "an isolated event." Then her friend was gone. Lost in a sea of ordinary horror.

Ellen stood frozen in place, a dishtowel dangling from her hand. As if staying still would keep the news from being real. She hadn't seen Stephanie Lansdale in a very long time. They had been close as freshmen, but during their sophomore year Stephanie was accepted into the elite program that gave her access to the secret knowledge of Miskatonic University. Ellen was left behind. They tried to maintain their friendship, but as Stephanie moved deeper and deeper into her new world, she became distant. Their interaction trickled to a thin stream.

Now Stephanie was dead. Another Miskatonic casualty.

"I was just watching the news, and I could have sworn I saw your friend—" Her uncle Joshua startled her out of her shock. Ellen watched him roll his wheelchair into the room.

Joshua Logan adopted her when she was ten years old, rescuing her from an endless string of foster homes. He was her only family. At least the only family she knew.

"Stephanie jumped from the clock tower last night. She's dead," Ellen offered in a wobbly voice.

Her uncle winced. "Oh, Elle, I'm so sorry. Are you okay?"

"I think so," she replied, even though she knew the news hadn't sunk in yet. "I'm just . . . in shock. I thought Steph was okay. I mean, as well as can be expected in this place."

"Sometimes things catch up with people."

She considered telling her uncle about her strange encounter with Joey Richards but decided against it.

"How was your first day of school?" her uncle asked after an appropriate pause.

"The usual. Chaotic. Overwhelming," Ellen sighed, eager to change the subject. *Later*, she thought, *I'll deal with this later*. "I think my teacher in forensic anthropology is going to be a nightmare."

"What about Andrew?"

"Andrew?" Ellen echoed, confused.

"Andrew Carter. How was he? Do you think he recognized you?"

"What?"

"Did he recognize your name?" Joshua pressed her.

"You don't take roll in a three-hundred-person class," Ellen snorted, but she remembered the look Carter gave her in class. And the encounter she had with him after the lecture. "Why would he recognize my name? Have we met before?"

"Maybe once. When you were young. Just after I took you in," he replied, lapsing into vagueness, like he always did when he talked about her past. "What do you think of him?"

"I don't know. I've only had one class with him. It's too early to say."

"Try," Joshua urged her.

Ellen struggled to come up with an answer. "He's very passionate about what he does. When he teaches he has a way of connecting with you, of making you feel like you're the only person in the room. And those eyes . . ." She searched for a way to describe their cold fire. "Rasputin had eyes like those."

Her uncle chuckled. "Not bad for someone who doesn't have an opinion." He appraised her with a stare. "Are you attracted to him?"

"To Carter? No, he's too obvious. I don't go for obvious men."

"Good, because he won't take you seriously if he thinks you have a crush on him."

"Why should I care what Carter thinks?"

"Because you might need his help someday."

Ellen shook her head as Joshua returned to his study. The man was as unreadable as the Sphinx. When she announced that she wanted to attend Miskatonic University, he resisted with a fierceness that startled her. At the time she thought it was because he hated the school, but did his objections have something to do with Andrew Carter?

You might need his help someday. Her uncle's words were thick with resignation. As if contact between them was inevitable. Preordained.

Shared nightmares. Earthquakes. A dead friend. Joey. Now this.

It was only the first day of the quarter, and Ellen already had more than her fair share of mysteries.

There was no body at Stephanie Lansdale's memorial. No family to console. Stephanie's parents refused to attend the service. They arrived from their home in West Virginia and stayed only long enough to claim their daughter's body. They lashed out before they left, condemning Miskatonic as an evil place. They threatened to sue.

The local media had a field day with the story. Once again there were calls to regulate the university. Everyone at Miskatonic knew what regulation meant. The region had been a hotbed of persecution during the Salem witch trials. In fact, the witch hunt lasted twenty years longer in Arkham. It was a black cloud that never blew away.

When Ellen arrived at her friend's memorial, she wasn't surprised to see the church packed with university officials. *Damage control*, she thought as she slipped into a pew. The top brass even convinced Andrew Carter to make a personal appearance. He sat in the front row, trying hard not to look bored.

Ellen scanned the crowd for Joey Richards. Stephanie's boyfriend was nowhere to be found. At first she assumed he was late. But when the service ended and there was still no sign of him, Ellen knew something was wrong.

Her hand fluttered to the key hidden beneath her blouse as a man's voice thundered in her head. *There she is. It must be with her. There's no one else left.*

"Go in peace, and may God be with you on the dangerous path you tread." The priest concluded the ceremony with the traditional Miskatonic blessing.

The congregation rose, following the minister down the aisle. For all their expressions of grief and concern, the university officials were anxious to leave. They practically ran for the doors.

"Excuse me, miss?"

Ellen instantly recognized the voice in her head. The middle-aged man that blocked her exit had the potential to be handsome. But there was an irregularity to his face, a suggestion that something was off.

"Are you Ellen Logan?" he asked.

"Yes. And you're Dr. Pierce, right? Dr. Richard Pierce?"

The burly man frowned. "Now how would you know that?"

"I took a cryptozoology class from you last year. I really enjoyed it."

He acknowledged the compliment with a slight bow. "I'm glad you did."

They stood and stared at each other for an awkward moment. Ellen decided to play a wild card. Joey Richards loved to study animals, so it stood to reason . . .

"Wait a minute. Aren't you Joey Richard's advisor?"

Richard Pierce wilted at the mention of Joey. "Yes, I am," he replied.

"I expected him to be here. Do you know where he is?" Ellen asked.

"He went home to his family in Texas. I guess Miss Lansdale's death was too much for him."

Ellen knew Pierce was lying. Anyone even casually acquainted with Joey knew he would never go back to Texas. His father threatened to kill him if he returned.

"I heard you ran into him the day Stephanie died," he continued.

Ellen's heart lurched. She struggled to keep her voice level. "Ran into him was right. He practically knocked me down when I was walking across campus," she admitted, seeing no point in denying an incident so many people witnessed. "At first I didn't recognize him. He was so dirty and out of it I thought he was a homeless guy. He ranted about Stephanie being dead. At first I thought he was joking. It wasn't until I got home that I saw it on the news."

"Did he, um, give you anything?"

"Like what?"

Pierce ignored the question and stepped closer. "Did he tell you about taking something? Maybe hint at where it was?"

She willed her face and mind to stay perfectly still. "No," she replied. "All he said was 'it got to Stephanie, it got to Stephanie.' Like I said, he wasn't very coherent."

His eyes narrowed. "You wouldn't lie to me, would you?"

Ellen shrugged. "I don't even know what you're talking about."

Slowly the sharp edge of his suspicion faded. He handed her a business card. "Okay. Here's how you can reach me, just in case."

"Dr. Pierce?" she called out as he turned to leave. "Do me a favor, would you? If you hear from Joey, send him my sympathies."

"I will. Take care of yourself, Miss Logan."

As soon as Dr. Pierce retreated, she let out a deep breath. Her eyes drifted to the front of the chapel. Another person was watching her. Andrew Carter's eyes darted away when she spotted him, back to the colleagues gathered around him.

Ellen thought about what her uncle told her, how at some point she would need his help. She could feel the time fast approaching.

Deep. Down. Dark.
????-??-1945

My mother sold everything we had for a book.
A worn-out, moth-eaten book.
I tried to read the title, but the words eluded me.

I was mad at her. Not mad. Furious. She had given away our future, our only way out, for something that looked like it belonged in the garbage.

My anger barely registered. She stared at me with glowing eyes and babbled. Told me about the primal creatures she summoned with the book. Creatures that lived deep beneath the earth and pierced the darkness with their light. Angels who could build ladders. Paths to freedom.

Angels? From down below?
I knew of only one angel from the darkness below.
Lucifer.

My mother hissed when I mentioned demons.
"I don't care what it is. I'm still going to use it."
"Use it to what?"
She leaned forward, eyes dancing. "I'm going to break into one of their camps. Show those Nazi bastards what they're up against."

What could I do?
I had to go with her.
I am my mother's son.

The sorcerer's apprentice.

———————— ⌇ ————————

Ellen rushed to the bookstore as soon as she changed out of her funeral clothes. She knew she was taking a risk. Dr. Pierce might be following her. Or having someone else follow her.

She couldn't wait.

Joey's voice drummed in her head. *If something happens to me. If something happens to me . . .* The words pushed her forward, into the crowded bookstore.

Ellen's heart raced as she approached the locker. *Everyone knows what you're doing,* she thought. *Any second someone's going to grab you and take you away.*

A line from a Shirley Jackson story popped into her head. "Nothing is hard to do unless you get upset and excited about it," she whispered to herself.

The locker door swung open on silent hinges. Inside was a worn canvas backpack. As Ellen looped her arms through the straps, she relaxed. No one was paying attention to her. People streamed by, their minds buzzing with everyday concerns—student loans, work schedules, the high price of textbooks. A guy that bumped into her was a premed student who was convinced he had lycanthropy. Two students gathered at a nearby locker were going over plans to rob a grave. Her nervousness was lost in a general tide of anxiety.

Ellen didn't open the bag until after dinner. Once her uncle retreated to his study, she escaped to her room and unpacked the strange parcel. There was only a single item—a large square object wrapped in a layer of protective cloth. She held her breath as she undressed it. It was an old leather-bound book, its title worn, bearing only the faint hint of language.

Ellen turned the book over in her hands. A letter fluttered to the floor.

Hey Ellen,

Remember how we used to joke about these types of letters? The "if you're reading this now I'm in deep shit" letters? I never thought I'd be writing one, especially to you. But things have gotten out of control and Stephanie . . . I'm afraid Steph has lost it.

The frat is into some really bad stuff. Some really, really bad stuff. It started a few months ago. You remember the cabin? The place where you, Steph, and I almost had a three-way? Well, the frat went up there for a little R&R, and we came across . . . it's hard to describe them without sounding stupid. They're fiery creatures. A cross between a squid and a worm. And they're big. Like monster-truck big.

We wanted to leave them alone, but one of the brothers (Butch. It's always fucking Butch.) said he knew a professor who might be able to help us. The professor was interested in our tale. He got a strange book out of the Miskatonic library and spent the summer translating it. He wants to control them. I have no idea why. Probably just a power thing.

Things didn't go well.

When do they ever, huh?

The best laid plans of mice and men.

I stole the book. I don't know if it will make a difference, but maybe you can take it to someone who can help, someone who'll find a way to undo the damage we've done.

I'm sorry to dump all this on you, but you're the only person I can trust. And you're smart. You're so smart. I never told you this before, Ellen, but I like you. I wish we had met under different circumstances. Maybe in another life.

Meet you there, okay? I'll save you a seat.

Joey

Ellen read the letter several times. Her skin crawled.

Reluctantly she opened the book. A burnt smell rose from the brittle pages. Drawings danced on the page. The figures were little more than frantic scribbles, as if the artist couldn't bear to look at the things he depicted.

Her eyes drifted across a language that looked like Latin.

"*Ialpon toltorn nanta. Iabes.*

"*Iabes. Iabes. Iabes.*"

The words swarmed her like angry insects.

Ellen woke up sprawled on the floor. She didn't remember falling. She groaned and turned on her side, looking at the book lying beside her. She had experienced a lot of strange things at Miskatonic, but the encounters were always fleeting. Nothing more than shadows. This was different.

I can't do this alone, she thought. *If I take this on by myself*. . . She knew her next step. It was time to pay a visit to Andrew Carter.

Chapter Five

"**D**o you think he'll notice I'm reading his favorite book?"

"I don't know. Do you think he'll like my Elder Sign tattoo?"

There was a line to see Andrew Carter. Ellen expected that. She brought along a book for what she assumed would be a long wait. What she wasn't prepared for was the chirpy chatter of the girls in front of her. No matter how hard she tried, their conversation pierced her skull. Most of her teenage years were spent moving from place to place. She never had time to develop friendships with people her age.

Ellen always wondered whether the constant motion robbed her of important adolescent experiences. *If this is any indication, I haven't missed a thing*, she thought.

Carter seemed to share her opinion. He ejected the girls from his office in less than five minutes. "Good luck," one of them sniped as she left.

Ellen gathered her things and set the timer on her watch. She was curious to see how long she would last.

Andrew Carter's office wasn't what she expected. She imagined a world of darkness, a place decorated with gruesome artifacts. Instead the walls were emerald green and covered with tasteful art. It was clear this place was meant to be a sanctuary—the muted, indirect light, the miniature stone waterfall perched on the windowsill, the worn leather couch that seemed to invite an afternoon nap. Even the air was relaxing. It smelled of sandalwood.

The atmosphere had no effect on its occupant. Andrew Carter stood at his desk and shoveled papers into a leather bag. An hour remained for student consultations, but it was clear he was done for the day.

"Dr. Carter?"

He shot her a sour look. "God, not another one," he muttered to himself.

Ellen stiffened. "*Excuse me?*"

He gave her a second look. "Wait a minute. Aren't you one of Dr. Pierce's students?"

"One of Dr. Pierce's stu—?" she echoed before she remembered. Carter saw her talking to Pierce at Stephanie's memorial service. "Oh, no. Hell no!"

His eyes returned to his bag. "If this is about the test, they're not graded yet. You'll get them from your teaching assistant next week."

"This isn't about the test. It's about something else."

"I'm late for a meeting."

"I won't take up too much of your time," she promised.

When he said nothing she closed the door behind her. He jumped like a shotgun blast had gone off.

"Open it! Now!" he barked.

"What?"

"The door! Open the door!"

"What? Why?" Ellen blinked before she remembered the troop that paraded through his office. "Oh, the girls. Those silly girls. I'm not one of them."

He rolled his eyes. "Yes, I know. You're *different*." He grabbed her by the elbow and marched her to the door.

"Hey, wait a sec . . . I need your help!" she protested.

"Everybody needs my help. I don't have time for this."

She jerked free from his grip. "Then tell me who does," she demanded.

"What?"

"Tell me who has the time. I need help identifying a book. An old book. Almost certainly stolen from the Miskatonic library."

She saw a flicker of interest in Carter's cold blue eyes. Then a colleague popped out of a nearby office and broke the spell.

"Dr. Blake. Dr. Connie Blake in linguistics should be able to help you. He's at the—"

"There you are," a voice growled.

A man stood at the end of the hall. For a moment Ellen thought her nightmare had come to life, that one of the miners had risen from the earth. The man was covered in mud. A rank smell filled the air, a stench that hinted at something far worse than human neglect. The odor brought people out of their offices. Students and teachers clustered in anxious pods.

"You have something the big guy needs. Hand it over."

Ellen squinted, trying to get a better look at the man. He was a fair distance away and camouflaged in mud, but she knew who it was.

A line from Joey Richard's letter popped in her head. *Butch. It's always fucking Butch.*

Butch pointed a gun at her. Ellen's world collapsed, narrowing to a single, sharp point. No one else was there. The people in the hall. Andrew Carter. It was just her and Butch, facing off like two gunslingers. And she had no gun.

"Butch? What the hell are you doing?"

"Where is it, Ellen?"

Out of the corner of her eye she saw a ripple part the crowd. A deafening alarm split the air. When Butch turned to see what happened, a man tackled him.

The crowd broke like a wave, scattering in all directions. Carter yanked Ellen into his office and slammed the door. He pushed her to the floor, and they scurried under his desk.

Ellen thought she heard a gunshot and a scream, but she couldn't hear much over the blare of the fire alarm. She tried to zero in on someone in the crowd, to see the scene through their eyes. It didn't work. All she saw was Butch. And a gun pointed at her.

"Are you okay?"

Ellen blinked. She wasn't sure how much time had passed. The alarm was still blaring, but things felt quiet. *Quieter,* she corrected herself. *Maybe Butch made a run for it.*

Carter crawled out from under the desk and helped her up. The weight of Ellen's backpack shifted, making her wobble.

"Are you okay?" he asked her again.

Ellen made a quick physical inventory. "I think so."

"Then would you mind telling me what's going on?"

She rubbed her neck. "I don't even know where to start."

"Why don't we start with the lunatic who just tried to kill you?"

"His name's Butch. Butch Stillwell. He's a frat boy from Delta Delta Tau. One of Joey's friends."

"Who's Joey?"

"Do you remember the first day of class when that weird guy ran into me?"

Carter stared at her for a long time. "Oh, yeah. You're the Mote It Be girl," he finally replied.

The Mote It Be girl, she thought. *Terrific. Just terrific.*

"That weird guy was, *is*, a friend of mine. Joey Richards. He slipped me a key to a locker in the bookstore. If anything happened to him, I was supposed to retrieve what was inside."

"And did something happen to him?"

She nodded. "He disappeared. Either that or he went into hiding. All I know is that he didn't show up for his girlfriend's funeral, and he would never do that."

"Wait a minute, are you talking about that suicide? The one we had a big send-off for?"

Ellen gritted her teeth. "You make it sound like she went off on a cruise."

Carter shook his head. "I'm sorry. It's just . . . I get trotted out to these things all the time. Expected to show emotions for people I don't know."

"I can imagine," she blurted before she caught herself. "No, scratch that. I can't imagine. I have no idea what it's like to be you."

"Go on," he replied, rejecting her sympathy.

"Anyway, when I was at her funeral, that guy approached me. Dr.—"

Carter's lips twisted in distaste. "Dr. Pierce. Dr. Richard Pierce."

"You know him?"

"I was on the board that disciplined him, yes."

"What was he disciplined for?"

He looked at her coolly. "I can't tell you. That information is confidential."

"He's a dangerous man, isn't he?" Ellen asked

"I guess it depends."

"On what?"

"On whether you have what he wants."

Ellen's cell phone chimed. She cursed at the screen.

"Are you late for something?" Carter drawled.

"No. It's a Miskalert."

Ellen showed him the message from the campus alert system.

Be advised: police activity.

Barlow Hall closed until further notice.

Carter scowled. "Fabulous. Fucking fabulous."

"I have what he wants, but it's not with me," she told him. "I hid it in a friend's house before I came here. She has no idea it's there."

"Is she a civilian?"

Ellen cringed. Miskatonic frowned on involving outsiders. *She* frowned on involving outsiders.

"I need to get it back before she gets hurt. Do you know a way out of here? One that doesn't involve the police?"

Carter stared at her. "Are you part of the program?" he asked.

Ellen bit her lip and made a weak joke. "Always the bridesmaid, never the bride."

"What?"

"No. I'm not part of the program. Not yet," she replied, a blush heating her cheeks.

The fire alarm stopped. Ellen heard the distant thump of feet on stairs. Carter continued to stare at her.

"Please, Dr. Carter. I need to get out of here. I need to get the book."

"Close your eyes," he said.

Ellen had no choice but to play along. She heard the scrape of furniture, followed by the jangle of keys. When she opened her eyes, a rug had been pulled back to reveal a trap door. A metal ladder descended into darkness.

"You're kidding," she blurted as she stared at the open hatch.

"It's the only way out."

"No. No. It's not that," she edged toward the black opening. "Is that what I think it is?"

"What do you think it is?"

"It's the secret passage Nathaniel West used. When he needed to get rid of his failed experiments."

He gave her a tight little nod. *So the legend is true*, she thought.

"Follow me," Carter said as he mounted the ladder.

"You don't have to go with me. I can manage."

"I'm stuck here, too," he reminded her. "And I have no intention of staying a moment longer."

<hr />

The tunnels under Miskatonic were a terrible place to be a psychic. The place reeked of pain and despair. Arkham Asylum may have been a thing of past. There were no physical remains of Nathaniel West's terrible kingdom. No wheelchairs or gurneys. No rusting beds. But Nathaniel West's victims were still there. Their spirits hung in space, immobilized in both spirit and form.

No crossing over for them, Ellen thought as she stopped to look at a ghostly figure. He was pinned against the wall, wire jutting out of his head. Ellen jumped when he looked at her with dead, black eyes.

"What's wrong?" Carter demanded.

"I ran into a spider web."

"Uh-huh," he replied, sounding less than convinced.

"Can I ask you a question?" Ellen ventured after a long silence. She didn't want to talk to Carter, but it was better than looking at the ghosts. Their misery felt threatening. Toxic.

"I told you my office hours are over."

Ellen sighed and pulled her earbuds out of her pocket. She was about to pop them in when he relented.

"Fine. What is it?"

"You know Hieronymus Bosch's *Garden of Earthly Delights*?"

"Of course I do."

"In one painting there was a scene where a demon wrote music on some poor guy's ass."

"Yes."

"Has anyone ever tried to play it?" Ellen asked.

"Excuse me?"

"Has anyone ever tried to play what was on the guy's ass? You know, orchestrate it?"

Carter stopped and stared at her. "Butt music," he replied. "Someone's trying to kill you, and you're asking me about six-hundred-year-old butt music?"

Ellen looked away, stung. The ghosts around her seemed to absorb her mood. They swarmed her like mosquitoes. A doe-eyed woman plucked at Ellen's sleeve like a needy child.

Ellen kept her eyes on the ground as they continued down the tunnel. She wasn't sure how far they had come or how far they had left to go. There were no landmarks in places like this. At least nothing that could be trusted.

Keep talking, she thought. *It's all you can do. Keep talking.*

"You're not the slightest bit curious what it would sound like?"

He snorted. "You're nuts, you know that?"

She trained her flashlight on a nearby wall, trying to drive the ghosts away. *I'm scared*, she thought. *Why can't you just play along?*

"To be honest, I've never thought about it before," he replied quietly.

"I'm not saying it would be a hit or anything," Ellen offered. "Nothing you could hum along to."

She fell silent as they reached another ladder.

The ghosts were thicker here. Ellen kept an eye on them while Carter fumbled with his keys. They climbed out into the Department of Psychology. She supposed it was someone's idea of a grim joke to put behavioral psychology where the worst of Nathaniel West's medical atrocities took place. Or maybe it was a reminder to the faculty to never forget their history. Either way, the place disturbed her more than the underground passage. The brightly painted walls screamed at her. Forced cheer packed the bulletin board of the office.

Ellen studied the cat pictures tacked to the door. *They think they're holding back the darkness, but they're not.*

Carter paused in the hall. "You coming?

Ellen looked down, at the blue and red light painting her sneakers.

"Dr. Carter?"

"What now?"

"That passage took us across the campus, didn't it?"

"Yes."

"Then why are the police still outside?"

Her cell phone lit up.

Be advised: Gunman seen on campus.

Police standoff on Curwen Street.

Ellen's heart lurched. She showed the message to Carter.

"Joey's frat is on Curwen Street," she informed him.

"All right. Now you've got my attention."

Ellen gawked at him. "A maniac pointing at gun at me wasn't enough?"

"People have faked getting shot in front of me."

"You're kidding. Someone's faked getting shot to get your attention?" She shook her head. "No offense, Dr. Carter, but you're not worth it."

"I'm glad you think so."

"Fake blood is way too expensive these days," she added.

"You think that's funny?"

Ellen shrugged. "It's all I've got right now."

He looked at her, his eyebrow spiking. "What's your name?"

"I'm Ellen. Ellen Lo—"

"Dr. Carter!"

A young man ran toward them before Ellen had a chance to introduce herself.

"Jesus, Miller. How did you find me?" Carter marveled.

"Who's that?" she demanded.

"My personal assistant," he replied. "The university hired him. To keep an eye on me."

The student looked at Ellen and broke into a big, sloppy grin. "Hey," he gasped.

She smiled back. "Hey."

Carter rolled his eyes. "What is it, Miller?"

"There's a situation at Delta Delta Tau. Some lunatic ran into the frat house with a gun. He's holding hostages."

"Butch," Ellen breathed. "I don't think they're hostages."

Carter shot her a sharp look. "You think the entire frat is behind this?"

"That's what Joey said. That's why he turned to me. I was the only person he could trust."

"Can he?"

"Trust me? They're shooting at me! What do you think?"

An uneasy silence settled between them.

"Hayley wants to talk to you, boss," Miller informed him.

Carter sighed. "Of course he does."

"Who's Hayley?" she asked.

"The president of Miskatonic," Carter replied. "You should know that."

Ellen shrugged. "The only official I know is Lisa from Student Loans."

"Fucking bitch," Carter's assistant spat.

Ellen smirked at Miller. "You too, huh? And I thought she saved all her venom for me."

"Are you two done? Because we have a situation out there!" Carter interrupted them, gesturing at the news van pulling up across the street.

Just what this place needs, Ellen thought. *More attention.*

Carter rubbed his face. "Okay. What we need to do is simple. We need to get to your friend before he—"

"She," Ellen corrected him.

"She gets hurt. And Miller?"

His assistant perked up. "Yes?"

"You need to keep President Hayley away from me. Because so help me God, if that man gets in my way one more time—"

"You'll skin me alive. Got it, boss."

⁕

Most of Miskatonic was in the streets. A festive, carnival-like atmosphere filled the air. The neighboring fraternities dragged out kegs. People watched the scene from collapsible lawn chairs. There was even a Hacky Sack game on the edge of the crowd.

The scene was in sharp contrast to the drama being played out on the other side of the tape. A Kevlar-clad SWAT team surrounded Delta Delta Tau. They tried to make contact with the people inside. Ellen could hear sounds over the loud-speaker, but she was too far away to make out any words.

"Watch it!" Carter hissed when a drunk student plowed into him.

Ellen hugged herself as they waded deeper into the crowd. Childhood memories flared to life. Lying on the playground with a mob surrounding her, their faces hidden by the glare of the sun. Gravel digging into her skin. *I never knew*, she thought. *I never knew who landed the first blow. Was it one of my friends?* She rubbed her arms, trying to erase the memory.

"I know a place near here," she announced, a little too loudly. "We might get a better view of what's happening."

"What about the owner?"

"Maria lives alone. I check on her from time to time. She won't mind me dropping by."

"What about me?"

"You'll be fine. She's a sucker for handsome men."

Carter stopped and gave her a sideways look.

"Ellen?" a female voice called out.

Maria Vargas stood on the edge of the crowd, plucking at the collar of her blouse. Ellen was stunned. Her friend stayed close to home. To see her anywhere near Miskatonic University was unusual.

Not just unusual, Ellen corrected herself. *Unheard of.*

When Maria spotted her, she rushed over and threw her arms around Ellen. Carter mouthed over the woman's head, "Is that her?" Ellen nodded.

"Thank God, you're here. Thank God!" Maria babbled.

Ellen withdrew to look at her friend. "What's wrong? Why aren't you at home?" she asked. "Have you been evacuated?"

The woman shook her head. "I just couldn't stay there anymore. The loud music and partying are bad enough, but the chanting. Those boys are driving me mad."

"Chanting?" Carter echoed.

Maria looked up, noticing him for the first time.

"Maria, I'd like you to meet my friend Andrew Carter."

He took her hand, gently pressing it between his. "It's a pleasure, Ms. Vargas." Maria offered him a weak smile.

"Would you take us back to your house so we can hear what you're talking about?" Ellen asked.

Her friend took a step back, fear blooming in her eyes. "We'll make sure nothing happens to you," Carter reassured her.

The prospect of protection from a tall, dark stranger was hard to resist. Maria threaded her arm through Carter's and let him guide her away from the crowd. Toward the real action.

DARKNESS BELOW

Deep. Down. Dark.
????-??-1945

It was easy to get into one of their camps. The look on the guard's face when my mother marched up and surrendered . . . well, it was one of the few times I remember laughing.

I have no idea how we managed to stay alive and stay together. So many families were separated. Sent to their deaths. Maybe my mother was more powerful than I gave her credit for.

Of course they suspected us. One of the officers watched my mother and me as we moved back and forth from the factory where we were forced to work. I hated being a cog in the machine. Part of the German war effort. I vented my frustration every chance I could. We were imprisoned, living like livestock. They marred our flesh, branding us with their mark. And for what?

My mother was unmoved by my protests.

She looked at me with calm, distant eyes. "In time. Everything in time."

She called for me a few weeks later. I bribed the guard with some cigarettes and snuck out to meet her at the parade ground where we gathered for roll call.

It was a clear, cold night.
My mother drew a magic circle and began to chant.
The words rose in a plume of steam as the ground
beneath us hummed.
I knew then we weren't alone.

Chapter Six

Ellen stood in the dark, looking out her friend's picture window. Maria's house, although small and modest, was perched on a prime piece of real estate. It offered panoramic views of the lowlands of Arkham. And of the fraternity below.

Ellen picked up the binoculars on the coffee table and peered into the backyard of Delta Delta Tau. The place was a disaster. Red cups lay scattered in the overgrown grass. A couch sat on the back porch. Trash cans overflowed in the alley behind them. She wasn't surprised to see huge rats crawling over the garbage. Their inky figures swarmed the darkness.

She lowered the binoculars. *Not huge rats. SWAT.*

"I asked Mrs. Vargas to make us some tea," Carter said as he joined her by the window. "What's going on down there?"

She offered him the binoculars.

"Where did you get those?"

"They were on the coffee table. I guess Maria does a lot of birdwatching," Ellen replied, putting the last word in air quotes.

Carter raised the binoculars to his face. Even though the old woman was in the kitchen and well out of hearing range, he dropped his voice. "She's the one you left the book with, isn't she?"

A low thrum shook the picture window, making the air vibrate around them.

"Oh, that's not good," Carter murmured as he cracked open one of the windows.

The sound of chanting drifted up to them.

"*Niis Zamran Ciaof Caosga.*

"*Zorge.*

"*Niis Zamran Ciaof Caosga.*

"*Zorge.*

"*Torsvi.*"

Carter scowled.

"What is it?" Ellen asked.

"I'm not sure, but it sounds like . . ."

An orange light flared in the windows of the frat. "Oh God. They're setting the place on fire," Ellen whispered.

Carter took a step back. "No, they're not."

The fraternity spat out a mouthful of glass as fire erupted from the windows. The inferno licked the sides of the house. The flames looked alive. Intelligent. Orange tendrils groping for something.

A moment later a wormlike creature burst through the roof. It reared up, bucking and thrashing, as if bound by an invisible chain.

Ellen stood in place, transfixed, as it crashed back into the house. "Get away from the window!" Carter yelled at her.

When she didn't respond, he threw her to the floor, shielding her with his body.

There was a deafening roar. The room shook as an explosion rocked the neighborhood. The windows flexed but held.

Maria Vargas dashed into the living room, a tea bag spinning in her hand. "What happened? Oh my God, what on earth happened?"

Carter scrambled off Ellen.

"The frat exploded," Ellen gasped as she sat up.

"What?"

"Delta Delta Tau just exploded, Maria."

Maria rushed to the window. Ellen tried to intercept her, but she was too late. It didn't matter. There was nothing left to see. The frat house was nothing but a smoldering crater. There was no sign of the creature. Car alarms howled all around them. Emergency vehicles cried in the distance. As she squeezed Maria's shoulders, Ellen wondered if the blast showed up on the local seismographs.

The woman raised a trembling hand to her lips. "Oh my God, those poor boys. Those poor, poor boys. I didn't mean for this to happen. Honestly, I didn't."

Carter looked at her, confused.

"What are you talking about?" Ellen asked.

Maria shot Ellen a panicked look. "The spell. I bought a spell from one of those places near the university. I didn't go to your store because I knew you wouldn't sell me one. Oh God, I should have listened to you when you told me not to mess with magic. What have I done?"

Ellen guided her friend to the couch. "Maria, calm down."

"All I wanted was some peace and quiet. I never meant to hurt them."

Carter sat beside her. "Do you still have the spell?" he asked. She nodded and pointed at a wadded-up piece of paper. He plucked it off the coffee table.

"Oh God, what if—"

"Relax, Maria, relax," Ellen soothed her friend. She was almost certain the spell was useless. Still . . . She held her breath while Carter examined it.

"It's not real," he finally announced, flicking it on the table. "The only thing you'd kill with that is a fly. And only if you had good aim."

"Are you sure?" Maria pressed him.

"I'm sure."

"You're not just saying that to make me feel better?"

"Ma'am, I'm not the kind of person who says things to make people feel better."

The old woman looked at Ellen. "Is that true?"

"I don't know."

"You don't know?"

"Ellen and I haven't known each other for long," Carter offered. "That's why I'm going to tell you one more time. You're not responsible for what just happened. Okay?"

"Okay," she answered in a little voice.

Carter's cell phone broke the silence. He looked at the number and cursed. "I have to take this."

"He likes you, Ellen," the old woman announced after Carter left.

"Maria," Ellen groaned.

"How long have you known him?" she asked.

Ellen remembered the stopwatch she started when she walked into his office. She glanced at it. "About an hour. Fifty-three minutes to be exact."

"You seem like you've known each other much longer than that," Maria said, her eyes glazing over.

Ellen could see her friend retreating to her comfort zone. It was only a matter of time before she'd start quoting from the romance novels she loved. She would probably be retreating into one of her bodice rippers tonight. Not that Ellen blamed her. What they just saw was . . .

"Look, I'm going to call Mrs. Brody and ask her to stay with you, okay?" Ellen squeezed Maria's hand as she moved off the couch.

"Okay," the woman agreed vaguely.

Carter occupied the kitchen, so Ellen ducked into Maria's guest room to make the call. The place was immaculate. The bed was neatly made, the surfaces dusted and polished. A water carafe sat on the nightstand, ready to quench the thirst of the visitor who would never arrive.

As Ellen spoke with Maria's neighbor, she wandered around the room, looking at the photos clustered on the shelves. She picked up one of them. She studied a young man's image, hoping to get a message, a clear reason for her friend's pain. There was nothing. There was always nothing.

Carter appeared in the doorway. "Where's the book?" he demanded.

"Do you know how I met Maria?" Ellen asked as she put the photo back on the shelf. "She came into the bookstore, hoping to find a spell that would let her speak to her son. She wanted to know why he killed himself."

"Jesus."

"I've sold a lot of spells. Most of them don't bother me. But selling a fake spell to a grieving mother? No way. I became her friend. I look after her. It's not very hard. She's a lonely woman. All she needed was someone to talk to."

Carter reached out and ran his finger along the table. "This is her son's room, isn't it?"

"Yes."

"She must clean it every week."

"No. I do."

Ellen watched as realization spread across his face. "This is the place she never goes," he replied.

"She can't bring herself to come in here. It's too painful."

"Why are you telling me this?"

"Because I need answers, too. Maybe not as desperately as Maria, but they were my friends, you know?"

"You think they're dead?"

"Stephanie is. And Joey?" Ellen fixed her eyes on a spot beyond the door. She could almost see Joey hovering like a ghost over Carter's shoulder. Tears choked her throat. "I need to be part of this," she said in a husky voice.

"This? There is no this!"

"A fraternity just exploded. There will be a this."

"What makes you so sure they'll come to me?"

She nodded at his phone. "I think they already have."

Carter looked away, his jaw tightening. "I suppose you won't give me the book until I agree to let you tag along," he grumbled.

Ellen opened the closet and retrieved the book from behind some old boxes. She offered it to him. "I won't play games. Not with this."

Carter gave the book, and her, a cool, appraising stare. He let her hang for a moment before he took it. He nodded at the wrapping. "What the hell is this?"

"Protection," she said. "Don't touch it with your bare hands. It packs a powerful punch."

"You speak from experience?"

"Yes."

"You know, I should cut you off right here. You're haven't been admitted to the program yet."

"I know," Ellen replied. She looked at the photos of Maria's son and waited.

"All right. I'll let you come with me," he relented. "But I decide how far you go. Understand?"

"Yes."

"And if you ask me a single question about the class while we're—"

"I won't," she assured him. He didn't look satisfied. He was about to say something else when she cut him off. "What do we do next?"

"I call Connie Blake and set up a meeting."

"Connie Blake? She's real?"

"He. He's real," Carter corrected her. "What made you think he wasn't real?"

"I thought you just made up a name. You know, to get rid of me."

Carter acted like he didn't hear her. "We need to meet with him, but the entire campus is locked down."

"What about a coffee house or something?" Ellen suggested.

Carter's lips curled into a smile. "You don't talk about forbidden knowledge at a Starbucks."

Ellen blushed and looked away. "What about my place?" she suggested.

"I am not stepping foot in a sorority."

"I don't belong to a sorority."

"You certainly look the part," he replied.

She stared at him for a long time, trying to decide if she had been insulted. In the end she let it go. "I live with my uncle."

"And he won't bother us?"

Ellen paused, wondering whether she should introduce herself. *Would Carter recognize my name?* She decided not to tell him. After all, he only just agreed to let her join him.

"He spends most of his time in the study, so I think we're good," she assured him.

Carter shrugged. "Sure. Why not? Your uncle's place it is."

Chapter Seven

Someone spray-painted the street sign again. River Runs Drive now read "River Runs Dry."

Ellen's home was the most famous unhaunted house in Arkham. A mock Tudor mansion, it hugged a bend in the Miskatonic River. It originally belonged to Jonathan Trelawney, a nineteenth-century tycoon who tried to force the industrial world on Arkham. The residents fought him. Their resistance, coupled with the Great Panic of 1873, ended his crusade.

Trelawney never forgot his failure. He condemned Arkham as a colonial backwater, a place hopelessly mired in the past. The citizens took pride in Trelawney's defeat. His Tudor house was allowed to stand, a lonely beachhead for an invasion that never came.

Ellen nodded at the man pacing in front of the wrought iron gates.

"Is that Dr. Blake?"

"About time," the man greeted them as they crossed the street. "I was ready to give up on you."

Angular, with a lanky body and a shock of blond hair, Connie Blake was right out of Carter's art history course. He looked like the Norman Rockwell portrait of Ichabod Crane. Carter's colleague was less stern than his fictional counterpart. There was a softness to his mouth, a hint that he was capable of kindness. She saw that kindness mirrored in his dark-blue eyes. They were as warm and murky as Carter's were cold and clear.

When he looked at her, she couldn't help but smile. The friendly expression stunned Blake.

"Andrew, who is this gorgeous girl?"

Carter snorted. "Gorgeous? Her?"

"You get the most beautiful women in your class."

"The weight of celebrity, I suppose."

"That and the fact that your class is required," Ellen added.

Blake rewarded her effort with a lopsided smile. He stepped forward, extending his hand. "My name is Connie Blake."

"I'm Ellen Logan," she announced.

Carter jerked as if he had been shocked. His eyes locked on her. "What did you just say?"

"She said her name is Ellen Logan," Blake offered.

Carter didn't hear him. "Would you excuse us for a minute, Con?"

He grabbed Ellen's arm and towed her down the street. As soon as they were out of earshot, he whirled around and hissed, "Let me see some ID."

"I beg your pardon?"

He snapped his fingers. "Identification. Now."

Ellen bristled. She considered refusing. But his anger was so strong, she knew she needed to defuse it. She handed over her wallet. Carter pawed through it, fishing out her driver's license, her Miskatonic ID, her ATM card. She tensed when he pulled out a picture of her and Joshua.

It was taken when she was ten years old, shortly after he adopted her. They were at the beginning of their grand tour around the world, visiting a Buddhist temple in Nepal. Ellen treasured the photo. It was the first time in her life she felt safe.

"Can I have my wallet back, please?" she demanded, her voice reed thin.

Carter looked at her. For a horrible moment Ellen thought he would refuse. Her hands curled into fists. Just as she was about to lunge for it, to snatch it out of his hands, he returned it.

Ellen glanced at the picture as she stuffed her wallet in her pocket. Trying to pretend it didn't matter. *They're just things,* she scolded herself. *Don't get attached to anything.*

"Did you know about me?" Carter asked.

"About your connection with Joshua? Only a week or so ago," she replied. "He told me when I came back from the first day of class."

The blood drained from Carter's face.

"What's wrong?" Ellen asked.

"Joshua's alive?"

"You thought he was dead?"

Carter pursed his lips. "I heard he was in a car accident a few years ago. I tried contacting him, but he never responded, so I just assumed . . ." The words trailed off in a shrug.

"Oh God, you don't know," Ellen breathed.

His eyes latched on to her. "Don't know what?"

Ellen hesitated, unsure what to say. Carter grabbed her arm again.

"*Don't know what?*"

"He's paralyzed. From the waist down. He's in a wheelchair," she blurted, watching as Carter absorbed the news. "I'm sorry. I didn't know you thought Joshua was dead. I would have told you everything up front if—"

Carter released the viselike grip on her arm.

"Are we good?" Connie Blake called out as they returned, eyeing Ellen suspiciously.

"We're good," Carter reassured him. "You remember Joshua Logan?"

Connie's face split into a smile. "He was quite the character."

"This is his niece," he paused to look at her again. "You are his niece, right?"

"Jeez, what do you want now? A DNA swab?" Ellen thought she saw him blush as he looked at the house.

"Oh yeah, he used to live here, didn't he?" Connie blurted. "I heard he threw some pretty wild parties."

"Wild parties, huh? I'll have to a word with him about that," Ellen smiled as she rummaged through her backpack.

"Wait a minute. He's here?" Carter replied.

"Yes. I talked to him after the first day of class, remember?"

"I thought you spoke to him on the phone or online or something."

Carter bit his lip. For a moment Ellen saw the mask of reserve slip. "Are you sure you want to go in? We could meet somewhere else if . . ."

Carter's expression hardened. "Let's get on with it, shall we?"

Ellen set her backpack in front of the wrought iron gates. She rifled through it until she found a massive medieval-looking key. She pushed it into the lock, tugging and twisting, engaging in an intricate dance. The gate surrendered with an agonized squeal.

Carter stopped her before she crossed the threshold and nodded at her feet. Broken glass littered the ground.

Ellen groaned. "Oh, terrific. We've had a fresh attack."

"Attack?" Connie Blake echoed.

She brushed the debris aside with her hiking boot. "This is why I can't wear nice shoes. Students throw beer bottles at the house whenever they drive by. I guess they see this place as the enemy. A challenge to everything Miskatonic represents."

"I don't see why they would. Jonathan Trelawney was a well-known spiritualist," Carter pointed out.

"I think subtle distinctions are lost on the drunken masses, Dr. Carter."

She scanned the street for would-be vandals. "Just once I'd like to catch one of them in the act."

Ellen led them down a narrow path bordered on either side by a dense, overgrown garden. Stone figures in various stages of decomposition poked out of the jungle. A headless cherub here, an armless demon there, an angel lying broken on the ground—they all served as silent guardians to the stone-gabled house at the end of the walkway.

Andrew Carter and Connie Blake exchanged uneasy glances. Ellen didn't blame them. From the outside the house looked menacing. The windows facing the street had been broken so many times that they kept them boarded up. The heavy wooden door was old and equally battle-scarred. No doorbell. No brass knocker. Nothing to suggest the presence of people to summon.

Blake tried hard not to look appalled. "You actually live here?"

"You sure this isn't a sorority house?" Carter teased her.

They fell silent as Ellen opened the door. Hidden behind the wrecked exterior lurked a home of surprising warmth. The entryway led to the main hall with wood floors and ornate furniture.

A grandfather clock ticked solemnly in the hall. No one could hear it. Loud music blasted in the hall. Katrina and the Waves, "Walking on Sunshine."

Ellen smiled. "Sounds like Joshua made a sale."

Carter shook his head. "In my day it was 'September.' Earth, Wind and Fire."

Ellen stopped and looked at him. *This is someone who knows Joshua,* she thought, *someone who might be able to tell me . . .*

The song cut out midchorus.

"Elle, is that you?"

Carter stirred at the sound of Joshua's voice.

"Why don't you go ahead?" Ellen offered as she set her things on the bench in the entryway. "His study is the third door on the left. Connie and I will wait for you in the kitchen."

Connie Blake's behavior changed the moment Carter left. The man who seemed so self-assured became uneasy. His eyes roamed around the room, sliding across the clock, the polished wood floors, anything but her. As she watched him squirm, she realized he had spent most of his life in Carter's shadow. Feeding on the scraps of his friend's celebrity. Blake's vulnerability intrigued her. Most professors at Miskatonic were cold and remote, their emotions hidden beneath thick layers of reserve. Not Connie Blake.

Visions steamed off him. Ellen saw him as a young boy sitting beneath a tree, watching Carter lead the other students on an imaginary expedition. She saw him hiding in the library, a skinny, miserable teenager plagued by acne. She saw him looming over a naked woman who beckoned to him and Carter—

"Stop. Right there."

The visions vanished so suddenly Ellen lost her balance. Connie Blake grabbed her as she stumbled. Her cheeks flared.

"Oh God, I'm sorry. I'm so sorry."

Blake flashed her a lopsided grin. "Carter didn't tell me you were psychic."

"He doesn't know."

"That's probably for the best. Carter hates psychics," Blake replied as he let her go. "You know what he calls us? Red shirts. From *Star Trek*, yeah?"

"Of course."

"He says that hanging out with a psychic makes about as much sense as swimming in shark-infested waters."

"Us? You mean—"

"What do you think just happened?"

"I don't know. I mean, I . . . I've never met another psychic before."

"You and I should find a time to talk."

"How about now? Over tea?" she offered as she gazed at the closed study door. "I think we have plenty of time."

Chapter Eight

"The Eibon Institute?" Ellen turned over Connie Blake's business card. They sat side by side in the breakfast nook in the kitchen, the table piled high with her textbooks. "What's the Eibon Institute?"

"It's a think tank for psychics. An independent organization that consults with the government on some of their more, um, challenging cases." Connie Blake tapped the business card. "*Post temporis, spatium ultra.* That's our motto."

"My Latin is a little rusty."

"Beyond time, beyond space."

Ellen tried not to roll her eyes. Arkham was full of psychics who claimed they could travel to other worlds.

"The human mind is an amazing thing. But the mind of a psychic? Awesome." Connie Blake's eyes glowed as he sipped his tea. "Think about H. P. Lovecraft's most important characters: Randolph Carter, Etienne de Marigny, King Kuranes. They all possessed the ability to travel between worlds. They could use their minds to cross over physically."

"That doesn't mean they're psychic. Some of them used magic items. Meditation," Ellen replied.

Connie waved off the suggestion. "Lovecraft made that up. That's pure fiction. I mean, meditation? Give me a break."

"Why would he lie?"

"Can you imagine what would happen if all the psychics in the world knew about the power they had? If they joined forces and concentrated on one thing? They could tear a hole in the world." Connie Blake paused to consider the possibility. Ellen couldn't decide whether he looked pleased or horrified.

"You should join us."

"What? The institute?"

"Yes."

"I'm not part of the program."

"Your status at Miskatonic doesn't matter. Like I said, we're an independent organization."

"And what exactly is it that you do?"

"I told you. We consult."

Carter and Joshua burst into the room before she had a chance to ask Connie Blake anything else. She snatched his business card off the table. Ellen thought Joshua would notice her pocketing the card. He had a sixth sense when she tried to hide things from him. But her uncle was oblivious. His attention was on Carter and only Carter.

The golden boy, she thought with a surge of jealousy. *Another world I'll never be part of.*

Connie's voice whispered in her head: *All the more reason to be part of mine.*

Carter looked at the tea and cookies on the table. "Having a good time, Connie?"

His friend leaned back in his chair. "I'm having a great time. Thanks for introducing us, Andrew."

Joshua scowled at her companion. "Who are you?"

"This is my colleague, Dr. Connie Blake," Carter offered. "Ellen found something he needs to look at."

Ellen's uncle turned to her for an explanation. "Oh, really?"

Ellen shifted under his gaze. "You know my friend Stephanie Lansdale died." Joshua nodded. "Well, now her boyfriend is missing. Right before he disappeared, he told me about a book. A book a lot of people are looking for."

"And I suppose you have it?" he demanded. When she said nothing he started to scold her. "Ellen, how many times have I told you——?"

Carter cut Joshua off. "She doesn't have the book. I have it."

Now it was Connie Blake's turn to be outraged. "Are you serious, Andrew? You have the book with you? You're actually carrying it in that beat-up old bag of yours?" He speared his friend with a glare.

"You prefer I leave it in an old lady's house?"

"Old lady?" Joshua echoed.

Ellen buried her face in her hands. "I'm so glad I handed this to the professionals," she moaned. "Would you guys please stop fucking around and get on with it?"

All three men looked at her, stunned.

"From the mouths of babes," Carter announced after a long, awkward silence.

Ellen batted her eyes. "Dr. Carter. You flatter me."

Her uncle snickered. Carter folded his arms. "I see you've taught your niece to be a pain in the ass," he observed.

"Just like I taught you, my boy."

Carter said nothing as he slid into the breakfast nook, joining Ellen and Connie. Joshua rolled up to the table.

Blake pulled out a pair of wire-rimmed glasses. "What do you have for me?"

"I suppose I should bring you up to speed on what's happened," Carter leaned in to get started.

"I'd rather you didn't," Blake sniffed.

"I'd certainly appreciate an update," Joshua said, flashing Ellen a look she chose to ignore.

"You'll have to excuse my friend. He's a bit of a purist." Carter sneered the last word. "He discounts anything that comes from the real world."

"I don't discount field research," Blake snapped.

"You don't pay much attention to it either," Carter pointed out.

"I value your research. Just because I'm not the romantic Indiana Jones type like you—"

"If you thought what I did was important, you'd do it, Connie," Carter growled.

"Would you two please get on with it?" Joshua chided them.

Carter put the book on the table and opened the cloth-wrapped shroud. Connie moved in for a closer look.

"Jesus Christ. Is this real?" he blurted.

"I don't know. You tell me," Carter challenged his friend.

Blake glared at him. "Only one way to find out."

Connie touched the book with his bare hand. He brushed it with his fingertips, stroking the cover with a soft, almost loving caress.

The book was in no mood to be gentle. Connie Blake's head jerked back. He collapsed against Ellen, his body twitching, his face a frozen mask of pain. His hands flailed at his face. She grabbed them, trying to keep him from clawing his eyes out.

"It's coming," Blake wailed. "Oh God, it's coming!"

Carter unhooked his friend's glasses and set them on the table. "Connie, Connie, can you hear me? Come on, Con, snap out of it!"

"I'm calling an ambulance," Joshua declared.

The moment Joshua pulled out his cell phone, Connie Blake snapped out of his trance. He sat up. He blinked and looked around the table. "What happened?"

"You had a fit. You touched the book and passed out," Carter's relief quickly passed. "You fuck. You dumb fuck. What were you thinking, touching a book like that with your bare hands?"

Joshua cut off Connie before he could respond. "Ellen, would you excuse us? I need a private word with these gentle-men." His tone was low. Lethal.

She scurried to her feet, relieved to be excused. She retreated to the backyard, to the edge of the Miskatonic River. She was glad she didn't have to witness her uncle's anger. The one time she truly provoked him he'd become so enraged she expected him to rise out of his wheelchair. She wondered whether he would manage that miraculous feat tonight. Connie and Carter had given him enough fuel.

She had never seen grown men act so immature. Picking fights, egging each other on . . . it was behavior straight out of grade school. At the same time their bickering touched her. There was a familiarity between them, the kind of intimacy only a lifelong friendship can produce. An intimacy that apparently involved sharing a woman. As Ellen stared at the twinkling lights on the other side of the river, she wondered what having such a close bond would be like.

"Joshua sent me out here to apologize," Carter announced, startling her out of her speculation.

"Is your friend okay?"

"He's fine."

"You know, the same thing happened to me when I touched the book."

He looked at her. She could see him making the connection. "You're psychic, too," he murmured

"I'm afraid so."

He cocked his head. "What's that supposed to mean?"

"Connie Blake told me you don't like psychics."

His lips curled into a smile. "Of course he did."

The playful expression didn't last long. Andrew Carter's face fell. His eyes locked onto a spot above her head. Ellen turned, following his gaze. All she saw were trees swaying in the wind.

"There's no wind," he said in a low voice.

"What?"

"Do you feel any wind?"

Yes. It was a single word, so easy to say. It was also a lie. The trees around them shuddered violently, in a way Ellen knew she should feel. But there was no wind.

A low thrum rose from the ground. The sound ran up her legs, freezing her where she stood. It filled her skull. Rattled her bones. Her heart vibrated like a plucked string.

Connie Blake's warning blasted in her head. *It's coming. Oh God, it's coming.*

Carter's mouth moved but she couldn't hear him. Ellen watched as he ran. She didn't see much point. There was no escape from whatever was coming. She could see it churning up the earth on the other side of the river. No matter what they did, they were both dead. They were all dead. Uncle Joshua. Connie Blake. Maybe the entire town of Arkham.

It wasn't until the thing crossed the Miskatonic and the water boiled that Ellen finally moved. Running after Carter.

I'm going to die, but I won't die alone. I won't, I won't, I won't.

Carter jumped onto the picnic table and held out his hand. Out of the corner of her eye she saw a huge bow wave of earth racing toward her. Opening like a zipper.

A blast of heat hit her body, pitching her forward. Carter grabbed her hand just as it closed on her. She jerked out of his grip, looking into his eyes as she fell. "I won't take you," she whispered. "I won't take you with me."

An inferno engulfed her, shooting over her head. Heat rose all around her. Then the world shifted. It tilted wildly on its axis.

Ellen plummeted down a steep hill, tumbling in a blur of arms and legs. She rolled, and rolled, and rolled. She spun until direction lost its meaning. Just when she thought it was over, that she would shatter into a million little pieces, there was . . .

Peace. Quiet. Cold.

Ellen opened her eyes to a sky dusted by the Milky Way. Trees swayed in the wind. *A real wind*, she thought as dead leaves skittered around her.

She rolled onto her side, peeling herself off the asphalt road. A man stood a few feet away. "You have to stop them," the shadowy figure announced.

Ellen scrambled to her feet. Her left hand burned. She clutched it to her chest.

"Stop them? Who?"

The man stepped closer. He wore filthy overalls and twirled a pickax. A gob of mud spattered on the ground.

The man nodded at an object lying on the road. Ellen didn't want to take her eyes off him. She was afraid if she did he would bury the pickax in her back. But she had no choice. Reluctantly she looked down and studied a weather-beaten sign.

A name was etched on the worn wood, with an arrow pointing the way. Ellen squinted, trying to focus. The word was slippery. She had to spell it out, the way she did in grade school.

"*B . . . E . . . N . . . T*—," she started. Before she could get any further, the man grabbed her and lifted her off the ground.

Ellen howled in outrage. *Why?* she wondered. *Why ask me to help and then—*

"Ellen. Ellen!" a voice called out. Familiar smells came rushing back. Mud. Grass. The damp funk of the riverbank. She opened her eyes. Carter loomed over her. He held her arms to her sides.

Something hard was wedged in her mouth. A piece of wood. She spat it out and gulped for air.

Carter loomed over her. "Ellen, relax. Do you hear me? Deep breaths. Slow d-e-e-p breaths," he commanded.

"Did you see? Did you see what—" she gasped as soon as she could speak.

Carter shook his head. At first she thought he was denying what he saw on the riverbank. Then his eyes flicked to the side. Uncle Joshua was beside him, looking pale and stricken. Connie Blake stood a few feet away, arms crossed. He watched her with a strange mix of curiosity and coolness.

Carter leaned forward and whispered in her ear. "Just relax, okay? Help is on the way."

There was nothing left for Ellen to do. She closed her eyes and waited.

Deep. Down. Dark.
????-??-1945

It all went to hell.

Would I be here if everything went off without
a hitch?

There were only two of us in the circle. At the very
least we needed four people to cover the cardinal
directions. But my mother didn't trust the other
prisoners. They would sell their souls for a scrap of
bread, she insisted.

The way you sold everything for a book? I wanted
to remind her.

I bit my tongue.

We no longer had the book, but the spells were lodged
in her head. They spilled out of her as she danced
around the magic circle. The ground hummed. The
earth shimmered. Vibrating like water in a glass.

I thought it was a hallucination. We were being
starved and worked to death. Being light-headed
was a normal part of life, so I thought . . .

I could never have imagined the thing that erupted
out of the earth. A creature of light and darkness.

It reached out, groping for my mother with long, fiery tendrils.

One of its arms touched her.
Her body filled with light.
She collapsed to the ground, convulsing.

That's when the officer stepped into our circle. The Nazi who watched us trudge back and forth from the camp. His insignia winked at me in the light. A skull with wings. He held a whistle in his hand, which he brought to his mouth and blew.

It broke the magic circle.

The creature exploded, body parts flying in every direction.

I thought the whistle was an ordinary thing. Until I saw the broken parts of the creature quiver. You know how metal filings stand up and move toward a magnet? That's what the creature did. The whistle attracted it. It lured it into a different kind of prison.

My mother was still unconscious, but I saw her move to her feet.

Her spirit left her body.

I'm sure you know what happened next.

My mother dove in front of the creature to protect it.

She was pulled into the whistle, along with a part of the creature.

The moment she was sucked in, the spell was broken. What was left of the creature rebelled. It burrowed back into the earth and started tearing up the camp. Trying to rip it from the ground like a noxious weed.

I rebelled, too. I rushed the Nazi and knocked him to the ground. My strength surprised him. At least that's what I like to think. He was probably too distracted by the creature destroying his camp to pay much attention to me . . .

I tore the whistle off the necklace that dangled from his throat. It was too late for my mother. She was already dead. All around me the world exploded. The Nazis had lost control, but they would quickly recover. I could already hear reinforcements arriving. Dogs barking.

A few hundred feet away I saw a hole in the fence.

With the thing in my pocket, I fled.

Chapter Nine

MYSTERIOUS EXPLOSION, FIRE DESTROYS FRATERNITY

ARKHAM – The calm of Curwen Street was shattered yesterday afternoon when a powerful explosion rocked the Delta Delta Tau fraternity house. Five policemen were injured, two critically. Several members of Delta Delta Tau are missing and presumed dead.

The drama started earlier in the day, with reports of a gunman on the campus of Miskatonic University. The man retreated to the fraternity, which prompted a lockdown of the neighborhood. Shortly before the explosion, eyewitnesses reported "chanting," followed by a "hum that shook the ground."

Officials at Miskatonic refused to comment on the case. The incident is only the latest in a series of tragic events to strike the school. Last month a female student jumped to her death from the university clock tower. Her parents have filed a wrongful death suit against the university. Karla Lansdale, the young girl's mother, insists that Miskatonic is "an evil, foul place, a blight that should be wiped off the face of the earth." Many people in Arkham share her opinion. According to a man who asked not to be identified, "the asylum may be gone, but the lunatics are still there. We as a community need to lock them up."

A smaller story ran beneath the headline: "Violent Windstorm Downs Trees in New Arkham." Ellen pushed away the newspaper. "Windstorm. Yeah, right," she muttered.

She stared at the tray on her table. If she wanted to get out of the hospital, she needed to eat. The doctors subjected her to a broad spectrum of tests. They came up with nothing except a burned hand. The lack of a firm diagnosis spooked them. She heard them arguing in the hall, weighing the risk of a relapse with the need to free her bed.

Ellen knew if she acted normally for the rest of the day, they would release her. So she tried her best to look normal. She ate her bland lunch. She watched television.

After enduring what seemed like an eternity of talk shows, a young resident entered the room. She recognized him. He was the one who admitted her. The doctor who saw her at her worst.

"How are you doing today, Miss Logan?" he asked as he scanned her chart.

"Okay. I have a headache, but it's not too bad."

"And the hand?"

"It hurts, but the pain medicine is keeping it under control."

He jotted more notes on the chart. Ellen wondered how long her paper trail was.

"Doctor?"

"Yes?"

"What happened to me?" she asked.

His pen froze in midair. "I need to get some readings first. Then we'll talk."

He examined her for a long time—taking her vital signs, shining a light in her eyes, testing her reflexes. She knew he was stalling, hoping to find the pattern, the diagnosis that eluded his superiors. There were no easy answers. In a hospital connected to such a dark university, there never were. As he pulled up a chair she wondered how many bizarre injuries he had seen. Torn limbs, gaping wounds, strange bite marks, massive internal injuries.

"Miss Logan, I have to be honest. I have no idea what happened," he finally admitted. He skimmed his notes one last time, just to be sure.

"Can you tell me what you saw?" Ellen asked

"When the paramedics brought you in you looked like you were having a seizure. All the classic signs were there. Involuntary movement. Trancelike state. Muscular rigidity." The doctor looked at her as if she was hiding the answer. "But the readings don't support the seizure theory."

"What do you mean?"

"I don't know how much you know about neurology, but there is a certain randomness to the way the brain functions. Seizures occur when electrical impulses all try to take the same route." He doodled a traffic jam on her chart. "When we hooked you up to the machine, nothing suggested you were having one. Now, either you can manipulate your body in unheard of ways or it was something else."

"What else could it be?"

He set her file on the bedside table. "Well, another explanation is that when you knelt on the ground you touched some sort of underground power line. That would explain your convulsions and your burned hand, but it doesn't explain the pattern of the wound." He lowered his voice. "Have you seen it?"

"No."

He solemnly removed the gauze, peeled away the dressing like he was unwrapping a mummy.

Circles were branded into her palm. Marks that looked almost like— "Tentacles," she whispered.

"Whatever you grabbed onto, it wasn't a power line," the doctor said.

No. It's something buried much deeper. Ellen didn't share the thought. She waited a long time before she spoke.

"But besides that, I'm okay?"

"Besides that, I have nothing."

"Does that mean I can go home?"

He returned to doctor mode. "Do you have someone who can keep an eye on you tonight?"

"I live with my uncle."

He consulted her chart. "And the nurses said you can walk on your own."

"Yes," Ellen replied. She thought the guided walks up and down the hall were a waste of time. Now she was glad she agreed to them.

"I see no reason to keep you here." With a quick flourish he signed the warrant for her release. "Just let me have a nurse rebandage your wound, and we'll send you on your way, okay?"

Time stood still after he left. At first Ellen thought it was her imagination. Hospitals had a way of slowing down time, of making every minute drag. But when Ellen measured out the time in TV shows, she realized that it *was* taking them a long time to discharge her. Two and a half talk shows passed before a nurse came in and rewrapped her hand.

When the nurse departed, Ellen changed into her street clothes and waited on the edge of the bed. She called Uncle Joshua, reminding him to open the pedestrian gate to their home.

Then she waited some more.

Only a doctor checking on the patient in the next bed broke the monotony. They brought the woman in the night before, under cover of darkness. Since then Ellen heard nothing. Whoever the person was, she wasn't well enough to use the bathroom. Ellen stifled the urge to peek around the curtain.

"Ready to get out of here?" a bright voice startled her out of her thoughts.

A hospital orderly stood before her with a wheelchair. "Am I glad to see you," she sighed.

"I bet you say that to all the staff."

"Yeah, but I mean it with you."

As he helped her out of her bed she caught a glimpse of the patient in the next bed. The woman was her age. She lay motionless, her hands curled against her chest. She stared blankly into space.

Ellen waited until they were out of the room before she asked the inevitable question. "What happened to her?"

The orderly leaned closer. "This is between us, right?"

"Of course," Ellen replied. Privacy laws made getting anything out of hospitals difficult. But information still had a way of escaping.

"They found her on the riverside."

The riverside. The hair on the back of Ellen's neck stood up.

"She was gibbering when the paramedics reached her. After that, nothing. Just a frozen statue in a bed." He punched the button for the elevator. "We've had a few like her come in. Circuits fried."

The orderly fell silent as a middle-aged doctor joined them. The man turned and sized them up. "Working hard, are we, Jenkins?"

"Oh, sir, yes sir!" the orderly exclaimed, mocking the man with his own formality. The doctor looked away, satisfied with the answer.

"Who was that?" Ellen asked as soon as the man exited the elevator.

"Dr. Peter West, the director of the hospital."

"Is he—"

"A relative of the infamous Dr. Herbert West," Jenkins finished the thought for her. "And a world-class prick."

"I believe it," she murmured as he wheeled her out into the lobby. The news blared in the waiting room. The smoking ruin of Delta Delta Tau filled the screen.

Jenkins rolled her out to the front entrance. The orderly insisted on helping her out of the wheelchair. The attention made Ellen uneasy. She was afraid he would wait with her until her nonexistent ride showed up. But the moment she was out of his chair he sped off to his next assignment.

Even though she was relieved, his sudden departure hurt. All the other discharged patients had family and friends at their side. Their laps overflowed with flowers, balloons, and stuffed animals. All she had was a plastic bag with her wallet and keys.

She tucked her hands under her arms and headed toward the parking lot.

"Miss Logan," a voice called out. Ellen looked up to see Richard Pierce striding toward her.

Well, you wanted someone to meet you, she thought. *Be careful what you wish for.*

"Dr. Pierce. What a—" she chirped.

He seized her injured hand. The pain was so intense it almost drove Ellen to her knees.

"Spare me the pleasantries," he hissed. "You have something I want. Give it to me."

"I don't know what you're talking about," she gasped.

"Oh yes, you do. Where's the book?" He tightened his grip on her hand. Tears flooded Ellen's eyes. "Where's the book?"

"Hey. *Hey!*" Andrew Carter ran up to them and shoved Pierce. Hard. Pierce stumbled backward with a surprised yelp.

"A knight in shining armor. Really, Andy?" Pierce chortled. "That's playing against type."

"Don't you have anything better to do than scare schoolgirls, Dick?"

"She has something of mine. I want it back," he spat. As he stared at Carter another thought bloomed in his head. "Or maybe you have it. Maybe she gave it to you."

"What the hell are you talking about? You think she has something valuable? Look at her." Carter shot her a quick glance. "She's a bimbo."

"Excuse me?" Ellen blurted. Neither man heard her.

"You're grasping at straws. Like you always do," Carter continued with a coolness that made the other man seethe.

"You better watch yourself, boy," Pierce snarled.

"That's rich, coming from a man who's still on academic probation. By the way, how's that working out for you?"

Richard Pierce's face turned a deep shade of red. He spluttered and stormed off.

Ellen looked at the hand she held against her body. It felt like a claw. Slowly, reluctantly, she unfolded it. Spots of blood dotted the bandage.

Carter winced at the fresh wounds. "You should go back in and have that looked at."

"And spend another six hours in the hospital? No thanks." She looked at the dead-eyed people smoking outside the hospital entrance. "The doctor gave me a prescription for pain meds. And ointment for the burn. I'll take care of it myself."

"Burn?"

"Second degree." She tucked her hand back under her arm. She decided not to tell him about the tentacle marks. "Thanks for coming to my rescue."

"Wait. Where are you going?" he asked when she started to walk away.

Ellen frowned. "I told you. I'm going to the drugstore. To get my prescriptions filled."

"Let me give you a ride."

"It'll take a few minutes, miss. Do you want to wait?"

"Guess I don't have much choice." Ellen moved away from the counter, yielding her spot to the next person in line.

Ellen didn't expect Andrew Carter to stay while she filled her prescriptions. She assumed he would drop her off and move on to more important things. But he followed her into the brightly lit store and took a seat as she talked to the pharmacist. He checked email on his phone, his long legs spread out in front of him. His height impressed her. She was five feet five, average for a woman. He had at least half a foot on her.

She stepped over his legs and plopped into the plastic chair beside him.

"You know, you don't have to stay. It might be a while."

"I'm fine," he insisted.

She saw a flash of movement on his phone. He wasn't checking email. He was playing a game.

"Aren't you a busy man?"

"Excuse me?" he asked without looking up.

"Don't you have better things to do than wait with me?" she asked.

He gave up on the game and put his phone away. "Not really," he admitted as he stretched. "I'm tenured, so I don't have to worry about job security. I've taught the same classes so many times I could do it in my sleep. And then there's Joshua."

"I knew it. He told you to look after me."

"Joshua is making his homemade lasagna," he replied. "To celebrate your return."

"Oh, I see. Now I understand." She laughed—an outburst that startled the people around her. An old woman glared at her from the blood pressure machine. "And you think you're getting some?"

"You're planning to eat it all yourself?"

"I thought I might."

He looked her up and down. "A little thing like you?" He snorted. "You wouldn't make it through a second piece."

"Wanna bet?" she challenged him.

Even as she spoke, the words lost their sparkle. There was something about the way Carter was staring at her. The way he went along with her teasing.

He's too eager, she thought. *Way too eager.* A cold fog settled on Ellen.

"You have something to tell me, don't you? Something bad," she breathed as she slumped into her chair.

His genial expression vanished. "I've been trying to figure out how to tell you the whole way over here."

"Just say it."

"Joey Richards, the guy who gave you the book? The police found his body this morning. On the banks of the Miskatonic. He'd been tortured."

Ellen slapped her hand to her mouth and bent over. The tears came out in rough, choppy waves. *Don't do this, not now, not in front of him*, her rational mind pleaded.

Ellen couldn't stop. She couldn't hold it back anymore. *Dead, they're both dead. Stephanie. Joey. Joey tortured.* The thought that someone brutalized Joey . . .

"Miss? Are you all right?" the pharmacist called out from behind his glass wall.

"She just got some bad news," Carter assured him. His voice dropped to a low murmur. "I'm sorry. I know the two of you were close."

Her body jerked. "What?"

"There was a note in the book you gave me. I knew it was personal, but I thought there might be some clues," he started.

The three-way, she thought with horror. *Carter thinks I had sex with Joey and Stephanie.*

Ellen sat bolt upright. "That wasn't me. The person he went to the cabin with. I don't know who he was talking about, but it wasn't me."

"Your personal life is none of my business," he insisted.

"It wasn't me."

She fixed her eyes on the allergy medicine kept behind the counter. The *Breaking Bad* section, Joey once joked in a rare moment of wit.

She swiped at her tears, forcing herself to calm down. "It was that book, wasn't it? The book got him killed," she sniffed.

"I think it did," Carter finally replied.

"What is it?" she demanded. When he didn't answer, she rephrased the question. "Do you know what it is?"

Carter relented after a few moments of silence. "Not at first. The cover was hard to read, so we looked at it under ultraviolet light. The title is *De Vermis Mysterious*."

"Which means?"

"Mysteries of the worm."

"There's a shocker," Ellen made a grim joke, even as she shivered.

"Your friend had a very rare book. We don't know much about it. Very few people do. Some of the original is in Latin, but the rest was written in cipher."

"Like the Voynich manuscript?" she offered.

He looked at her, surprised. "Similar," he replied. "A few years ago they discovered a translation of *De Vermis* that was written in Enochian."

"Enochian?" Ellen echoed.

"It was a language invented in the fifteen hundreds that supposedly allowed people to communicate with angels," Carter continued. "When researchers found Enochian in the book they got really excited. They thought they found their Rosetta Stone. That they could translate the book using Enochian. They only managed to crack one section."

"What was that one section about?" she asked.

Carter said nothing.

"Did it have anything to do with the thing on the riverbank?"

They stared at each other for a long time—the silence broken only by the clack of pills going into bottles.

"Dr. Carter, what did you see?"

"Miss Logan, your prescription's ready," the pharmacist's assistant announced.

Ellen closed her eyes and cursed. She thought Carter would use the opportunity to escape. If she was in his position, confronted by a student who demanded answers, she would flee. He had probably told her too much already. But when she turned around, with her bag of drugs in her hand, he was still there. Ellen felt a rush of gratitude. It was then she decided to back off.

He saved you from Pierce. He gave you a ride, she thought. *Just leave him alone. Let him have his lasagna in peace.* Her stomach rumbled an enthusiastic response.

"Let's go eat," she announced as she walked by him.

Carter fell into place behind her. Ellen could sense his confusion. He was clearly used to people pushing, taking as much from him as they could.

He stopped her halfway down the seasonal aisle. This time of year it was Halloween. Witches and ghosts peered over his shoulder as if they were trying to listen.

"I'm going to tell you two things. That's it. Okay?"

"Okay," she agreed.

"The only reason— The only reason I'm still with you is that you let go."

"What?"

"We were on the riverbank. That thing was chasing you. I held out my hand. Do you remember?"

"Yes."

"It hit you as I grabbed onto you. You could have pulled me under, but you didn't. You let go."

Ellen frowned. "Pulled you under?"

"That thing opened a space and yanked you underground. Deep into the earth. For a few minutes, we couldn't . . ." he trailed off. "Then you popped up. Like a little gopher."

He stared at her as the shoppers moved around them.

"What was the second thing you were going to tell me?" she asked.

"You should be dead. You should be dead, and I have no idea why you're still here."

Chapter Ten

You should be dead. The words haunted her as Carter searched for a place to park. For some reason the streets around her house were packed. They had to settle on a spot a few blocks away. Ellen tried to focus, to figure out why things were so tight. *Was it Pledge Week? Homecoming? Parents' Weekend?*

Time suddenly seemed as slippery as ice. Ellen stared out the windshield. The night was dark, the streets poorly lit. *I could be anywhere*, she thought. *Any time.* She shifted in her seat.

"Ellen?"

She looked at Carter, surprised. It was the first time he spoke her name since . . . well, since ever.

"I'm sorry. It's been a long day," she said, responding to the concern in his voice. "No, it's been more than that. It's been a long, terrifying, epically shitty day." Her vision blurred. "This is the first time I've lost close friends," she croaked.

"Well, if you're going to stay at Miskatonic, you better get used to it."

She glanced at him. "How do you manage?"

"I don't have friends," he replied.

Ellen thought he was joking, but his expression was grim. "What about Connie Blake?"

"He's not my friend."

"What is he then?"

He fixed her with a stern look, one he used on students cheating on a test. Ellen slumped in her seat. "I'm sorry. I didn't mean to . . . I was only trying . . ." She stopped. *What exactly are you trying to do?*

Carter gave her a gentle shake. She lurched out of the stupor. "I'm sorry, Dr. Carter. The painkiller is making me feel a little . . ." Ellen circled her finger around her head.

Carter smiled into the dashboard. "Stop apologizing. And stop calling me Dr. Carter," he replied. "Carter is fine."

"Just Carter?"

"Just Carter," he said as he opened the driver-side door.

A blast of cold air hit Ellen when she stepped onto the street. The weather changed since she first arrived at the hospital. Summer was a distant memory. She wrapped her arms around her body, trying to fight the chill.

"You're cold," he announced.

When Carter took off his leather jacket, she backed away. "Oh no, I couldn't. I still smell like that thing."

"Smell?"

She offered him her arm. "I smell like smoke."

Carter looked at her suspiciously, as if he expected a trap. He bent down and sniffed the inside of her wrist.

"I don't smell anything."

"You're sure?"

"Yes," he assured her.

This time when he offered his jacket she accepted. She blushed as he helped her into it. The men in her life (even her boyfriends) treated her as an equal. And while she preferred it that way, sometimes she wished . . .

Carter interrupted her thoughts. "So you're the one Joshua left me for."

"I beg your pardon?"

"Joshua took off about ten years ago. Told me he had something important to attend to. I assume that was you."

"Probably," she said as they walked toward her house. "He showed up at the foster home around that time."

"Foster home?"

"I'm an orphan. Straight out of Charles Dickens."

"Or Harry Potter. Or Peter Pan. Or Tarzan . . ."

"A living, breathing trope." Ellen smiled, her face brightening. "Joshua blew into my life like a tornado. He marched into the foster home where I was staying, looked me right in the eye, and said he was my uncle. That's when my life really began."

"How old were you?"

"Ten," she said.

"Ten? You spent ten years in foster homes?"

"I'm not sure. I don't remember much before—"

Carter stopped dead in his tracks. He motioned for her to be quiet. Ellen looked up at the trees. They were still. After a few moments he shook his head and started walking again.

Ellen continued the conversation. "Did he tell you anything? About me?" she asked.

"No. He just said he had business to attend to," Carter replied. "I'm sure he was trying to spare my feelings. He's been like a father to me since I was fourteen. Maybe he thought I'd be jealous if I found out about you."

"But you were . . ." She paused to do some quick mental math. "You were in your twenties when he adopted me. An adult."

"You never stop needing your father, Ellen," he said softly.

"I'm sorry. I didn't mean to." She turned to look at him, but he was a couple of paces behind her, frozen in place. "Carter, what in God's name?"

"We're being followed."

Ellen glanced over his shoulder. All she saw was an old man shuffling toward them. "That guy? He's nothing to—" *Worry about.* The words died in her throat.

The man passed under a yellow streetlamp. He was younger than she thought. And naked. Two deep cuts crossed his chest, meeting in the middle.

A Y incision, she thought. *The kind coroners make.*

Ellen gasped. "Joey," she whispered. "Oh my God. It's Joey."

The thing stirred at the sound of the name.

"What's he doing?" Carter asked.

"Just standing there. Watching us."

"How far is it to your house?"

"I— I—"

Carter snapped his fingers in front of her face. "How— far— is— it?"

She pointed down the street. Away from Joey. "Three blocks." *Three long blocks,* she thought.

"Ellen."

"How?" she spluttered, asking the question that had been on her mind since the trees shivered on the riverbank. "How can it be? *How can any of this be?*"

Carter put his hands on her shoulders. "I'm going to tell you something, and you need to listen, okay?"

"Okay," she squeaked.

"That thing you're looking at is no longer your friend. Your friend is dead. That? That's an empty shell. A dried-out husk."

"A dangerous dried-out husk," she added. "We need to get back to the house. Behind the gates."

Carter looked at her, relieved. He didn't need to waste any more time explaining.

"We need to make a run for it. You lead the way, okay? On the count of three. Ready?" He waited long enough for her to nod, then screamed, "*Three!*"

Ellen jumped off her mark like an Olympic sprinter. The sudden motion startled the Joey creature. It roared, making a sound that would have paralyzed her if she wasn't already running. She glanced over her shoulder. Carter was right behind her, his face tight with fear.

She lifted her eyes to see where Joey was. "Concentrate. Concentrate!" Carter snarled.

His words snapped her back into focus. Ellen counted down the houses on her block.

355, 353, 351 . . .

Ellen skidded to a halt. *Be unlocked,* she thought as she wrestled with the latch. *Please, please, Joshua. I told you to unlock the gate.*

The gate yielded with an angry screech. Carter shoved her through the opening just as the Joey thing reached them. He dropped into a crouch and flipped the creature. It tumbled through the air, landing hard on a patch of broken glass.

Carter howled in delight as the thing struggled to get up. It squirmed on the ground, grinding glass deeper into Joey Richards's body. He advanced on it, fists clenched. Energized by his small victory.

Ellen grabbed Carter by the coat and yanked him inside. The thing roared, throwing itself against the iron gate just as she slammed it shut.

Ellen heard bones snap. The thing snarled and paced, an arm dangling uselessly from its body.

An image bloomed in her head. A man on a lonely country road, twirling an ax.

"You're not Joey. You— you—" Ellen stammered. "You were in my head. Trying to show me something. A sign. B—"

Carter clamped his hand over her mouth. "Not. Another. Word," he ordered her.

"Set it free. Set it free and it will spare you," the man rasped.

"Yeah. Sure, it will," Carter shot back.

The man nodded at Ellen. "It could have killed her. It could have killed her on the riverbank, and it didn't."

Joey's body twitched. The thing inside looked down at the naked body, at the damaged arm and carved-up chest.

It locked eyes with Ellen. Her mind flared.

"Weak," it rasped. "I've forgotten how weak flesh is." The corpse crumpled, landing on the ground with a sickening squelch.

Ellen turned away. *Dried-out husk, dried-out husk, a dried-out husk*, she chanted.

Not so dried out, another voice chirped.

Ellen's head spun. She felt like an astronaut spiraling out of control. Unsure which way was up. She dropped to her knees and threw up.

Carter stood by the gate, peering at the ground. *Keeping an eye on It.*

Bile rose in her throat. She kept it down this time. "Is it dead?" she croaked once she recovered. She tried not to look at the corpse.

"Dead enough." He fixed her with a stare. "We need to get rid of the body. In the river."

She bit down on her lip, drawing blood. "Uh-huh."

"Ellen?"

"Yeah?"

"I really need your help. You have to keep it together, okay?" She nodded.

"There's a blanket in the shed," she said once she found her voice. "We can use it to wrap up the body."

They said nothing as they went about their grim task. Carter protected her from the worst part of the job. He insisted she keep an eye out for the police while he piled what was left of her friend into the blanket. Ellen knew it was busywork. Routine patrols of her neighborhood were rare. Still, she appreciated the gesture.

When the time came to move the body, she was determined to pull her weight. Her injured hand throbbed as they dragged Joey Richards to the river. It pulsed so hard she almost threw up again.

They managed to get him to the wooden pier that jutted out into the river. A lone boat thumped against the dock as it rode the swift-moving waters of the Miskatonic. Ellen fished out the oars and handed one to Carter.

"If we can push him out a few feet, the current will carry him out to the ocean."

"Do you want to say anything before we let him go?" Carter asked.

Ellen wracked her brains for something appropriate. A sad little singsong slid off her tongue.

> *"Met Agwekote u yet?*
> *"U pa we mwa na resif?*
> *"Agwe tarayo, kote un ye?*
> *"U pa mwe su la me.*
> *"M'ge z'aviro na me mwe.*
> *"M'pa sa tune deye.*
> *"M'duva deja.*
> *"M'pa sa tune deye.*
> *"Met Agwe-woto kote u ye nu.*
> *"U pa we mwe na resif."*

Ellen fell silent as she watched the remains drift away.
"What did you just say?" Carter demanded.
"Huh?"

"Those words. Where did they come from?"

She shrugged. "I don't know."

"You . . .don't . . .know?" Carter's voice rose with each word. "Do you mean to tell me you have no idea what you just said?"

"No. Do you?" she asked, hoping he could translate for her.

Carter was no mood to be an academic. "Have you lost your mind? Have you lost your fucking mind? Didn't you see what happens to people who chant spells they don't understand?"

"It's not a spell. And it's not evil," she insisted.

"How do you know?"

"I just know."

"Oh, it's a psychic thing, is it?" he snapped. "Don't think your powers will protect you. The graveyards are full of people like you."

People like you. The words seared into Ellen's brain. She was used to prejudice from people on the outside. But to hear them from Andrew Carter, from the man who embodied everything Miskatonic University was . . . It made her mad.

Not mad. Furious.

"We also burn well, Carter. Don't forget that."

For a moment all he did was stare. Something dark bloomed in his eyes, a weed wedged deep. "Oh, fuck you. Don't make this into a political thing," Carter growled.

Indignation raced through her body like wildfire. "No, fuck you! It is a political thing. It's a political thing when you write off an entire group of people. How can you say such a thing? People look up to you. What you say influences the way they feel. The way they treat me."

"That's it! We're done!" he erupted. "Do you hear me? Done!"

Her anger retreated as quickly as it came. Ellen watched Andrew Carter storm off. She fought the urge to run after him. She knew he could destroy her—all it would take was a bad grade or a word in someone's ear to end her college career. But she refused to apologize to him just because he was powerful. If that meant ruining her chances to graduate, so be it.

Besides, she thought as she drifted to the house, *you have other options. You could tell fortunes. Run a New Age store like Norm's. Dress like a witch and be the lead singer of a rock band.*

The thought of being the next Stevie Nicks kept her together long enough to reach the house. The moment she entered the kitchen and saw Joshua pulling the homecoming lasagna out of the oven, her brave façade crumbled.

"I screwed up, Joshua. I really screwed up."

<hr>

"You know, I heard he's a direct descendant of Jack de M . . . M . . . Moulin. A great—great-however-many-times— grandson or something."

Jacques de Molay, you moron, Ellen thought as she waited outside Andrew Carter's office. *And it's hard to be a great-however-many-times grandson when the guy didn't have any children.*

Ellen pressed her fingers into her eyes. She was jittery. She needed to apologize to Carter and had no idea how she was going to do it. Two days had passed since their fight. She knew she had to act quickly before his anger had a chance to harden. Ellen didn't know why she cared. She should have been thinking about other things—Joey, or the creature, or Richard Pierce, the malevolent professor who was after her.

Ellen hoped the long line of admirers would buy her some time, give her the chance to figure out what to say. Carter mowed through them with the same efficiency as the first time she visited. Before she knew it she was in front of him, an unprepared actor thrust onto the stage.

"Umm, hi," she greeted him in a shaky voice.

Carter didn't look up. He flipped through a large book spread out on his desk. Ellen wondered whether it was the one she gave him. She edged closer to get a better look. He slammed the book shut.

"What do you want?" he demanded.

At that moment Ellen knew Carter had already written her off. *Just say you're sorry and get out of here*, a voice whispered in her head.

"I wanted to return this." She offered him the leather jacket draped over her arm. When he didn't respond, she hung it on a nearby chair. "You might want to get it dry cleaned."

"Do you still think you smell like smoke?" he replied.

Ellen couldn't tell if he was being serious or sarcastic. She gave him the benefit of the doubt. "I don't know."

"You don't know?"

"I can't tell. I smell smoke all the time," she admitted as she pulled out a carefully wrapped loaf pan. She set it on the edge of his desk.

"What's that?"

"Joshua's lasagna. Bake it at three hundred fifty for about twenty minutes."

Carter rolled his eyes. Just as he was about to say something, she cut him off.

"Look, I want to apologize. I went off on you, and I'm sorry. I just . . . I flipped. I held you responsible for something that—"

"Something that what?"

Ellen wanted to tell him about the mob that attacked her when she was a child. He might understand. He might even feel sorry for her. She resisted the urge.

"Something that has nothing to do with you."

"Playing the mystery card. Nice. I haven't seen that one in a long time." Carter leaned back in his chair. He reminded Ellen of a petty bureaucrat. The kind you found in corrupt countries.

"Ruler of your own little kingdom," she murmured.

"What did you say?"

Ellen couldn't hold her tongue. "You're a real prick, you know that?"

He gave her a bored, dead-eyed look. "It has been brought to my attention, yes. Are we done?"

"Yeah. I think we are." *You screwed up again*, Ellen thought as she stormed out of his office.

This time, she didn't care.

Deep. Down. Dark.

????-??-1945

I ran. I fled across countries. Across continents. Across the seething gray fury of the Atlantic. I was always on high alert. Waiting for the inevitable hand to land on my shoulder. To drag me back to the camp.

I reached America just as it entered the war. I took a job at a munitions factory. Ironically, it was the same work I did for the Nazis. It didn't bother me. It kept me busy. Idle hands and all that.

I no longer believed what I saw that night. My mother's spirit sucked into a whistle . . . Ridiculous! A fever dream and nothing more. But I kept the whistle, even though I didn't want to. Deep down I knew it was true.

The thing she summoned was in it. With her. Two genies in a bottle. It was trapped. And furious. I felt its rage. Sometimes, at night, the whistle thrummed with strange energy, making it impossible to sleep. I needed to free it. But where on earth could I safely do that? I saw the way it tore apart the camp.

Just as I was about to hike deep into the woods and take my chances, the factory foreman made an announcement. Business was expanding. They needed to manufacture parts for the things they produced. To do that they needed raw material. Iron pyrite. And there was a place not too far away, a mine deep in the hills of Massachusetts that needed more workers . . .

My hand shot up before he could ask for volunteers.

Chapter Eleven

"Although many artists provided us with brief glimpses of the underworld, Dante was the first to make hell political."

A print by Gustave Dore loomed over Carter. A grim-faced man stood in the twilight of a thick forest. A huge lion blocked his path. Ellen immediately recognized the image. When she lived in Florence, Italy, the school she attended spent a lot of time on Dante. The students translated his poetry, analyzed the art he inspired, and learned about his years as a politician. By the time Ellen left the school she was sick of him. As she stared at him now, cowering before the mighty creature that threatened him, Ellen felt a twinge of sympathy. She remembered things about Dante she had forgotten—how he was an orphan like her, the victim of a fierce civil war, a man who died alone and in exile.

"Dude, you wouldn't believe how drunk I got Saturday night," a man boasted, severing her connection with the poet of the underworld.

Ellen looked at the men sitting next to her. She considered saying something, but there was no point. She was in their world now—the balcony. Andrew Carter was a distant, almost otherworldly, presence.

Unlike Dante, her exile was self-imposed. In the days following her botched apology she avoided Carter. Even though Joshua insisted Andrew Carter wasn't the kind of man to bear a grudge, Ellen was skeptical. Joshua hadn't seen Carter in ten years. How did he know nothing had changed?

The conversation they had echoed in her head. *You're the one Joshua left me for.* He passed it off as a joke, but Ellen wondered. *Does he resent me? Does he hate the fact I exist?*

She didn't want to find out, so she retreated to the very edge of the class. Carter didn't notice. The moment she left her seat in the front row, another eager young student took her place.

"The monsters Dante encountered in the Inferno are twisted creatures, a mix of man and Other. An expression of what we now call body horror."

The image shifted to a more disturbing scene—another brambly forest where the souls of the damned were imprisoned in the trunks of twisted trees. The men struggled to free themselves, even as their limbs turned to wood.

Men trapped . . . struggling to break free.

Something stirred inside her. It raced up her stomach, wedging in the back of her throat. Ellen gagged. She leapt to her feet, stumbling over people as she ran for the exit. The ripple reached the front of the class.

"Is everything alright up there?" Carter called out.

"It's nothing, Dr. Carter," one of the frat boys shouted, delighted to take the spotlight. "It's just that hell is hard for some of us to take on a Monday morning."

The roar of laughter followed Ellen into the bathroom. She locked herself in a stall and hunched over the toilet. She threw up so hard she saw stars. And that image . . . she kept seeing that image.

Men imprisoned in the earth, limbs twisted, reaching out for help.

"Those men," she whispered. "Those poor, poor men."

A voice hissed in response. *They knew what they were doing. They had it coming.*

The shrill voice of a classmate jolted Ellen out of her stupor. "Can you believe someone got sick over those old pictures? I mean, God, get a grip."

She didn't remember passing out on the cold stone floor. She moved slowly to her feet, clutching her head. Something was wrong, deeply wrong, but going to the hospital wasn't an option. They had no clue how to help her. And the last thing she needed was another trip to Herbert West Memorial. If she went back, she wasn't coming out. They would send her to the psych ward for an observation that might never end.

Ellen waited for the between-class rush to end before she ventured to the sinks. As she splashed cold water on her face she stared at herself in the mirror. The face that gazed back at her was paler than usual. Her eyes were slightly dilated. Except for those slight surface changes, there was nothing to suggest her inner turmoil. No sign of the flickering inside her. Or the nightmare tattooed on her mind.

Tattooed, she thought with a jolt. *Does that mean it's permanent?*

"Don't think about it," she whispered to her reflection. "Just don't think about it."

Ellen pushed her way through a lab and two more classes, fueled by a potent blend of caffeine and fear. By the late afternoon her exhaustion caught up with her. She needed to crash. Going home wasn't an option. Her uncle Joshua was entertaining a client. As soon as she walked in Joshua would expect her to entertain them.

There was only one place left to go.

Ellen felt for the key hidden in the lining of her denim jacket. After casting a nervous glance around the commons, she changed direction. Her destination was a run-down house a few blocks off the town square. The home once belonged to a politician whose promising career ended in scandal and disgrace. The man killed himself a short time later. The property bounced around for years until the present owner converted it into a mini-dorm. Eight students lived there, sharing a communal kitchen and bathrooms.

The house was quiet when she arrived. The only sound that greeted her was muffled music coming from the basement. She crept down the hall and listened at the stairs.

The thumping beat of electronica meant only one thing. Martha Pickman was hard at work on one of her paintings. Ellen smiled, vowing to drop in on her friend before she left.

Her room was at the very top, in the sloped attic of the house. It had been a few weeks since she'd been there. She could tell by the thin layer of dust that no one had disturbed her lair. Not that anyone would. No one knew about the room. Not even Joshua. And the people who lived in the house were afraid of the space. It was where the ghost of Charles Montgomery lived. There were all the classic signs—cold spots, misplaced items, sheets torn off beds. But when the landlord offered to rent it to her furnished and at a ridiculously low rate, Ellen didn't hesitate.

Ghosts didn't scare her. They were a regular part of her life. A welcome presence, even.

"Hello, Charlie," Ellen greeted the portrait on the wall as she sat on the bed.

Charles Montgomery was a handsome, intense-looking man, a young Daniel Day-Lewis. Ellen experienced a wall of hostility when she first moved in. Then she discovered his picture. The moment she hung it on the wall the mood shifted. He became friendlier. Sometimes when she studied he would stand behind her. She would feel a puff of breath on her neck, fingers running down her back.

Once, after a party on New Year's Eve, she stripped off her clothes and offered him her body. Even though she was drunk, she remembered the bed groaning beneath her. A cold presence entered her, whipping her into a frenzy that defied description. Her hand drifted to her breast as she remembered the vague pleasures of that evening.

She flashed the portrait a mischievous smile. "Not now, Charlie. I need to concentrate."

Ellen looked at the whiteboard propped up on her desk. For the past two years she spent her spare time reconstructing the Logan family tree. Her eyes wandered across the product of her research. *Another dense forest*, she thought as she traced the branches of Joshua Logan's immediate (and not so immediate) family.

Ellen searched for something, anything that would challenge what she already knew. There was no sign of her missing family. All of Joshua Logan's brothers and sisters, both dead and alive, were accounted for. At first she thought she overlooked someone. But when she went back to the genealogical archives to check the connections, it confirmed her research was accurate.

For some reason her family had been pruned from the Logan family tree. The question that haunted her was why.

She tried to pry information from Joshua. In the ten years she had been with him he told her only three things. She was born in New Orleans. Her real name was Jessica, not Ellen. And her mother loved Duke Ellington. This last bit of information proved to be the most valuable. When she put "Take the A Train" on her headphones, she experienced a potent tug of memory. For a fleeting moment she heard a familiar voice, a flash of a smile. The sweetness of the memory lingered like perfume. Whenever Ellen felt lost or vulnerable she would escape to her room and play Duke Ellington.

There were no memories for her that blustery autumn afternoon. She collapsed on the bed and fell into a deep, oblivious sleep.

Ellen woke a few hours later, lulled out of the darkness by a strange sound. She sat bolt upright, squinting into the gloom. "Charlie? You there?" she whispered, even though she knew it wasn't him.

Probably seeing other women, she thought with a grin. Her smile was cut short by the sound that woke her from her sleep. Light accompanied it this time. Ellen stared at the blinking object for a long time before she recognized her cell phone.

"Ellen, where the hell are you? You're late!" a voice barked when she answered the call.

"Late?" she echoed. She was just about to ask the man who he was when everything came rushing back. "Oh my God, Uncle Joshua, I'm so sorry. I, um . . . I must have fallen asleep in the library."

"Well, hurry home. Dinner is almost ready, and I don't want to keep our guest waiting."

Guest? Was I supposed to have dinner with his client? Joshua didn't mention anything about it. She was sure she would have remembered if he told her about a dinner date. *Or maybe not,* she thought. *Let's face it. If you're passing out in bathrooms, the odds of forgetting a dinner date are pretty high.*

Ellen grabbed her backpack and vaulted down the stairs.

Chapter Twelve

"Honey, we're in the dining room," Joshua announced as she came through the front door.

Ellen dropped her backpack in the hall and sighed. She was in no mood to entertain.

"I'll be right there. Just let me wash up."

She ducked into the guest bathroom and put on her mask. She brushed her hair, straightened her clothes, splashed water on her face. But there was no hiding the fact that she raced across the length of Arkham. In a last-ditch effort to look normal, she tried removing her sunglasses. Even the mellow glow of the bathroom lights made her eyes burn. She put them back on, hoping that Joshua would let the breach of etiquette slide.

Her uncle sat at the head of the table, waiting for her like a Middle Eastern sultan. Ellen felt a twinge of anger as she walked into the room. If there was one thing that bothered her about Joshua, it was his insistence on maintaining old-world customs. Being a woman at Miskatonic was hard enough. She was used to dealing with discrimination at school, but to come home and see it in the eyes of her uncle . . .

Ellen pushed away the thought. *He rescued you when no one else cared. He gave you a place to stay. Show some loyalty.*

She bent down and kissed him on the cheek. "I'm sorry I'm late. Those leather chairs in the library should be outlawed."

Joshua's dinner guest chuckled. When Ellen turned to greet him, she froze.

Andrew Carter sat at the end of the table.

Ellen straightened, suddenly feeling out of place in her own home. Carter's words rang in her head. *The graveyards are full of people like you. People like you.* The words made her skin crawl.

Her eyes dropped to the floor. "Hello, Dr. Carter."

"Miss Logan." His voice was soft and civil, without the slightest hint of anger. It was hard to believe he was the same man who lashed out at her.

Her uncle motioned toward the chair between them. Ellen took her place at the table. She took her time smoothing out her dinner napkin.

"Ellen?"

"Yes?" She fidgeted, feeling both men staring at her.

"Please take off your sunglasses."

"Do you mind if I keep them on tonight? I have a bad headache."

"Tell you what, sweetheart—I'll turn off the chandelier. We can dine by candlelight." Joshua rolled back in his wheelchair and switched off the lights.

Ellen waited until the room was dark before she slipped off her sunglasses. The flickering candles still bothered her, but she could live with the pain.

All she wanted to do was eat dinner in peace, but Joshua insisted on including her in the conversation. He encouraged her to tell Carter about their travels around the world. The places they stayed, the people they met. Ellen respected her uncle's wishes, but it made her feel like a performing animal. She got the feeling Joshua wanted to prove something to Carter.

She had no idea what.

Carter behaved oddly as well. Several times during dinner she caught him staring at her intently. Whenever she did, his eyes darted away. He offered no explanation. No apologies for his bold gaze. Ellen was relieved when dinner finally ended.

As soon as the two men retired to Joshua's study, Ellen stepped outside for some much-needed air. She drifted to the river's edge. After everything that happened—the terrifying contact with the monster, the dumping of her friend's undead body—she should have hated the river's cold, silver glint. But she felt connected to the Miskatonic. She felt a bond with all rivers, an attraction so deep she knew it was part of her past. No matter where she was in the world, she sought out rivers, even if they were only feeble brown trickles.

The Miskatonic was no feeble brown trickle. As she sat at the picnic table she remembered the one and only time she ventured into the water. The river's pull impressed her. And it was cold. Ellen had never swum in a river as bone-chilling as the Miskatonic.

She thought about the fantastic stories—that the Miskatonic was cold because it was a tributary of the Styx, the mythical river that ran through the underworld. Like most urban legends, the story had a fundamental flaw. If the

Miskatonic sprang from a river that made people immortal, no one should die if they swam in it. But people did. Every year the Miskatonic claimed a fresh batch of souls.

"Hey," a voice greeted her.

Carter stepped out of the darkness. He carried two mugs of steaming liquid. He sat beside her and slid a mug across the table.

"What's that?" she asked.

"It's the tea my aunt used to make when I had migraines," Carter replied.

"*You* made this?"

He raised his eyebrow. "You don't have to sound so surprised. I am capable of functioning in the real world."

"I didn't— it's just— I thought— you know—" she spluttered before she gave up. "Thank you."

"You're welcome."

He watched as she took the first sip.

There was no medicinal taste, none of the bitterness she expected in an herbal remedy. The tea was creamy and sweet, with a faint aroma of cherries. She took another sip.

"They found Joey Richard's body. It washed up on the riverbank again," she announced. There were no tears this time.

"Did it?"

"The police are blaming the frat. Said they stole his corpse from the hospital as part of a sick prank."

"That's what they usually say," Carter sighed as he scanned the dark waters. "You've been skipping class."

"I've been up in the balcony," Ellen corrected him.

He gave her a sharp look. "Hiding from me?"

"Yes."

"Why?"

"I called you a prick. I figured I'd better lay low for a while."

He gave her a tight little smile. "If I flunked everyone who called me a prick . . ." The playful expression evaporated. "Joshua told me what happened. About almost being beaten to death because you were psychic. I wouldn't have said anything if I'd known."

"You just would have thought it." Ellen regretted the words the moment they spilled out of her mouth. She grabbed his hand and squeezed. Carter's fingers twitched, curling into his palm. "I'm sorry. I didn't mean it," she blurted. "I have . . . I have a lot of pent-up anger. What do they call it? Sublimated rage."

"They?"

"Therapists," she said as she released his hand. Even the word made her tired. "It probably won't surprise you to hear that I've seen a lot of psychiatrists."

"Most people at Miskatonic have seen psychiatrists."

"Have you?"

"Yes," he admitted after a long pause. "That fact's not for public consumption, okay?"

"Of course," she agreed. It touched her that he revealed something so personal.

"Have you ever tried to read me?" he asked.

"You mean, psychically? God, no."

"You think it would be bad?"

She yawned, feeling a wave of drowsiness. The nap in her attic room had done little to refresh her.

"It's more of an ethical thing. I don't read people without their permission. Unless I'm in grave danger or something."

"You're better than most of the psychics I know. Even if you do work at Mote It Be."

"Hey. A girl has to eat."

He smiled and put his arm around her. Ellen tensed. The gesture seemed odd after his reaction to her touch.

"What are you doing?" she asked.

"Putting my arm around you."

"Why?"

"Because I don't want you to bang your head."

Another wave of drowsiness hit her, this one much stronger than the last. She stared into his light-blue eyes. They suddenly seemed as cold as the Miskatonic.

"*You bastard.* The tea. You spiked the tea."

"I'm sorry, Ellen. Truly I am," he murmured as he lowered her onto the picnic bench.

Ellen tried to fight the approaching darkness. The moment her head touched the wood, she blacked out.

Chapter Thirteen

Ellen woke up in the middle of a road. Warm asphalt pressed into her cheek. It held the heat of a day that had long since passed. She sat up, waiting for a wave of panic to pass. There was no need to hurry. She was in the middle of nowhere, dumped on a lonely country road. The only things moving on the blacktop were dead leaves.

Their dried husks skittered across the road. Ellen watched them dance as she weighed her options.

"Think, girl, think," she said. Hearing her voice kept the darkness at bay. "Carter slipped something in my drink; I passed out. He put me in a car and dumped me here. How long would that take? An hour? Two hours? How long could I be gone without Joshua noticing?"

Ellen lapsed into a gloomy silence. If Joshua was on the phone doing business, Carter could take her halfway around the world before her uncle realized she was gone.

Another wave of panic hit. *I'm lost.*

Her rational voice took over. *Then look around. Try to figure out where you are.*

Ellen wobbled to her feet. Whatever Carter slipped into her drink still coursed through her veins. She had a hard time focusing on the landscape. Slowly, with great effort, the world sharpened. A narrow path branched off the road and curved into a forest. Behind her, barely visible in the fold of a valley, she saw the distant twinkle of lights.

"A town," she gasped.

She glanced at her watch. Eleven o'clock. People were watching the news, brushing their teeth, getting ready for bed. If she hurried she might be able to reach them before they fell asleep.

The path forward was clear, but every time Ellen headed toward the town she drifted deeper into the mountains. Her body refused to change direction. Up and up she went, drifting along the mountain path like a lost spirit. As the forest closed in on her she thought about Dante. His poetry followed her, falling into rhythm with her feet.

> *I found myself within a forest dark,*
> *For the straightforward path had been lost,*
> *So bitter it is, death is little more.*

Death.

The word stopped her in her tracks. She hiked for a long time, but she wasn't thirsty or hungry. She didn't feel fatigued. She felt . . . what exactly did she feel?

She raised her hand and punched herself hard in the stomach. Nothing. No pain, not the slightest hint of discomfort.

"Am I dead?" she wondered aloud.

The dense forest swallowed her question.

Ellen tried to remember the beginning of her journey. When she turned to start her journey, did she see her body lying in the road? Everything seemed vague. *She* seemed vague. A shadow.

She crumpled to the ground and cried out, "Oh my God, I'm dead. I'm dead. I'm dead. I'm dead."

"Well. You certainly know how to make an entrance."

A man in long crimson robes loomed above her. He wore a creepy plague mask—with a beak almost eight inches long. Most of it concealed his face, but she could see his eyes. They glowed with kindness.

He wasn't the cold miner, twirling his axe. Demanding that she see.

"Who are you supposed to be?" she asked the new arrival. "Dante?"

"Dante? You think I look like . . ." The man looked down at his garb and laughed. "I guess I do."

"Who are you?"

"It's not important," he insisted. "Not yet."

He headed deeper into the woods. Ellen followed.

"Am I dead? Is this a dream?" she asked.

The man turned and fixed her with sparkling eyes. A vision filled her head. She saw her body tied to a bed, with shadows looming over her.

"W-what? W-what's happening?" she spluttered.

The man lay a hand on her arm. "Don't worry. You're perfectly safe."

Doesn't look like it to me, she thought.

The man tilted his head. "They are taking care of your body. Your spirit is with me. In the Dreamlands."

She stopped in her tracks. "The Dreamlands? Lovecraft's Dreamlands?" she blurted. "The place with all the terrible monsters?"

The man stiffened. "That's only part of this world."

"This doesn't make sense," she murmured. "None of this makes sense."

The strange man chuckled. "My dear, why does it need to?"

He led her to a clearing at the top of a hill. In the middle of dead yellow grass was an opening in the earth—a hole ringed by a small circle of stones. At first Ellen thought it was the remains of a well. As she moved closer she saw mist rising from its depths. She thought of the Oracle of Delphi, where people went into a mystical trance by breathing vapors from the earth.

She inched closer.

The vision returned, of her bound to the bed. Chanting filtered up from the depths. The ghostly words tugged at her, luring her closer to the edge. The man in the plague mask appeared beside her.

"I don't understand. I don't understand at all," she sighed.

He put his hand on her shoulder. "Very few people do their first time, but you will. In time you will," he reassured her. "The only way out is through. Always remember that."

The man's hand tightened, and he pushed her into the well. Ellen tumbled into the abyss. Her head spun as it hit cold stone; her hands fluttered in front of her like startled birds. Her fingers clawed at the slimy walls, searching for something, anything to stop her fall.

The man gazed down at her. His words fell with her. "You will understand, my dear. In time, you will understand."

She fell and fell and fell. She fell for so long that distance ceased to have meaning.

Ellen slowly relaxed. She let her body yield to the pull of gravity. She even managed to drift off as she plummeted to certain death. She dreamt of the hell that awaited her. She tried to prepare herself for it, for that horrible moment when she finally hit bottom.

I wish I could stop this.

I wish there was a way out.

Her body jerked. It felt like someone was reaching into her. Pulling out her insides.

She looked down and saw a hook attached to a rope that was unspooling from her body.

She groaned. Now she really wished she were dead.

"Get it out. Oh God, get it out," she wailed, her voice splintering, her terror bouncing off the walls.

The rope wedged in her guts tightened. It pulled at her insides, threatening to yank her organs out. She curled into a tight ball and tried to grab onto the rope, to keep herself from unspooling.

Her body refused to move.

The chanting grew louder. It was getting closer. Growing in intensity. Crawling across her body.

"Somebody help me!" she screamed. *"Please, please, help me."*

"*WAKE UP!*" a voice thundered.

Her entire body arched, lifting toward the sound of the voice. She knew she had to move, to make one final effort before—

Ellen woke up drenched in sweat. She was back home, in her room. Her arms and legs were tied to the bedposts. Andrew Carter lay beside her, panting.

Cold terror seeped through her body. *Oh my God, he slipped a drug into my drink. He slipped me a drug and raped me in my own bed.*

But when Ellen looked around, the explanation didn't make sense. They were both fully clothed. She wasn't in her bed. She was in Joshua's room. And her uncle was with them. Hovering on the other side of the bed, he tapped out a nervous beat on the arm of his wheelchair.

"What happened?" she croaked.

Carter slowly rose from the bed, staring at her with dazed eyes. "You remember when I told you I had no idea why you were still alive?" he said, his voice low and husky.

"Yes."

"Well, now I know."

"What do you mean?"

"You were possessed," Joshua replied as he edged closer.

"How did you know about—"

"Carter told me what happened. How your behavior started to change: you were mumbling about smoke, refusing to look him in the eye—"

Ellen groaned. She wanted to hide her face in her hands, but they were still bound to the bedposts.

"You invited him to dinner to watch me. Why didn't you just ask?" she demanded.

"Why didn't we ask what? If you were okay?" Carter snorted. "We couldn't."

"Why not?"

"Because the thing inside you would have known. It might have burrowed deeper into you. And I had a hard enough time digging it out as it was."

Digging it out? Ellen glanced at the bedside table, half expecting to see her insides piled there.

"It wasn't physical," Carter told her. "Although you might feel like I tore your guts out."

Joshua backed away from the bed. His face was as pale and sweaty as Carter's. "I'm going to get you something to drink, Ellen. A nice cup of tea," he said in a quiet voice.

"Oh, shit. Joshua, I didn't—" Carter rose from the bed, but the old man was already gone.

He plopped down with a sigh and reached for the straps that bound her to the bed. "I'm going to free you. Don't hit me anymore, okay?"

"I hit you?"

He showed her the red welts on his arms.

Mortification shot through Ellen. "Oh my God, Carter. I'm sorry. I'm so, so sorry."

He shrugged off her concern. "It's my own fault. I haven't performed this ritual in a while. I should have tied you up first."

Carter loosened the knots with an ease that surprised her. *He's done this before*, she thought. *Many, many times.*

He freed her arms and turned his attention to her feet. Ellen propped herself on her elbows, watching him untie her. A warm flush coursed through her, surging between her legs.

Crush.

The word, like the sensation, struck like a bolt out of the blue.

Oh God, do I have crush on Andrew Carter?

"You know, I saw Dante. Or someone dressed like Dante," she blurted, trying to retreat from the thought. The feeling that . . .

"Did you?" he said without looking up.

"He wore a long crimson robe and had a plague mask on, but I could tell it was him." She recited some of his poem. "*Nel mezzo del cammin di nostra vita mi ritrovai per una selva oscura, Tant e amara che pocp e piu morte.*"

"I cannot well repeat how there I entered. So full was I of slumber at the moment," Carter translated.

"Pretty apt, huh?"

"A little too apt," he said as he helped her sit up.

For the first time Ellen noticed the dark circles under his eyes. She rubbed her wrists and took a deep breath. "I owe you an apology, Dr. Carter. You were right. I shouldn't have said those words that night on the river. Everything started happening after that."

Carter studied her for a long time before he spoke. "It was a coincidence. You did nothing wrong."

"What?"

"The words weren't a spell." He pulled out a three-by-five card. "I wrote down what you said."

"You remembered it?"

"I have a photographic memory. Part of what makes me the walking freak show I am." The blast of self-loathing stunned her. "A colleague of mine in African Studies recognized it," he continued. "He translated it for me. It's a prayer to Agwe, the god of the sea."

The moment Ellen looked at the words, she felt a rush of recognition. An image floated up from the depths, so clear it took her breath away. Of her as a child, out in a garden, squishing mud between her toes. And a woman at the kitchen window, singing as she washed the dishes. Her reedy voice filled the space between them.

> *Maître Agwe, where are you?*
> *Don't you see I'm on the reef?*
> *Master Agwe, where are you?*
> *Don't you see I'm on the reef?*
> *Don't you see I'm on the sea?*
> *I've a rudder in my hand.*
> *I can't go back.*
> *I'm already moving forward.*
> *I can't turn back.*

Dazzled by the new vision, Ellen didn't hear Carter at first. "Hmm?"

"I said do you recognize it?"

She nodded and clutched the card to her chest, her eyes wet with tears. "God, I could hug you. I could really, really hug you."

"Well, don't. You smell like a mule," he shot back.

Ellen burst into laughter. It felt good. Like bubbly champagne. "You really need to work on your bedside manner, doctor."

Joshua rolled back into the room, bearing a tray with a teapot and some mugs. Ellen quickly stuffed the card under her shirt. Carter scowled at her sleight of hand.

"Care to join us, Andrew?" Joshua asked.

Carter moved off the bed. "I can't. I have an early flight tomorrow. A conference on death cults in Chicago."

Ellen felt a stab of disappointment. She didn't want him to go. He turned back to her. "May I have a word with you, please?" he asked.

"Of course."

Carter took Ellen's arm and helped her to her feet.

"Do you think that's wise? She only just, um . . . woken up . . ." Joshua's voice trailed off, stuck between concern and suspicion.

"Don't worry, old man. I'll take good care of her," Carter assured him.

He said nothing until they reached the hall.

"What's going on?" he demanded.

"What do you mean?"

"You hid that card pretty damn quickly."

"I just didn't want him to see it. Joshua doesn't like it when I find out things about my past," she explained.

"What are you talking about?"

"The poem you gave me. About Master Agwe and the sea. For a moment, for one brief moment, I saw a place. A dock on a river. Maybe the place I was born. Where my family came from."

"And Joshua doesn't want you to know about your family?"

"It sounds bad when you say it."

Carter studied the door to Joshua's bedroom. "It *is* bad." His stare was intense. Laser-like. "Are you safe here? With him?" he demanded.

"What?"

"Are you safe?"

"Yes, I am," she replied without hesitation. Still, the look, Carter's uncertainty, frightened her. *Does he know something about Joshua?* she wondered.

He slung his leather bag over his shoulder. "Stay out of trouble until I get back, okay?"

"I can't make any promises," she replied.

She hated the words the moment she said them. They were too light. Not the way she wanted to end the conversation.

"Dr. Carter?"

"Just Carter."

"Thank you for what you've done. Truly. I'm grateful."

"Sure," he shrugged, brushing off her words. He suddenly looked shy. Boyish. "Say goodbye to Joshua for me."

"What was that all about?" Joshua asked when she returned.

She sat down on the bed and watched her uncle pour tea.

"Carter chewed me out for not being more careful. He didn't want to do it in front of you."

She picked up her mug, taking a deep breath of the steamy liquid. She missed the smell of cherries.

"You're lucky."

"What do you mean?"

"He only chews out the people he cares about."

Cares about? Ellen pushed away the thought. *Not there. We can go a lot of places, but we are* not *going there.*

Deep. Down. Dark.
????-??-1945

The mine they sent us to was a very bad place.
A place where negative energy gathered. I saw it
in the faces of the men we worked with. Miners
are superstitious people. They are familiar with the
darkness. Attuned to it. This felt different. Their
eyes darted to the necklace that hung from my
neck. They asked pointed questions. Wondering if
it was connected to the strange creature they saw
in their dreams.

What else could I do?
They knew.

I told them everything. Shared my secrets. They
were quiet for a very long time. Then one of them
finally spoke. He suggested we could "harness" the
creature, get it to help us in the mine.

Like it was nothing more than a pack animal.

All for the "good" of the war effort.

I laughed in his face.

You want to summon this thing just to get out
of work?

No one smiled.

I knew at that moment that these men were doomed, as doomed as my mother the day she laid eyes on that goddamn book.

But I was outnumbered. And tired. Sick of the shadows that ruled my life.

I went along with them.

I led the men to their doom.

Chapter Fourteen

It took time for Ellen to recover. She didn't realize how much the creature changed her until it was gone. The thing did no permanent damage, but the strain of hosting it took its toll. Every muscle in her body ached. Then there was the depression, the deep sense of loneliness that plagued her. She missed the creature. Sure, it threatened her. It flooded her mind with nightmarish images of death and destruction. But she sensed no malice. Just frustration. It tried to communicate with her the only way it knew how—in dreams. And she didn't understand. No human could.

We moved to speech, she thought on her first day back to class. *When we moved to speech, we left so much behind.*

The occupation (her uncle refused to call it possession) had physical side effects as well. She caught herself leaning forward to compensate for the weight of a presence that was no longer there. She stumbled on sidewalks. She fell into some hedges on the way to work. Her room was littered with ruined pens, torn books, anything that required manual dexterity. What frightened her the most were her eyes. The creature was gone, but a strange afterglow remained. At first she thought it was her imagination. Then she noticed that other people avoided her eyes. They kept their eyes fixed on the ground when they talked to her.

Ellen's sense of isolation deepened.

She found herself longing for the company of the monster. She wanted to understand the thing, and the dreams that haunted her. She considered going to Andrew Carter. He was with her that night on the riverbank. He expelled the thing from her body.

Ellen didn't want to bother him.

Andrew Carter saved her life.

He had already done enough.

Besides, this was *her* investigation.

These were *her* friends.

She felt a fierce obligation to find out what happened.

On her own.

In the end there was only one solution.

A creature + psychic communication = the Eibon Institute.

She had to find Connie Blake.

Finding him was a challenge. He gave her his business card when they first met, but there was nothing on the card except the name of the institute and a catchy logo. Ellen assumed it was some sort of test, that to be considered she had to prove her psychic abilities by tracking them down. She resented having to perform such a cheap parlor trick. She dropped by the linguistics department, where Connie Blake supposedly worked. He wasn't there. He didn't have an office or a mailbox. He wasn't listed in the class schedules or the university catalog. He wasn't even on the department website.

She turned her attention to the Eibon Institute. No luck there. It was as shadowy as Connie Blake.

In the end she asked a hacker friend for help. He texted her the physical address in less than an hour.

All for the price of a beer, she thought with a smile.

———————⌁———————

The Eibon Institute wasn't what she expected. High-security gates, surveillance cameras, private security—it looked more like an armed compound than an intellectual think tank. She couldn't just walk into the place. There was no clear entrance, no way to visit. In fact, as she stared at the menacing building she noticed people walking by as if it didn't exist. Like some invisible spell cloaked it.

She closed her eyes and fell into the stillness that made her more receptive to communication. "Are you in there, Connie Blake?" she called out. She heard nothing except the white noise of the people on the street.

The Institute would be a hard nut to crack.

She dropped by whenever she had time between classes. She couldn't resist the allure of a building no one else saw. Fortunately there was a bench across the street—all that remained of an old bus line. Every afternoon Ellen sat on the bench and studied while sending psychic messages.

A few days into her vigil, while working on some sketches of the creature, she glanced up to see Connie Blake marching toward her.

He looked different than the last time she saw him. He was no longer the sweet, open-faced man she met. When she rose from the bench to greet him, he knocked the sketchbook out of her hand.

"What the hell do you think you're doing?" he shouted. "Are you spying on us?"

She looked at him, stunned. "Spying on you? I'm not spying on you!"

"Do you have any idea how dangerous this is? How do we know you're not still infected by that . . . that thing?"

"We?" Ellen echoed as she picked up her drawings.

She glanced over Connie's shoulder. A gang of people stood behind him. Their needlelike stares pierced her body.

Psychics.

Ellen always dreamed of the day when she would meet people who shared her talent. She imagined the scene countless times—the sense of belonging, the unspoken camaraderie she would feel.

There was nothing like that here. Her fellow psychics were just another angry mob. And Connie was their leader.

Ellen backed away, clutching her sketchbook to her chest.

"We have important work to do. Vital work. We can't get anything done when you're out here *broadcasting*." He tossed out what was obviously some sort of psychic insult. The crowd behind her laughed—a mirthless outburst that hurt more than their harsh stares. "So why don't you do yourself a favor and get out of here!"

"I've got a better idea, Blake. Why don't we take her inside and show her what we do?" a man in the crowd shouted. Another round of laughter followed.

Ellen shivered. The mood of the crowd was shifting, the way it had on that autumn day long ago. The kids that cornered her in the schoolyard had been joking. Even the first rock they threw was tossed out lightheartedly. But the moment they drew blood, the moment they sensed their power, things got ugly. The memories came rushing back—the barrage of rocks, the sting of blood in her eyes, the snarls and grunts as her classmates held her down and kicked her.

"Ellen?" Connie Blake called out before she remembered the blow that plunged her into darkness.

His face was as white as chalk. Several of the people around him looked sick. One woman cried, her sobs amplified by the dead silence.

It took Ellen a moment to realize they picked up on her visions. They served as silent witnesses to her anguish, to the persecution they all feared.

Rage flooded her body. She didn't want their pity.

"Fuck you. Fuck you and your fucking . . . cult," she spat, focusing her anger on Connie Blake. "You're no better than they are."

Ellen grabbed her things and ran. They felt sorry for her now, but there was no guarantee the crowd would stay that way. She sprinted for the safety of Miskatonic University. She vaulted up the stairs of the chemistry building and hid in an empty lab.

Ellen slid to the floor and clutched her knees to her chest. Her eyes wandered across a poster of the periodic table. The sign calmed her. There was an order to this world, a measured regularity she found soothing. The borders bent and warped with new discoveries, but they rarely broke.

Potassium was always potassium; calcium was always calcium—

"Scandium is always scandium," a voice named the next element on the chart.

Connie Blake stood on the other side of the lab table. Ellen scurried to her feet. She snatched a can of mace from her bag and pointed it at him. He ignored the weapon.

"How old were you?"

"What?"

"How old were you when it happened?"

"Thirteen," she replied.

He rolled up his sleeve to expose a long white scar that ran along the inside of his arm. "I was twelve. I tripped when I ran away and landed on some broken glass. I think that's what saved me. The guys chasing me freaked out when they saw blood."

"Then you should know better," Ellen replied after a long silence. "You shouldn't be the leader of a mob."

"They're not a mob," Blake snapped, then took a deep breath. "You have to understand. They were protecting me. We had no idea if the exorcism was a success."

"Exorcism?" she echoed. Even though she knew what happened, the word still shocked her. "You knew about it?"

"Of course I knew about it. What, did you think Carter the boy wonder did it all on this own?" Blake snarled.

The burst of anger spooked Ellen. *Issues,* her mind whispered as she put her mace away, *the man has issues.*

"Give me your hand," he asked her.

"No."

"Please. I want to make sure that you're okay. That the creature's gone."

He held out his hand. Ellen looked at the scar on his arm and relented.

The moment he touched her, he let out a startled yelp.

"What is it? Is it the creature?" Ellen gasped.

He stared at her in disbelief. "I think it's you. Jesus, you're strong. It's like touching a live wire."

"But the creature's gone?"

"Yes," he replied.

His eyes glazed over. Ellen tried to pull away, but his grip tightened on her. *Power surge*, she thought, *he's feeding off the power surge.*

"What do you know about the creature, Dr. Blake?"

"Why don't you ask Carter?"

"I'm asking you."

"Why?"

"Because I want to find out if this institute of yours has anything to offer," she replied as she freed her hand.

"I'm not giving out free samples. Eibon isn't a candy store."

"Then I'm not interested."

"What?"

"I'm not interested." She slid her backpack over her shoulder. "I need information. *Now.* And if your institute's not willing to help me—"

"Do you know how prestigious the Eibon Institute is? Do you know how many people would die to be in your position?"

"I'm sure your institute has a lot to offer. And I'm sure you'll have no trouble recruiting someone else."

"You're bluffing."

"Do you think so? After what I just went through?" she challenged him.

His eyes locked on hers. He held her gaze for only a few seconds.

"Oh, for Christ's sake," he said as he shook his head. "Let's go to the Garden. I need a cigarette."

Chapter Fifteen

The Botanical Garden was the only place on campus where people were allowed to smoke. A narrow strip of land wedged between the chemistry and biology buildings, the Garden was meant to be an oasis, a peaceful spot where faculty and students could take a break from the world.

The soil at Miskatonic was not conducive to tranquility. The roses, gardenias, and the sweet-smelling flowers originally planted there withered in the hostile environment. The students responded by replacing them with more sinister varietals—belladonna, nightshade, angel's trumpet, foxglove. The Garden thrived, becoming a valuable resource for pharmaceutical research. And it was here that smokers won one of their few public victories. They argued that since the Garden was full of poisonous substances (including tobacco), they should be allowed to light up. After a long and heated debate, university officials gave in.

Ellen visited the Garden before, but always in the safety of a group. Even with a teacher leading the way she felt uneasy being in the presence of so many dangerous plants. As she ventured into the dense thicket with Connie Blake, Ellen tried to remember what she learned in botany class. She drew a complete blank. She stopped in her tracks, suddenly aware of how exposed she was—not only to the vegetation but to Connie Blake. Less than half an hour ago he was the leader of a threatening mob. Now she followed him to a secluded spot where the deadly overgrowth would muffle her cries for help.

What the hell do you think you're doing?

"I was wondering when you were going to ask yourself that question," he said as he turned to face her.

"Don't do that."

"What?"

"Don't get into my head. Not after everything that's happened," she replied, trying to push away the image of the crowd that almost killed her.

"It was bad, wasn't it?

"I was in a coma for a week. They thought I had brain damage, that I wouldn't . . ." Her mind slammed shut like a steel trap. "Well, you know what they thought."

"Come here," he said gently.

"I'm fine," Ellen insisted.

Connie Blake pulled her into his arms. He smelled of old cigarettes and musty books. The rich, familiar aroma comforted her. Her body slumped and she relaxed into the embrace.

"You're not fine. How can you be fine after something like that?" he murmured, his voice a warm buzz on the top of her head. Ellen started to cry. "It's happened to most of us at some point in our lives. It's not your fault. You realize that, don't you?"

"But—"

He pulled back to look at her. "*It's not your fault.*" His eyes blazed with anger. "Don't you understand? That's why we have the institute. To protect us from the people who don't understand."

Ellen wrestled free, swiping at her tears. "Look. I didn't come here to be lectured. Or converted. Or whatever the hell you're trying to do," she told him. "If you're not going to help—"

"All right. All right. Jesus."

He led her deeper into the garden. After a few more minutes of slogging their way through dense jungle, they emerged in the central courtyard. Like the rest of the garden, it started out bright and cheerful. Now it was a dark, Gothic place slowly losing its battle with time. Ellen drifted past a fountain full of stagnant rainwater. A wood nymph perched on the crumbling structure, the host of a party that ended a long, long time ago. Connie sat on one of cracked stone benches. He twisted and turned, contorting his body. At first Ellen thought he brushed against one of the more hostile plants. Then she saw the cigarette dangling from his lips.

An itch of a different kind, she thought. Ellen joined him.

"And I thought our garden was a mess," she murmured.

"Yeah. This place is straight out of 'Rappaccini's Daughter,'" Connie observed.

"What?"

"'Rappaccini's Daughter.' One of Nathaniel Hawthorne's short stories," Connie replied as he lit his cigarette. "It was about an alluring woman who lived in a poison garden. She was immune to all the deadly plants, but if she touched any-one, they died."

"Do you suppose the students were aware of that when they built this place?"

He took a fierce drag on his cigarette and exhaled slowly through his nose. He reminded Ellen of an angry dragon.

"I don't know. I don't work here, remember?"

She retreated to safer ground. "What's Connie short for?"

"Excuse me?"

"Connie. It's short for something, right?"

"That's not what we're here for," he inhaled so sharply the cigarette crackled.

"Fine." She dug into her backpack and fished out her sketchbook.

"Connor," he replied after a long silence. "My mother named me after a famous writer."

"Flannery O'Connor?"

"How did you know?"

"I'm a southern girl. New Orleans. At least that's what my uncle tells me."

"You don't have an accent."

"I suspect I lost it."

"How?"

"I don't know." She watched the doomed fountain spring another leak. She shifted her feet as a trickle of water headed her way. "Dr. Blake, what did you see that night? On the riverbank?"

"You mean besides Andrew jumping in to save you?"

A hot blush crawled up her neck. "Carter jumped in to save me?"

"Yeah, he leaped right in the thick of it for you. Like some middle-aged action hero."

He flicked his cigarette at the fountain. It landed on the ground with a angry hiss.

"I wouldn't be alive if it wasn't for him," she reminded him.

Blake gave her a sharp look. "Don't get used to it. He's not exactly hero material."

"What did you see on the riverbank, Dr. Blake?"

He placed something on the bench between them—a small figurine, the kind Ellen used when she played Dungeons and Dragons. Except it wasn't a fighter, a wizard, or a thief. It was a monster. *Her* monster.

Ellen picked up the tiny replica and ran her fingers over its outstretched tentacles. "Where did you get this?" she asked.

"You know how Carter says that we communicate our knowledge through art."

"Yes."

"Well, we also communicate our knowledge in other ways. Through role-playing games. Graphic novels. Music and video games. Carter doesn't acknowledge it. He considers it low culture."

Ellen turned the figure around, trying to look at it from as many angles as she could. "Is this from 'Call of Cthulhu'?"

"Yes."

"What are they?" she asked as she handed it back.

"We call them chthonians. The name reflects our ignorance. Chthonians, from the Greek *chthon*, of or relating to the underworld."

"The underworld?"

Ellen thought about her dream with the man who re-minded her of Dante, the explorer of the underworld. Suddenly his appearance made sense. *What did he say to her after he pushed her into the well? You will understand. In time, you will understand.*

"Chthonians are in-between creatures. They dwell in the twilight world, far from humans," Blake continued. "They're like giant squid, except they propel themselves through the earth instead of the water. They're solitary creatures, but they sometimes make psychic contact with humans. It's extremely rare. They avoid it unless it's absolutely necessary."

"Why?"

"Can you imagine how much it would hurt to squeeze their bodies into a human shape? To transmit to such an insignificant creature?"

She winced, shifting on the bench. "Actually, I can," she replied.

Connie Blake tensed. "I'm sorry I didn't—" he started.

She ignored him. "I think it's still trying to communicate with me. I've been having the same dream, night after night. Men trapped in the earth. Reaching out for me from the walls. And a man standing on the outskirts of a town, twirling a pickax. He's always pointing at a sign. 'Bent' something."

Connie Blake finished the vision for her. "Bentham. That's what the sign said. Bentham."

She looked over at him. "You saw it, too?"

"I had no choice," he replied. "I was with you on the riverbank. Some of its energies transferred to me."

"Transferred?" she repeated, remembering what he told her earlier about the creature infecting his people. "Did it hurt you?"

"Let's just say it's an experience I'd rather not repeat."

"What did it show you?"

His cell phone rang before he could reply. Connie retreated to the far corner of the courtyard. She could tell by his nervous glances the phone call was about her. She watched him smooth down his hair and straighten his tie. *Going back into professional mode*, she thought with a sigh.

"I have to go," he announced when he returned.

She nodded at the phone. "I hope I haven't gotten you into trouble."

"Nothing I can't handle." He reached into his pocket and produced another chthonian figurine. "Here. A gift."

Ellen's cheeks flared as she put the statue in her pocket. She couldn't remember the last time anyone gave her a gift.

"Thank you."

"And here." He offered her another business card. "My personal cell phone is on there. That way you won't disturb the others if you need to get in touch."

"I *am* sorry about that. Really. I didn't know I was bothering you," she started to apologize, but a thought stopped her short. *You should have known better. You've should have started learning how to behave like a psychic a long time ago . . .*

"Look, Ellen, I'm not trying to recruit you. Just let me say one thing. Miskatonic isn't the only way. There are other paths. Ones that don't require so much sacrifice."

"But all true knowledge requires sacrifice, doesn't it?" she said, repeating the unofficial motto of Miskatonic.

"What I'm talking about is different," he insisted as they headed out of the grim garden. "When the time comes, you'll feel the difference. You'll know the difference. And I hope you'll remember then that there are alternatives."

* * *

Bentham.

Now that she had a name, Ellen was sure she had the answer. The moment she got home she raced to her room, past Andrew Carter and her bewildered uncle. In the week following her possession Carter had become a regular fixture in their household. He showed up after his afternoon classes. They all had an early dinner together. Then the two men retreated to the study, where they spent the rest of the evening.

Ellen knew Joshua mentored him early in his life. That Carter's instruction was interrupted when Joshua raced down to New Orleans to rescue her. And she knew Joshua loved her. Still, as she stood outside the closed door and listened to their muffled conversation, she wondered whether her uncle preferred Carter.

Her doubts didn't bother her tonight. In fact she was glad to see Carter. His presence meant she could devote the time before dinner to her research.

Bentham.

She was anxious to see where the name would take her. As she waited for her computer to boot, she put the chthonian on the keyboard. She felt another rush at the sight of the creature. This time the sensation was weaker. She saw inaccuracies she hadn't noticed before. In an attempt to make the model look more conventional, the creator imposed squid-like features on it, putting a beak in the middle of the outstretched tentacles and saucerlike eyes on either side of its "head."

The deliberate manipulation irritated her. *Just another example of human arrogance, the kind of single-mindedness that's destroying the planet*, she thought. *Scum. That's what we are. We feed off the crust of the earth. We multiply. We clog up the atmosphere. Nothing but scum.*

"Whoa," Ellen grabbed her head, startled by the sheer ferocity of her thoughts. The feeling faded the moment she became aware of it.

B-E-N-T-H-A-M.

She pounded on the keyboard so hard that the monster fell off the desk. *Serves you right, buddy*, she thought as she hit the Return button.

Bentham Kentucky Vacations, Bentham Dental Groups. The search revealed nothing.

When she came across Jeremy Bentham, a philosopher from the eighteenth century, her heart raced. But if Jeremy Bentham harbored any secrets, any link to her world, she didn't see it. He was a no-nonsense legal scholar. His world was rational, the actions of humanity reduced to mathematical equations. Hedonic calculation, individual utility, felicific calculus . . . The only whiff of peculiarity was what happened to him after death.

"Who's that?" a voice demanded.

Ellen yelped. For a moment, for one crazy moment, she thought the words came from Bentham.

Carter stood behind her, peering at the screen.

"Jeremy Bentham." She sat back and rubbed her neck. "Did you know that after he died he had himself preserved so he could be wheeled out for committee meetings?"

"You're kidding."

He moved in for a closer look. Ellen caught a whiff of cologne—spice and musk, a hint of exotic lands to be explored. *Don't go there*, a voice warned her.

"Listen to this." She read Bentham's will to keep her mind off Carter's alluring smell. "'The skeleton he will cause to be put together in such a manner as that the whole figure may be seated in a chair usually occupied by me when living, in the attitude in which I am sitting when engaged in thought. From time to time, cause it to be stationed in such part of the room as to the assembled company shall meet.'"

"And I thought death would be enough to get me out of department meetings," Carter grumbled as he sat on her bed.

In jeans, sneakers, and an untucked shirt, he was casual in a way the mummified professor would never be.

"Connie just called. He said you paid him a visit," he announced.

"Dr. Blake called you?"

"He likes to taunt me whenever he can. He thinks we're competing for you," he said, giving her a look that made it clear they weren't. "He said you had a rough time at the institute."

"I went there to talk to him. I waited for him outside, thinking about the thing. I didn't know I was . . . what do they call it?"

"Broadcasting," Carter offered.

"I didn't know I was broadcasting until I looked up and saw a crowd at the gate."

"Jesus."

"I freaked out. God, what does my shrink say? They *triggered* me. I turned and ran. Connie found me hiding in one of the biology labs."

Carter's eyes flooded with rage. "That bastard. That fucking bastard."

Ellen knew his reaction had nothing to do with her. *It's between them*, she thought. *A piece of ancient history.*

"Why did you go to the institute in the first place?" Carter demanded after a long silence.

"I needed answers about what I saw on the riverbank. I figured Connie might have something to offer."

"And did he?"

"He and I had the same dream or vision or whatever you call it," she answered. A wave of self-consciousness hit her. She didn't like talking about her abilities. "When that *thing* possessed me, I saw a town in the woods. And a sign. 'Bent.' That was all. Connie saw more. 'Bentham.' That was the name on the sign. Bentham."

Carter nodded at the computer screen. "Is that why you're so interested in Jeremy Bentham?"

"I hoped there might be a connection between him and this." She picked up her toppled figurine and offered it to him. He plucked it out of her hand.

"Ah, *architeuthis infernis*."

"You know them?"

"Not personally, no," Carter replied. Ellen looked up, convinced he was mocking her. There was no humor, no telltale sarcasm in his voice.

"Can I offer you some friendly advice?" asked Carter.

"Please."

"Your thinking is too linear. Don't waste your time with straight questions. Our world doesn't function that way." He returned the figurine to its perch. "If you want to understand the message, don't obsess on the words. Consider the subject itself."

"The chthonians?"

"Find out everything you can about them. I'm willing to bet you'll find another reference to Bentham. One that makes more sense."

"God, I hope so. 'Professor in a box' really creeps me out."

His eyes lingered on the picture. "You and me both. I pity the poor graduate student that has to wheel him out for meetings."

"Another line on the vita, I suppose," Ellen replied, amused by the thought of some poor student wrestling with Bentham and his box. "I wonder how you would describe the job. Corpse wrangler?"

"No, more like administrative liaison for the recently retired."

"Did you ever have to do anything like that, Carter?"

"That's another straight question," he teased her. He smiled as he left the room to head back downstairs to her uncle. "Happy hunting."

Deep. Down. Dark.

????-??-1945

They laid out a magic circle. The men offered sac-rifices, painting the ground with the blood they thought would protect them.

I watched them prepare and felt a glimmer of hope.

Maybe it will be different this time, I thought. Maybe this time, with enough men, enough preparation . . .

It all went to hell. Again.

Why did I think it was going to be so simple?

Because I didn't think about my mother. It didn't occur to me that being trapped with a monster changed her. Her spirit curdled. The only thing left was rage. It was her rage, not the creature, that I felt at night. And I didn't warn her. I didn't tell her what we were trying to do.

The moment I blew the whistle, she leapt out in all her fury. Time had stood still for her. She was still locked in a moment that had passed years ago. When she saw the men in the magic circle, she thought they were Nazis. And when she saw me, in the middle of it all . . .

She thought sacrifice.

She released the creature that had been bottled up with her for so long. It attacked the world around it. Tearing down the beams that held up our world. And as the world collapsed around us, as men were crushed beneath tons of earth, she harvested them. Grabbed their spirits and crammed them into the whistle.

She spared me. I don't know how she did it. Maybe all that time with the creature allowed her to control it. To influence it somehow.

I will be alone soon. Hell, I'm alone now. The men who are still alive, well, they don't really want to talk to me, do they? When they die, they'll be sucked into the whistle. Trapped. And then, then . . .

It's only a matter of time before I join them.

Chapter Sixteen

"The king's son picked up the maiden's left slipper, and it was small and dainty, and all golden. Next morning he went with it to his father and said to him, 'No one shall be my wife but she whose foot this golden slipper fits.' The two sisters were glad, for they had pretty feet. The eldest went with the shoe into her room and wanted to try it on, and her mother stood by. But she could not get her big toe into it; the shoe was too small for her. Then her mother gave her a knife and said, 'Cut the toe off.'"

"Eeew, gross!" one of the girls in the reading group squealed. She scolded the librarian, "That's not the way the Cinderella story goes. Tell it right!"

Ellen wiggled her feet as she watched the commotion from a table in the Miskatonic Library. The children were used to the Walt Disney versions of *Grimms' Fairy Tales*—of bright, cheerful worlds where evil was only a fleeting presence. They didn't know the older, more gruesome versions of the stories. They didn't know that in the earlier tales the frog king turned into a prince not with a kiss but by being thrown against the wall. Or that Hansel and Gretel didn't lose their way in the forest—their starving parents abandoned them.

Even though these stories were more authentic, Ellen wondered whether it was a good idea to share them with children. Sure, this was an older group of kids, and they were the children of Miskatonic employees. Still . . .

The librarian seemed to share Ellen's concern. She abandoned the Grimm brothers and pulled out *The Wizard of Oz*.

Ellen stared at the books stacked in front of her. She had spent the entire day holed up in the library, searching for the answer she so desperately needed.

Bentham.

The name no longer rolled off her tongue. It stuck in her throat like a popcorn kernel. Ellen flipped through her notebook, retracing the path of her research. From cryptozoology to giant squid, from Bram Stoker's *Lair of the White Worm* to Frank Herbert's *Dune*, she followed every winding path.

She came back with nothing.

Ellen let out a frustrated huff. Her eyes drifted to a dog-eared *Call of Cthulhu Manual*. She remembered what Connie Blake said, that their knowledge was transmitted through video games, graphic novels, and role-playing games. She hoped so. She loved to look at art in museums, but reading monster manuals and stories about the Avengers . . . that was a lot more fun.

She found herself humming as she flipped through the role-playing guide. She stopped to read the article on Randolph Carter, Andrew Carter's grandfather.

Randolph Carter looked exactly like him. Except the older Carter had a beard. Other than that, they were interchangeable.

She smiled and shook her head. *I'm sure Andrew Carter loves that.*

Her upbeat expression faded when she reached the entry on the chthonians. The illustration was so realistic she pulled back her fingers. The written entry described the creature perfectly.

Ellen searched for the reference. Brian Lumley. *The Burrowers Beneath.* She quickly pawed through the books on her desk.

When she came up empty handed, her heart began to pound. *This is it. This must be it.*

She rose from the table, trying hard to contain her excitement. She walked over to the computer and typed the title into the database. The book was on the ground floor, in one of the few sections open to undergraduates. Ellen was glad she didn't have to ask someone to fetch the book.

The librarians were odd, even by Miskatonic standards. Severe, sallow-faced men who dressed like funeral directors, they exhibited an unhealthy attachment to their books. Hostility and intense suspicion greeted any request for a volume in their "exclusive collection." These gatekeepers even turned away esteemed professors. One of her friends joked that they reminded him of Gollum, the twisted creature in *Lord of the Rings.* Ellen disagreed. Gollum had some compassion left, a hint of the sunny hobbit he once was. The librarians reminded her more of the Ringwraiths, the cold, spectral army that hounded Frodo to the very gates of Mordor.

"As the Shadow grows once more, they too may walk again," Ellen breathed as one of the bizarre men passed her.

He gave her a sharp glare, but she didn't stay on his radar for long. No one ever did.

The book she needed was in the horror section, with the other works of "fiction." Ellen scanned the titles as she drifted down the aisle. Robert Bloch. Ramsey Campbell. August Derleth. Stephen King. H. P. Lovecraft. Ellen ran her hand over one of Lovecraft's books as she passed, paying silent tribute to the master. She continued down the alphabet to Lumley.

Ellen had read some of his work before. When she was a teenager she devoured the books that featured Harry Keogh, the psychic investigator. Even though she and Harry had nothing in common, Ellen loved reading about someone with her powers as the main character. All too often, "her kind" was relegated to sidekick status or worse, portrayed as comic relief.

A high-pitched squeal pierced the stillness of the library. *"Oh God! Oh my God!"*

Ellen lost her grip on the book as she pulled it off the shelf. Its spine cracked as it tumbled to the floor. Under normal circumstances the mistreatment of a book (even an unrestricted one) would have drawn the wrath of the librarians. They had more pressing concerns.

Someone had just lost their mind.

Ellen was close enough to see the unfortunate soul. The man stared down at an old book, his eyes wide, his face frozen in a grimace. Everyone in the library had seen scenes like this play out. Still, the people around her shuddered as the librarians descended. Dragging him off to an unknown part of the library. To a place and a fate they all feared.

"All the king's horses and all the king's men, huh?" a spiky-haired punk observed as the librarians escorted the man through a security door.

"I wonder what Humpty was reading," Ellen replied.

"I don't know. They snatched the book away before I could read the title."

The man flashed her an apologetic look that seemed out of place on such a severe face. Thin and angular with dyed-black hair, he was handsome in a grim kind of way. Ellen wondered what he looked like beneath the pale Kabuki makeup and the kohl-rimmed eyes.

"Given his reaction, that's probably a good thing," Ellen offered. She noticed the way his eyes lingered on her. "My name's Ellen."

He accepted her outstretched hand.

"I'm Stuart."

His handshake was warm and gentle, not at all the death grip she expected.

"Stuart? Is that your vampire name?"

He dismissed the practice with a wave of his hand. "No, it's my real name. I don't go in for all that alternate persona shit."

It was routine among people pretending to be other-worldly creatures to take on another identity. In fact, she knew some people who would respond only to their fictional names.

As if reality isn't weird enough around here, she thought.

"Hey, I know this may sound strange coming from some-one like me but, um, would you like to go get some coffee?" he asked.

"Why would it sound strange coming from someone like you? Vampires need caffeine too, don't they?"

He looked at her hopefully. "Does that mean yes?"

"Just let me get my book and we can go."

She picked up the book that lay broken and exposed on the floor. Her eyes wandered across the open page.

Yrs. sincerely,

R. Bentham

Ellen blinked hard, convinced she was seeing things. The name at the top of the page never wavered. R. BENTHAM. Raymond Bentham, to be more precise. His name appeared on letters addressed to Titus Crow. She forced herself to remain calm as she flipped through the "fictional" correspondence.

This could just be a coincidence, she reminded herself, *like old professor in a—* Her thoughts were interrupted by more words.

Big caves. Coal seams. Tunnels.

Men trapped underground. Struggling to break free.

"Mines. Miners," she murmured. "Miners."

Ellen experienced a strong urge to dump Stuart, to chase the lead like a bloodhound locked on a scent. She shut the book before she could get pulled in any deeper.

Take your time. Take your time or you'll melt down in the middle of the library.

"Are you alright?" Stuart asked her.

"Nothing a double espresso won't fix."

The agony was unbearable. Ellen twisted and turned, but the earth refused to release its grip. Tons of rubble pressed down on her body. It was only a matter of time before she died. She could feel the life leeching out of her.

"God, please forgive me, I had to do it, I had to," she whispered.

The words were hot and coppery in her mouth. Ellen didn't expect an answer (she was a long, long way from God), so she was surprised when she heard a faint mewling.

The plaintive cry was answered by the distant sound of rumbling. A man lay a few feet away. He stared at Ellen with big brown eyes, his face wide with terror. When she reached out to comfort him, she saw a tattoo on her arm.

Numbers.

The air around her grew hot. Ellen struggled to stay, but the man whose body she occupied turned inward. His life flashed before her. He slipped and slid in the mud, pursued by howling dogs and men shouting in German.

Something was in his hand. Something he had taken from them.

He headed toward the barbed wire fence, carrying her along.

The sharp points waited for them, glistening in the rain.

I don't belong here, she thought.

Oh, you do, the unseen man replied. *You do belong here. You* need *to be here.*

Ellen threw up her arms as her body hit the fence.

Wake up, wake up, wake up . . . Her eyes flew open.

Her hands scrabbled across her body, searching for shredded skin, for the deep grooves of the nightmare.

Nothing.

Slowly the real world returned. The room she was in was unfamiliar—full of strange shapes and long shadows. A man slept beside her. After a few moments she remembered.

Stuart.

She hadn't planned on sleeping with the man in the library, but the evening had been so comfortable, the seduction so smooth, Ellen surrendered to the moment. It had been a long time since she had been with a man. She reveled in the simple pleasure of making love. Stuart masqueraded as a vampire, but he had none of the usual hang-ups. No desire to bite or draw blood.

There had been only one odd moment. As she raced toward an orgasm, Connie Blake popped into her head. For a split second it felt like he pushed his way inside her, like he was trying to take over.

Ellen shook her head. "Impossible," she blurted into the darkness. *But was it?* she wondered. *How much do you really know about Connie Blake and what he can do?*

Stuart shifted in his sleep. "Katie."

The name that spilled out of his mouth was full of innocence. Ellen knew it wasn't an ex-girlfriend. Or a current one. Not that it mattered.

He was a one-night stand. A single-serving friend.

Ellen smiled at the man beside her. He let her wash the makeup off his face the night before—an act of trust that set the stage for everything that followed. His face was less severe without the mask. His features were fuller. In the light of day he looked like the Midwestern boy he was. Even the spiderweb tattooed on his shoulder seemed quaint. At least compared to other designs she had seen.

"Katie, don't go out there."

Ellen leaned closer. "I won't," she whispered in his ear.

She hoped the words would be enough to change the course of his dream. She pressed her lips to his cheek and saw a little girl running toward a tornado. Stuart's . . . sister.

The girl's thoughts were as ferocious as the twister bearing down on her. *Please, please, lift me up. Take me away. I don't want to be here anymore. I don't want my father to come into my bedroom anymore.*

Ellen jerked, started by the intimacy of the vision.

She was tempted to wake Stuart, to hear the rest of the story. There was no point. She knew what happened. He wouldn't be at Miskatonic if there was a happy ending.

She said a silent prayer for the lost girl, then she tumbled out of bed and searched for her clothes. Leaving Stuart to battle the dark forces that engulfed his little sister.

As soon as she was dressed she drifted down the stairs like a ghost. His roommates were fast asleep on the living room floor. All around them were the remains of a ritual—incense, candles, and empty bottles. They even burned a pentagram into the carpet. Ellen tiptoed around the magic circle and let herself out.

A powerful storm ripped through Arkham overnight. Ellen surveyed the damage. Roof shingles ripped off houses. Fences knocked down. The storm even toppled the city's sturdy garbage cans. They lay like a line of fallen warriors, their guts spilled on the streets. Ellen studied the contents as she headed home.

Anything to keep her mind off the little girl spinning in the vortex of violent winds.

Please. Take me away . . . I don't want my father to come into my bedroom anymore.

She focused on the garbage. Most of it was uninspiring—pizza boxes, cookie wrappers, empty prescription bottles. Old gun magazines and hardcore pornography.

Ellen bent down to examine the address label on the cover of *Sensual Sinners*. Steve Reigler. She wondered if that was his real name. *Why subscribe to a magazine you could pick up incognito at the local convenience store? Was he a shut-in? One of Miskatonic's walking wounded?*

Her cell phone buzzed before she could decide. Ellen stared at the screen in disbelief. There were twenty-two missed calls. Twenty-two calls since she left the library with Stuart.

A cold wave of panic gripped her. *Joshua. Something's happened to Joshua.* She straightened, moving so fast that her head spun.

"Hello?" Ellen squeaked.

"Ellen?"

"Uncle Joshua? Are you okay?"

"I'm fine. Why wouldn't I be?"

It was only then that she allowed herself to breathe.

"You didn't try to call me last night?"

"No."

"Must have been a wrong number then," she said, even though she knew it was a lie. If it was a wrong number, the caller would have tried once. Maybe twice. Not twenty-two times.

Her uncle brought her back to reality. "I just wanted to let you know Miskatonic is closed today. The storm that blew through here last night was pretty intense. Knocked out power at the university."

"Do we have power?"

"Yeah. I have no idea how we managed to stay on the grid. Most of Arkham is dark."

Ellen could hear him fighting the urge to grill her. *She's twenty years old; she's free to come and go as she pleases.*

After a long pause, he settled on a neutral question. "Where are you?"

"I'm on Stevenson Street looking through some guy's garbage," she half joked.

"Do you think that's a productive use of your time?" Joshua replied.

The pointed question made her wilt. Ellen stepped away from the garbage can, feeling a rush of guilt. "No," she replied.

"Well then, why don't you come on home?"

"I'll be right there."

Ellen stared hard at her cell phone, stung by Joshua's ability to manipulate her. She remembered how Andrew Carter and Connie Blake squirmed under her uncle's steely gaze. How Carter crept to the riverbank when Joshua "suggested" he apologize to her. *At least I'm not the only one*, she thought,

Her cell phone buzzed again. Ellen hissed, annoyed her uncle was bothering her again.

"I told you I'm on my way," she barked.

The person on the other end said nothing.

"Hello? Who is this?"

"Who do you think it is?" a flat, emotionless voice replied.

Ellen struggled to place the caller. "Are you the one who's been calling me all night?"

"Yes."

"Why?"

"Who were you with last night? Was it *him*?" The man spit out the last word with such spite that Ellen knew who it was. Not just who it was, but who he was talking about.

"Is that you, Connie Blake?"

"Answer the question."

"I'm not answering the question. It's none of your fucking business who I was with," she snapped, refusing to let Connie Blake intimidate her. She knew that if she showed the slightest bit of weakness, she would be answering to him as well.

"If it's none of my fucking business, why were you thinking of me when you were doing it?" he taunted her.

Ellen felt as if someone had reached in and twisted her insides. *He did it. He got into my head when I was making love to . . .*

She sat down hard on the curb. As Ellen struggled to recover, she heard the chitter-chatter of random thoughts. *She's rummaging around in the garbage. What the hell is she looking for?*

She looked down the wind-swept street, expecting to see Connie. A man in a Honda watched her from across the street. When their eyes met, he looked away, pretending to check mail on his cell phone.

An amateur, she thought. *Probably someone from the frat.*

The frat. Ellen had been so preoccupied (*possessed*, she corrected herself, *not preoccupied, possessed*) that she forgot about Delta Delta Tau. The brothers were still missing. No bodies had been found at the fraternity. People assumed they were hiding from the police. The current rumor circulating was the explosion came from a secret meth lab in their basement. Ellen knew it was bullshit. They were on the run, but it wasn't because of drugs.

"Where *are* they?" she wondered out loud.

"What did you say?" Connie Blake growled.

"I have to go. I don't have time for this." She cut him off midsentence.

Ellen tapped the phone to her lips and weighed her options. She had absolutely no interest in confronting the man in the car. The last frat member took a shot at her. *This guy might have a gun, too*, she thought. She looked around the empty street. *And if he decided to grab me, no one would see it.*

Ellen's heart hammered as she rose to her feet. She brushed the leaves off her pants, trying to act casual.

Miskatonic was closed for the day, but there would still be people. A skeleton crew at the very least. She slung her backpack over her shoulder and headed toward campus.

Behind her she heard the crunch of glass. The man sifted through the garbage. *God, they must be desperate if they're this obvious*, she thought.

She tried not to think about it as she took the long way home.

Ellen spent the rest of the day hiding behind the sturdy gates of Trelawney House. She was glad she had the day off. Her extracurricular activities (*possession, call it possession*) had taken its toll. She returned home to a mountain of homework. There were chapters to read, presentations to plan, quizzes to prepare for—even a five-page paper due in Carter's class. She considered asking him for an extension but quickly decided against it. She needed a practical challenge, something to keep her mind off the fact that someone was following her.

And off Connie Blake.

The man's behavior disgusted her. *To have somebody in your head was one thing. But while you were making love? Not quite psychic rape, but close,* she thought. *Real close.* The thought made her sick to her stomach.

"Enough," she whispered as she plopped down in her chair. If she let her mind wander now, she would spend the rest of the day catching it.

After fortifying herself with a cup of Turkish coffee, she tackled the more demanding work first—the subjects that required the most concentration. By the time her uncle called her down to lunch she felt stable enough to move on to Carter's paper. His assignment was simple. Describe the myth that frightens you and why. She knew the answer to the first part of the question—the kidnapping of Persephone by Hades, the god of the underworld. Explaining why was more complicated. She could offer the stock response: the horror of being snatched from the face of the earth, taken from everything and everyone you knew.

It ran deeper than that.

Deeper than the fear of hell.

Once she settled, Ellen's fingers flew across the keyboard.

Why did Hades choose Persephone as his bride? Why did the god of death choose the daughter of the earth? Why not the daughter of the ocean or the daughter of the sky? All elements in nature have their dark side. There are storms on the sea that tear apart ships. Wind and rain in the sky that wreak havoc on the world below. What did he see in her? Did he see an extraordinary darkness as he watched her playing in the fields with the other nymphs? Was she aware of it? Did she feel the darkness inside her, lurking on the edge of conscious awareness?

Am I a bad person?

The question startled Ellen, but it didn't surprise her. For years she begged Joshua to tell her about her past. He always refused. When she was younger she filled the silence with romantic fantasies. She imagined herself as Cinderella awaiting the arrival of her fairy godmother. As the years passed the bright picture faded.

Ellen wondered whether he hid things to protect her from herself. *Do I possess a darkness powerful enough to rip the ground open beneath me? Could I be the queen of a terrible world?*

The computer cursor blinked, waiting for an answer. Ellen closed her eyes. She tried to imagine herself as a fearsome death goddess. It seemed as likely as anything else did.

That's what frightened her. The ambiguity. The sense that she could be anyone. Or anything.

The sense of occupying another person's world intensified when she turned to *The Burrowers Beneath*, the book she checked out of the library. She expected to recognize some elements in Brian Lumley's story—the chthonian, Bentham, the mines. It was much more than that.

The tale reflected Ellen's experience in almost every detail. The nightmares, the ability of the creature to control humans telepathically, a dead person brought back to life. There was even a fierce windstorm.

It was all there, preserved in fiction more than thirty years ago. She wondered whether Lumley's story was inspired by an actual event.

Ellen turned to her computer. *Bentham* and *mines*. A moment later the screen responded.

"Oh my God," Ellen stammered.

Her search was over.

Chapter Seventeen

"A word with you, Miss Logan?"

Andrew Carter's clipped tone stopped Ellen in her tracks. Students drifted by her. Some of them glared. Jealous she was the center of attention. Even if Carter was furious.

He spent most of his lecture glaring at her. As she climbed the stairs to the stage she wondered what she had done. It wasn't the paper. She didn't ask for special treatment. She turned the assignment in at the beginning of class like everyone else. It wasn't the investigation. Carter offered her advice, but he expressed no interest in being involved.

By the time she reached the podium she had exhausted all the plausible explanations. Her thoughts drifted into the realm of the absurd.

Carter turned on her, eyes flashing. "I don't appreciate being used," he growled.

Ellen frowned. "Used?"

"Used." He spat the word back at her.

"I understand the word, but you need to use it in a sentence."

"I got a call from Connie Blake yesterday."

Ellen's heart lurched. *Oh God, he didn't, he didn't.*

"Let me guess. He thought we were together the other night."

"Is that what you told him?"

"No, but that didn't stop him from thinking it," she replied. "Look, Connie called me when I was with someone."

"*With* someone?" Carter echoed.

"Don't be dense," Ellen snapped before she reined in her anger. "I don't know how he knew, whether he picked up on some vibe, whether I broadcasted, whatever. All I know was that he called me twenty-two times. When I finally answered the phone he accused me of sleeping with you."

"And what did you say?"

"I told him it was none of his business. He must have taken that as a yes." She shook her head. "Jesus, he called you and accused you of . . . What a fucking shit!"

Carter's eyes darted around the room. "There's more," he said.

Ellen moved closer to the podium. "Is someone following you?" she whispered.

He cocked his head. "Now why would you say that?"

"Because someone's been following me."

He motioned for her to be silent. "We need to meet somewhere. Somewhere that's handicapped accessible."

It took Ellen a moment to figure out what he was talking about. She nodded and moved off the stage.

Later that day, as trick-or-treaters prepared for their assault on the neighborhood, Ellen and Carter sat in Uncle Joshua's study.

"An academic tribunal? Are you serious, Andrew?!" Joshua exclaimed. "The university called an academic tribunal?"

Ellen looked at her uncle. She knew things were serious when Joshua let them into his study. He never let anyone into his study.

Her eyes wandered around Joshua's inner sanctum, studying the books and statues, the mysteries that lurked in every corner. That and the dust bunnies. Ellen ran her finger along her chair. Joshua glared at her.

"Are we boring you, Ellen? Because if you'd rather be out trick-or-treating—"

She ignored her uncle's sarcasm. "What's an academic tribunal?"

"You remember that library in Spain, where people who didn't return books were subject to excommunication?" her uncle asked.

Ellen nodded. It seemed absurd to her at the time, but after coming to Miskatonic she understood the need for such drastic measures.

"This is worse," her uncle insisted. "The book your friend Joey stole was very rare. And a page is torn out of it."

"A page they'll assume *I* tore out of the book," Carter added. "At the very least I could lose my position at the university."

"And the very worst?"

Carter looked away. He pretended to pluck an imaginary piece of lint from his pants.

"Torture. Although it's a punishment rarely used," Joshua replied.

Ellen rose to her feet. "*Torture?* You can't be serious!"

"Why can't I?" Joshua asked her.

"Because this is America. Torture doesn't happen here!"

"You've never heard of waterboarding?"

"But that's— that's—" she spluttered.

"That's torture, Ellen. Right here. Our country."

The anger rushed out of her like a popped balloon.

"You'll have to excuse my niece. She's a bit of an idealist."

Carter watched her as she slumped into her seat. "There's nothing wrong with that," he insisted.

"Who did this?" she asked Carter.

"I'll give you one guess," he replied.

Ellen touched her injured hand. "Pierce," she breathed. "He's trying to frame you. To pin the theft on you. That bastard!"

"Language," her uncle warned her.

"What can I do to help?" Ellen asked.

Carter's head jerked up. "What?"

"I'm the one responsible for what's happening."

"You're not responsible."

"Yes, I am. I gave you the book. I need to get you out of this."

Carter looked at her like she had sprouted another head. "Are you for fucking real? You're so . . . decent." He made it sound like an insult.

"Andrew, language," Joshua snapped.

"I know. Decent? Give me a break," she said.

Joshua favored her with a smile. Now that she had his attention, Ellen pointed at him and pantomimed opening a book. The old man nodded.

"Not just decent. Smart as a whip," her uncle complimented her.

Ellen blushed to the roots of her hair. She didn't like to admit it, but she hungered for Joshua's praise. It was as essential to her as oxygen.

"Elle, would you mind taking me out to the river? I could use some fresh air."

"Sure." She got behind him and wheeled him toward the door.

When Carter moved to follow them, Joshua shook his head. "Not you, my boy."

"Why not?" Carter protested.

"Because I need to talk to her, and you can't listen."

The backpack dug into Ellen's shoulders as she walked across campus. The plan was to return the stolen book in broad daylight. That way she could lose herself in the crowd of students rushing to their next class. Still, she knew safety in numbers would take her only so far.

She broadcasted her intentions earlier, focusing on the business card Richard Pierce gave her at Stephanie's memorial. Now someone was following her. Their presence weighed her down as much as her backpack. She could sense the man's thoughts. And he could sense hers.

Keep it together, she urged herself as she popped in her earbuds. The white soul of "Never Gonna Give You Up" blasted from her phone. Her pursuer reeled from the psychic blast. Ellen smirked as she took a shortcut to the library. *Take that, you bastard.*

When she reached the return bin, she set her backpack on the ground. Her hands trembled as she rummaged through her bag. Out of the corner of her eye she saw the campus police approaching her.

Ellen sighed in relief.

Her biggest fear was that Pierce would take matters into his own hands. That he (and maybe some of his frat boys) would kidnap her. Snatch her up in broad daylight and take her God knows where. Pierce opted for the more conservative approach. He let officials do his dirty work.

One of the officers grabbed her arm. "Miss?"

She yanked out her earbuds. "I'm sorry. Did you say something?"

"I said step away from the bag."

"This bag? My bag?" She looked at the backpack as if it had done something wrong.

"It will only take a minute," the officer insisted.

Ellen shrugged and did what she was told. Only then did she see Richard Pierce lurking at the foot of the stairs.

"Make sure you search every inch of that bag," Pierce snarled.

The police officer glared at him. "We know how to do our job, sir."

"Is it all right if I sit down? I've had a busy day," she asked the officer.

"Go ahead."

Ellen watched the police sift through her backpack. They did a careful job. They didn't scatter her papers or worse, dump her things all over the ground. They inspected her belongings with calm thoroughness.

All while Pierce watched, pacing back and forth like an angry tiger.

The head officer handed her the backpack. "Okay, miss. Thank you for your time."

Pierce shot Ellen a withering look. "What? Do it again!" he demanded.

"Sir, there's nothing in her bag."

"Do it again! Have your assistant do it this time." He nodded at the officer's partner.

Both men tensed, offended by Pierce's choice of words.

She offered the backpack. "If it'll make him happy, go ahead."

Once she handed it off, she pulled aside the other officer. "Look, I don't want to cause any trouble. Especially when a professor's involved. But this guy's done nothing but harass me since the beginning of the semester. He's convinced I have something he wants. Some book. That's what you're looking for, right?"

"I can't tell you that."

"What is she telling you? What are you telling him, you bitch?"

Pierce approached her with alarming speed. If there hadn't been two officers beside her, she would have high-tailed it into the library. One of them stepped in front of her.

"There is no need for that kind of language, sir."

"You see?" Ellen exclaimed. "You see what I have to deal with? He's crazy!"

Pierce launched himself at her. "*You fucking bitch!*"

He took a swing at the police officer who stood between them. The officer's response was instant. He grabbed Pierce's arm and wrenched it behind his back. Pierce screamed, crashing to his knees. Ellen saw a flash of silver.

"You're under arrest for assaulting a police officer."

"You can't! You can't!" Pierce protested as the handcuffs clicked onto his wrists. "It's her. She's the one that's the problem!"

"Not from where I'm standing, sir."

He motioned for his partner to return Ellen's backpack.

"Are you all right?" the partner asked her.

"I think so," Ellen breathed. "Thank God you were here."

"You bitch! You fucking bitch!" Pierce continued to rant as he rolled on his stomach, trying to get up.

Ellen shuddered. It reminded her of the Joey thing, grinding glass into its body.

"Is this normal behavior, officer? I mean, even for Miskatonic that's strange, right?"

"Don't worry. He'll be getting a full mental evaluation," the officer assured her.

A psychiatric hold. That'll give me seventy-two hours before he's out again. Seventy-two hours, at most. Ellen slung her bag over her shoulder. *I better get moving.*

"Miss?"

"I'm sorry. Did you say something?"

"Would you like a ride home?"

"I would. Thank you."

Anything to put more time on the clock.

Chapter Eighteen

Carter waited for her at the front gates of the house. When she arrived in a squad car, he looked concerned. But when he saw her in the passenger seat, he relaxed a little. The officer rounded the car and opened the door for her. Thankfully, she didn't have to go to the station to press charges. Since Pierce took a swing at a cop, it was out of her hands. Ellen hoped a felony charge would be enough to keep the professor occupied.

Don't count on it, she warned herself. Richard Pierce was a well-connected man. He would find someone to help him post bail. Maybe even weasel his way out of the psychiatric hold.

"Jesus, what happened to you?" Carter asked after the squad car left.

"Do you mind if we wait until Joshua gets here? I don't want to tell the story twice. Besides, I need to talk to you about something."

Carter fidgeted.

"Relax. It's not about the class. I remember our deal," she assured him. "Besides, I know your teaching assistant grades my stuff."

"Actually, I grade your stuff."

"What?"

"I grade your stuff," he repeated.

Ellen remembered her essay. How she questioned her own nature. *He read that. God, he read that.*

"You look disturbed."

"I don't know whether to be flattered or terrified."

He shrugged. "Just satisfying my curiosity, that's all."

"Am I living up to your expectations?"

He gave her a measured look. "What did you want to talk about?" he asked.

Ellen couldn't help but think about the girls he expelled from his office. The ones so desperate for his attention. *Don't be like them*, she reminded herself.

She put down her backpack and pulled out a piece of paper. "You were right when you said there were no straight answers. Bentham's not a person. It's a place."

She handed him a photocopy and stood beside him. Her eyes glided across the words she knew by heart.

ACCIDENT AT BENTHAM MINE

ARKHAM – Tragedy visited the small mining community of Bentham Corners yesterday. A major tunnel in the Bentham Mine collapsed, trapping fifty-two miners. All are feared dead.

The accident occurred shortly after three in the afternoon. According to the survivors, workers in the deepest part of the mine had just blasted a section of earth when they heard a deafening roar. "A rush of hot air knocked me down," Jonas Tobias recalls. "The impact drove the man next to me into one of the posts and killed him. I started running and yelling to the others to get out."

Michael Bradford, who was working in the shaft just above the mine, said, "I heard men screaming from below. Then I saw miners frantically scampering up the ladders." Only eight men managed to reach safety before the shaft collapsed. Among those presumed dead is twenty-five-year-old skip tender Ivan Leibowitz, who stayed at his post to warn the other miners. "I told him to get out while he could." Bradford insists. "But he refused to leave his post. He died blowing a whistle. Sounding the alarm so we could get out." Company officials and miners alike are calling Leibowitz a hero.

The tragedy is especially devastating to the small community of Bentham Corners, a village fifty miles west of Arkham. A company town of five hundred people, its existence revolves around the mines. Almost everyone in the town knew the fifty-two men who died. "They were our fathers and sons, uncles and brothers, husbands, students, and friends." Lily Graham, a local teacher, laments, "They can never be replaced."

An investigation into the cause of the accident is being conducted.

"When did this happen?" Carter asked once he finished the article.

"In 1945. Just after the war in Europe ended. In the narrow sliver of time between VE day and VJ day." She handed him a small glittering rock. "This is what they mined. Iron pyrite. The stone of protection."

"You keep one in your backpack?"

"I borrowed it from Mote It Be," she explained. "We sell a lot of them. They're supposed to ward off negative energy and shield a person from physical harm."

"They were also used as the igniter in old colonial guns."

Ellen chuckled, amused by the irony. *If the regulars at Mote It Be knew what else their mystical rocks did . . .*

"You ever see those ray guns that spark when you pump the trigger?" he asked.

"I had one when I was a kid."

"Well, iron pyrite was what produced the spark." Carter paused and looked at her. "What's the connection between this and the chthonians?"

"I don't know. That's what I'm hoping to find out," she replied as she stuffed her things back into her bag. "I'm going to interview one of the survivors of the disaster."

"Someone's still alive?"

"He's in one of the nursing homes in town. Edgewood Manor. I talked to him on the phone. He's eighty-six. He's got some health issues, but he's still as sharp as a tack."

"Mind if I come with you?"

"I was hoping you might," she admitted. "I'm still a newbie when it comes to all this."

The van carrying Joshua arrived. Ellen tried to look inside. She could always tell how things went by the way her uncle sat in his wheelchair. The tinted glass was too dark for her to see.

A man popped out of the van and shot her a bright smile. "Oh my God, it's an angel from heaven!" he exclaimed, clutching his chest. Ellen beamed. All the drivers at Arkham Paratransit were good, but Marshall was an old friend.

He was one of the few people she knew who survived his tenure at Miskatonic. Of course, it didn't hurt that he avoided the spooky stuff. His degree was in physical therapy.

Ellen ran up to him. Her friend lifted her off her feet and twirled her. She liked the way it made her feel. Weightless. Free of the burdens of the world, if only for a second.

"It's so good to see you, Marsh."

"Hey, why don't you and I blow this joint?" he offered when he set her down. "Run away and sip margaritas on a beach somewhere."

"I think your girlfriend might have a thing or two to say about that."

"Oh, she's coming with us," he winked at her as he opened the side door.

"I swear, a man could waste away while you flirt," Joshua groused.

Ellen watched Marshall unfold the ramp and lower Joshua to the ground. She glanced at Carter. His eyes sparkled with tears.

Ellen drifted back to him. "I keep forgetting you're a newbie, too," she murmured.

"Huh?"

"Joshua wasn't paralyzed when you knew him."

"No." He fell silent, his mind drifting. "The last time I saw him he was preparing to hike the Appalachian Trail."

Joshua. Hiking?

"God, I wish I had seen that."

"He used to be so . . . vibrant."

"He still is," she reassured him.

Still, she had to admit Joshua looked rough. She hoped the trip out had been worth it.

"Okay, sweetheart, I have to make tracks." Marshall rounded the van. "If you ever change your mind about Mexico, call me."

"I will."

"He's serious, you know," Joshua said as the van pulled away.

"He is not."

"If you called and told him you were ready to go, he'd drop his girlfriend in a heartbeat. I mean, wouldn't you, Andrew?"

"Do you mind?" Ellen blurted, horrified.

"I don't have a girlfriend," Carter murmured.

"Why not?" Joshua demanded.

"Joshua, that's none of your business," Ellen scolded him.

Carter gave her a pointed look. "You know, I am capable of speaking for myself."

She threw up her hands in surrender. "Then I'll leave you gentlemen to it."

"She's mad at us," her uncle said in a mock stage whisper.

"No, old man, I'm mad at you," Ellen snapped. "You know, maybe I *should* take Marshall up on Mexico."

She tugged hard on the gates. A bolt of searing pain shot through her injured hand. "Shit!" she hissed.

Carter instantly appeared at her side.

"What's wrong?"

She showed him the blood spots on her bandage.

"Let's go sit by the river," Joshua suggested. "Carter can take care of your wound while we talk."

"There's no need. I'm—" she started to protest.

Her uncle fixed her with a stern look. "Ellen."

The late afternoon sun was just dipping behind the trees when the two men settled on the weathered bench. Ellen went back to the house to fetch the first aid supplies. She knew they would talk about her while she was gone.

Ellen closed her eyes as she rummaged in the bathroom, trying to connect with Joshua. No luck. They had been together too long. Her uncle knew how to block her, to shield important thoughts.

For a moment she considered trying Carter. Then she remembered the flat look he had given her when she asked him how she was doing in his class. *Don't want to go there.*

"I was just telling Andrew I returned the book successfully," Joshua said when Ellen rejoined them.

She sat beside Carter. His head was down, resting on the picnic table. It was an oddly boyish gesture. Ellen fought the urge to rub his back.

"How was it, dealing with the librarians? Was it bad?" she asked.

The look on Joshua's face said it all. "No worse than dealing with dementors," he replied.

Despite her uncle's grim expression, Ellen smiled. They read Harry Potter as they moved from place to place. No matter where they were, her uncle would always find an English-language bookstore.

"I owe you," Carter said, lifting his head. "I owe you big time."

Joshua nodded in her direction. "You owe her, too."

"No, old man, he owes you," Ellen said before Carter had a chance to respond. "Let's not make this more complicated than it needs to be."

"No one followed you?" Carter demanded. "You're sure?"

"An old man in a wheelchair? Hell, people avoid looking at me." He nodded at Ellen. "And Pierce was focused on her, not me."

Carter turned, giving Ellen his full attention.

"Tell me, my dear, how did your part in the bait and switch go?" Joshua asked.

"Dr. Pierce was arrested for assaulting a police officer."

"What?" the two men blurted at almost the same time.

Ellen looked down, trying to hide her pleasure. "Not bad for a girl, huh?" she taunted her uncle. Whenever he felt she had to try harder, he challenged her with those words. They always worked.

"Pierce was convinced I had the book. He showed up with the cops at the library, all hot to catch me in the act. When they found nothing in my backpack, he went nuts. Of course, it didn't help that I psychically Rickrolled him."

Joshua frowned. "Rickrolled?"

"I planted an earworm in his head so he couldn't concentrate."

"What on earth is an earworm?" her uncle asked.

Ellen rolled her eyes. "Geez, grandpa, look it up on the internet. You know what the internet is, don't you?"

Joshua turned to Carter for an explanation. "Do you have any idea what this girl is talking about?"

The younger man smiled. "I've heard the song, yes. It stays with you for *days*."

Carter finally noticed her injured hand. He unwrapped the bandage and started to treat the wound. She expected him to be brusque, like the rest of him, but his touch was warm. Surprisingly gentle.

"You continue to amaze me, Carter," she said as he dabbed cream into her palm.

"I wasn't aware I amazed you at all," he replied, talking to her hand.

"Next thing you'll be telling me is that you've been to a rave."

Carter looked up. "Have you?"

"Kids, can we get back to the point?" Joshua demanded. Her uncle's impatience was mixed with hurt.

He doesn't like being left out, she thought as she looked at him. *Welcome to the club, buddy.*

"What happened?" Carter urged her.

"While they looked through my bag, I took one of the officers aside and told them Pierce had been stalking me all semester. Talking nonsense about having a book he wanted. He overheard me and lost it. I mean, completely fucking lost it."

"Language," Joshua warned her. Ellen pursed her lips.

"He lunged at me, right in front of the police. And when one of the officers stepped between us, he took a swing at the guy. The last time I saw Pierce he was on his way to a psychiatric hold."

"All right, Ellen, that's it. I want you to stop investigating this. Now!" Joshua ordered her.

Carter flinched as he wrapped her hand. Ellen wondered how many times he had been on the receiving end of Joshua's wrath.

"I can't," she insisted.

"Can't or won't?"

"Can't," she replied. "Look, I'm not happy about the situation, but I'm already on this lunatic's radar. If I stay where I am, I'm a sitting duck. If I keep one step ahead of him, if I find out what he's doing, I might have a chance. I might even be able to stop him."

Joshua turned to Carter. "Andrew, would you please talk some sense into her?"

Ellen waited for him to take the old man's side.

Carter finished bandaging her hand and sat back.

"She's right. She has the bull's attention. Now all she can do is run for the fence."

"And hopefully clear it," she added.

Carter gave her a skeptical look. "Yes, hopefully."

"How many of your students have died?" The question spilled out before Ellen could stop it.

"You don't have to answer that, Andrew" Joshua advised.

Carter stared at her for a long time. "Not as many as have died with *him*."

"Is that why he was disciplined?"

"One of the reasons, yes."

One of the reasons . . . Ellen shuddered as she thought about what a man like Richard Pierce might be capable of.

"I still want to help," she decided.

Joshua turned to Carter. "Okay, I'll let her go if you promise to look after—"

"No," Ellen blurted, a little too loudly. "You can't do that."

"Can't do what?" her uncle demanded.

"He's not my babysitter! If you're serious about protecting me, give me one of your guns. The Glock would be nice."

"You know how to shoot?" Carter asked her.

Her uncle hissed, offended by the question. "Please, Andrew. How many years have you known me? She knows how to shoot."

"Which makes not having my own gun embarrassing. I mean how can you expect me to—"

Joshua glared at her. "Now is not the time, my dear."

Carter stood and wiped his hands with a towel. "Well, I'd love to stay and listen to this family argument, but I have a graduate seminar in about twenty minutes."

"Always on the wheel, aren't we, my boy?" Joshua observed.

"Never stops."

Ellen felt something personal pass between the two men. A foreign language she would never learn.

"Elle?" her uncle called out.

"Hmm?"

"I asked if you would see Andrew out."

"She doesn't have to—" Carter started to object.

Ellen produced her set of medieval keys and rattled them. "Yes, I do. The keys to the kingdom, remember?"

Carter said nothing as they headed for the gate. Ellen appreciated the silence. Even though they talked for only half an hour, she was drained. She gazed out at the Miskatonic as they walked to the gates. The wind whipped the water into short, frothy waves. It was getting close to the golden hour, the time when even a place like Arkham seemed charming. Magical in a *good* way.

Ellen longed to walk the banks of the river, to soak up the rays of the setting sun. She couldn't. The investigation had come at the expense of her studies. An all-nighter loomed in her future.

"Is it Ellen or Elle?" Carter asked.

"Excuse me?"

"Joshua calls you Elle sometimes. Is it Ellen or Elle?"

"Ellen," she replied as she fiddled with the lock on the gate, using her good hand this time. "I made the mistake of telling him I wished I had a nickname. He came up with Elle. I hate it. I share my name with a fashion magazine."

"It could have been worse. He could have called you Lenny."

"The old man wouldn't have survived if he called me that."

Carter smiled, a rich, broad smile that lit up his face. He lingered at the open gate. "I haven't had a chance to thank you. You put yourself on the line for me. I don't forget things like that."

He offered her his hand. Ellen took it, clasping it between hers.

"I'm glad I could help. And it was fun. In a twisted sort of way. A nice break from classes," she admitted. "Except yours, of course."

"Of course," he agreed as he stepped through the gates.

Back to the normal world, at least for a little while, Ellen thought.

"I'll see you tomorrow at Edgewood Manor. Eleven o'clock, okay?" Ellen called out after him.

"I'll be there."

Deep. Down. Dark.
????-??-1945

Am I still alive? The line between life and death is so thin I don't know what side I'm on anymore.

I have seen her. The person who will come next, who will free me from this unnatural prison. A woman with blond hair and blue eyes, who has a Jewish name. Strange. At first I thought it was a delusion, a last gasp of hope from my dying brain. Except . . .

I saw her even before the accident.

In my dreams.

I woke up in the middle of the night and wrote letters to her.

I have tried to prepare her, to lay the groundwork.

I hope she finds the breadcrumbs I left her. That she picks up the trail.

Hurry, girl, hurry. Before I . . .

Chapter Nineteen

Ellen stood on the sidewalk outside Edgewood Manor.

The retirement home was old, at least by American standards. Ellen peered at the stone structure that squatted behind the old Victorian, the remnants of a family home that dated back to colonial times.

Over the years Edgewood Manor expanded from its original footprint until it assumed its present form—a private facility that housed forty senior citizens. The place was a crazy quilt of culture. An intersection of East and West. Old and new. Ellen paused to admire the onion domes, the cupolas and the minarets, the Victorian lead-glass windows.

Despite the bewildering mix, the place worked. Edgewood Manor wasn't a grim Winchester House. It was bright. Welcoming.

As Ellen climbed the stairs to the main building, her spirits lifted for the first time since her friends died.

The residents added to the atmosphere. Spread out on the wraparound porch, they enjoyed the cool autumn day. A few greeted her as she walked up the stairs. One man even whistled.

Ellen's eyes lingered on the plaque by the front door.

Historical landmark #544: Edgewood Manor was one of the last stops on the underground railroad. Between 1850 and 1865, more than 30,000 slaves reached Canada through this secret network.

"Cool," Ellen breathed.

Andrew Carter thundered up the stairs.

"Sorry I'm late," he gasped. "The president of the university showed up at my office. Wanted to talk to me about a stolen book that turned up in one of the library's return bins."

"And?"

"He's suspicious, but doesn't have proof, so . . ." His eyes settled on her black sweater and short herringbone skirt. "What's with the getup?"

"I thought I'd dress up. Show Mr. Graham a little respect," she explained as she smoothed down her skirt.

"You should tell her she looks nice," a man in one of the porch chairs suggested.

Carter shot the man a dirty look. "You look nice," he parroted as he looked away, his eyes fixing on a spot just above her shoulder.

"Thank you very much," she offered him a mock curtsy. When he continued to stare into space, she frowned. "What's wrong?"

"Nothing. It's just—" He moved closer so the residents wouldn't hear. "I hate these places. I'd rather put a bullet in my head than end up here."

"That's a little extreme, don't you think?"

"No."

He opened the front door and waited for her to go inside. Ellen ignored the cue.

"I guess I can't blame you for feeling that way," she ventured. "I bet you've seen a lot."

Carter's mouth curled into a smirk. "Save the charm for the inmates, Ellen."

The front parlor was just as crowded as the porch. Ellen looked at the residents relaxing in the sunlit room and felt a stab of envy. She couldn't remember the last time she had a day off. Between Stephanie, Joey, Pierce, and her studies, there was no time to stop. No time to even slow down. Ellen stared at a woman curled up with a book, a man playing chess with another resident. She wondered if she would ever have time to rest.

Harold Graham awaited them in the room he shared with his wife, Lily. She wasn't there, but Ellen saw her everywhere. Family pictures covered the walls. Nice, homey touches decorated the room—a wooden dresser, a couple of handwoven rugs, a chair, and a small loveseat arranged around a glass coffee table.

Mr. Graham sat in an old reclining chair. Just as she suspected, he dressed up for the occasion. He wore his best suit and a tie.

"Miss Logan?" The man struggled to free himself from his chair.

She extended her hand. "You must be Mr. Graham."

"In the flesh. At least for a little while longer."

Ellen nodded at the oxygen tank next to his chair. "Did the Bentham Mine do that?"

"No. Three packs a day did," he replied and looked at her hopefully. "You wouldn't happen to have a cigarette, would you?"

"No, but I did bring something else."

The old man's eyes widened when she dug a bottle out of her bag. He agreed to talk to her on one condition—that she smuggle in a bottle of whiskey. She knew he would be happy with a generic brand, but she bought a ten-year-old Glenmorangie single malt.

He gazed at her with such gratitude that Ellen had to look away.

She grabbed Carter's arm and urged him forward. "I'd like you to meet Dr. Andrew Carter."

"Dr. Carter?"

"Yes, sir."

"*The* Dr. Carter?"

Carter flinched. "*A* Dr. Carter."

"Are you the one who wrote all those books about mythology?" Mr. Graham pressed him.

Mythology, Ellen thought with a snort.

"Yes, I am," he answered.

Graham grabbed his hand and pumped it vigorously. "My wife is a big fan of your work."

He motioned for them to sit. Ellen joined Carter on the loveseat. It was a close fit. They were wedged together so tightly that she pressed up against him.

"I wish Lily could be with us, but she's gone to the outlet mall with the others. Can't resist a good deal." He paused, his expression darkening. "That and she doesn't like to talk about the past. Especially when it involves Bentham."

"Were you married at the time?" Ellen asked.

Carter shifted beside her, suddenly noticing their closeness.

"No, but we were dating when it happened. She was the schoolteacher in Bentham Corners. Trying to teach the kids something that would get them out of that godforsaken place."

"Is it true that Bentham was a company town?"

"Yes."

"In the 1940s? I thought they were a nineteenth-century thing."

"Darling, there were company towns in the 1970s." He eased himself back into his chair, letting out a soft grunt as he settled. "But before we go any further, I need a drink. Will you join me?"

"Of course."

"Dr. Carter?"

"Sure."

"There are some glasses under the table. Would you fetch them for me?" he asked Ellen.

When she bent to retrieve them the old man looked down her sweater. She considered covering up but saw no harm in letting him have a peek. He was harmless.

Graham filled the glasses and raised his in a toast. "To old friends."

"Old friends," she echoed.

Ellen felt a sharp twinge as she remembered Stephanie and Joey. She knocked back the whiskey to chase the pain. Her eyes watered as the liquid scorched her throat.

When she set down the empty glass, the two men were staring at her. A flush ran up her face.

"What?"

The old man broke the silence. "A woman after my own heart," he sighed. "My dear, if I was Dr. Carter's age—"

"And single," she reminded him.

He nodded. "And single."

The mention of his wife robbed him of his spryness. "Well, I'm sure you've heard it all before," the old man sighed.

She ducked down to catch his eye. "I'm still flattered."

The two of them shared a smile.

"You're a sweet girl, but I'm sure you have better things to do than flirt with a dirty old man." He sat back to nurse his drink. "What do you want to know about Bentham?"

"Let's start with the mine itself."

She bent down to retrieve some files. This time Graham didn't ogle her. He was already moving back in time, and his eyes took on a distant, dreamy look.

I hope he's up to this, Ellen thought as she unrolled the map of the Bentham Mine.

The old man leaned forward, digging in his pocket for his reading glasses. Carter leaned forward, too.

"My God, where did you get this?" Graham asked.

"From the curator of the Arkham Historical Society." She pinned down the document with some of his wife's knick-knacks. "Mrs. Lyles has a special collection of materials on the

Bentham disaster. Pictures, diaries . . . she even tape-recorded interviews with some of the survivors."

"I didn't know anyone cared," Mr. Graham replied.

Ellen heard the soft, wounded tone in his voice. "Mrs. Lyles does," she reassured him. "In fact, it's safe to say that it's a bit of an obsession with her."

"Why?"

"I think it goes back to her days as a labor organizer," Ellen ventured, wondering if it was wise to divulge the woman's militant past.

It didn't bother Graham.

"If there was ever a place that needed a union, it was Bentham," he said as he sipped his whiskey. "I've been a miner since I was fourteen. I come from a long line of miners. Father, uncles . . . practically everyone in my family worked underground. I knew what to expect. I went into the job with no illusions. But nothing, and I mean nothing, prepared me for Bentham.

"The mine was an evil place. I'm not just talking about the slave drivers who ran the site. They were bad enough. But there was something else, something in the . . . I could never quite put my finger on it. It was a darkness. A darkness that had nothing to do with light, you know what I mean?"

Even though he hadn't been underground for more than fifty years, Ellen could feel the fear wafting off him.

"Can you show me where you worked?" she asked.

He pointed to a level halfway down the mine.

"And where did the accident take place?"

He squinted hard and poked at the base of the map. "Here. A few levels below where I worked." His expression clouded as he studied the map. "I think there must have been some terrible air down there because the guys . . . Look, I don't want to speak ill of the dead. They were good men, even the ones who caused trouble. But in the weeks leading up to the accident they started acting strange. No, not strange. Batshit crazy."

Carter stirred beside her. "What do you mean?" he asked.

"Every level has its culture. When a group works together they develop a common language, share stories, experience things that other groups don't. But at the end of the day we're all still miners, you know? There's a bond there, a brotherhood." Graham paused as Ellen poured him another finger of whiskey. "In the weeks before the accident we lost that connection. They became secretive, refusing to talk to anyone outside their little circle. And then there were the animals."

"Animals?" Ellen was convinced she misheard him, but the old man nodded as he picked up his drink.

"You've heard of canaries in coal mines, right? Well, we used to take small animals underground as an early warning system for toxic gas. Nothing unusual about that—it's a common practice. But their animals didn't come back up. It was a one-way trip for all of them. That just didn't make sense. If there was gas where the men worked, no one would have come back up."

"Sacrifices," Carter breathed. The old man gave him an uneasy look.

"Was there anyone in charge of what they were doing?" Ellen asked.

"God, what was his name? Ivan, um . . . Liebowitz. Ivan Liebowitz."

Ellen felt the hair on her arms stand up. Ivan Leibowitz was the man in her dream. The man twirling the pickaxe. She was sure of it.

"He was with them on the day of the collapse, which was strange. It was supposed to be his day off. Jewish holiday or something."

"Was there anything else unusual about that day?" Ellen asked.

"What do you mean?"

"Any strange activity, sounds?"

"You mean besides the sound of men dying?"

Ellen glanced up at the old man. There was an edge in his voice. They were approaching the border of what he was willing to talk about.

"I meant no disrespect, sir. I just want to understand what happened."

"Why is it so important to you?"

Before she had a chance to respond, Carter spoke up. "We have reason to believe some students have taken an interest in the Bentham Mine. They may be down there as we speak."

Ellen looked at him, stunned. This was the first she heard of it. It made sense. She couldn't believe she didn't make the connection.

"Students? Students from Miskatonic?" Graham blurted once he got over his shock.

"Yes."

"No, that's impossible. He said he . . ." The old man stopped, but Ellen heard the rest of the sentence. *Took care of it. Ivan said he would take care of it.*

"Did you work with Mr. Leibowitz?" she asked.

Graham's mood shifted. He glared at them with open hostility.

"I want you to leave."

"Just one more thing, Mr. Graham, please." She didn't want to ask the question, but the last nightmare was too strong. When she was crushed under rubble, when she was looking out through someone else's eyes, she saw numbers on her arm. A faint tattoo.

"Did Ivan Leibowitz escape from a concentration camp?"

Graham was on his feet. "*Get out!* I said get out!" he thundered. The man's body shook with a rage that made him seem years younger. Ellen could see the tough, hard-drinking miner he once was.

So could Carter. He moved in front of her, protecting her as she gathered her things. But he couldn't shield her from Graham's words.

"Fucking university. They should burn it to the ground. It's because of people like you that evil thrives."

Ellen stepped away from Carter.

"No, it's because of you. It's because of you that history repeats itself."

Graham flinched. For a moment, Ellen thought he would relent. Tell her what *really* happened.

"Thank you for visiting, Miss Logan, Dr. Carter," he nodded, his words iced with fake civility.

Ellen marched into the hall, with Carter on her heels. She was angry. Frustrated. No one else would come to talk to Harold Graham. Not before he died. Before those smoke-addled lungs gave out on him.

All that knowledge. Gone . . .

"*You!*" a voice bellowed.

Ellen turned to see a man in pajamas and a bathrobe headed toward them. At first she thought he was talking to her. But the man's eyes never left Carter.

"I told you never to come back," the old man barked.

"No. You told me never to visit *you*. I'm not here to see you."

The man responded by punching Carter in the face. The blow caught Carter off guard, knocking him into the wall. Ellen yelped and grabbed the man before he had a chance to launch another attack. His strength impressed her. It was all she could do to hold onto him. After a few moments of wrestling, two burly male nurses arrived. They dragged the man away.

"Carter, are you—"

The question died in her throat. Carter was gone. After a few minutes of searching she found him on the porch. He held his hand to his nose. Blood seeped through his fingers. Ellen dug into her bag and handed him a Kleenex.

"You okay?"

Carter glared at her as he snatched the tissues. "What do you think?"

"Who was that man?"

"My father," he replied after a long silence.

"Your father? That man was your father?"

"*Is* my father," he corrected her. "In case you didn't notice, he's very much alive."

"What's he doing here? Is he sick?"

"I'm hiding him."

"Hiding him from what?"

"From people who might use him to get to me."

Ellen gawked at Carter. "You're kidding me, right?"

"'I have no idea what it's like to be you.' You said that when we first met. Remember? Well . . ." The words trailed off into a shrug.

"No one knows he's here?"

"Not even Joshua. You're the only one."

"I won't tell anyone," she reassured him.

"You're too kind," he replied, without much enthusiasm.

Ellen rested her head against the warm wall. "Tell that to the old man who just kicked us out of his room," she said.

"He doesn't count."

"Why not?"

"Because he's hiding something." Carter leaned back, unwinding now that the conversation changed direction. "I'm surprised you got as far as you did. Of course, it didn't hurt that you let him look down your shirt."

"You noticed, huh?"

"Trust me. I see it. *A lot.*" He shot her a pointed look. A don't-even-try-it-with-me look. "By the way, how did you get your hands on such fine whiskey?"

"Fake ID."

Carter blanched. "How old *are* you?" he demanded.

Ellen considered evading the question. Her age was always a touchy subject. "Twenty. Four months to go until
twenty-one."

"Jesus Christ!"

She glanced at him. "Why do you sound so surprised?
Most of your students are my age."

"Maybe so, but I don't fraternize with them."

"Fraternize?" Ellen echoed, the word irritating her. "Is that
what you think we're doing? Fraternizing?"

"What would you call it?"

"I thought we were on a case. You know, investigating?"

A bus pulled up to the curb, unloading a group of se-
niors from a morning expedition. They marched in formation,
shopping bags in hand.

Ellen consulted her watch. It was almost noon. "I don't
have time for this. The police have already had Pierce for eight
hours. I need to go."

Carter grabbed her wrist. "Hey, hey, hey. It's not personal.
You just need to understand that . . . I need to be careful, okay?
You think the punishment for stealing books is bad?"

He tried to pass it off as a joke, but the words hung heavy
in the air. He let go of her wrist, suddenly aware of the contact.

"Why did you ask him about a guy in a concentration
camp?" Carter asked. "Ivan, um . . ."

"Ivan Leibowitz." Something tightened inside her when
she said his name.

"Why are you so interested in him?"

"Because he may be responsible for what happened in the
Bentham Mine."

"In a good way or a bad way?"

"I don't know," she admitted. "It's no coincidence he was there on the day of the collapse. And on the level where all hell broke loose."

"What makes you so sure?"

"Just a hunch."

"Feminine intuition? Or are your Spidey senses tingling?"

Ellen smiled at the blatant attempt to bait her. "I won't even dignify that with a response."

She picked up her bag and slung it over her shoulder. "Let's get out of here before your father comes back for round two."

Chapter Twenty

The Headless Horseman.

That was all Ellen could think about as they walked up the road to Bentham Corners. She looked at the tightly clustered trees. Their skeletal branches loomed over them, poised to strike. Ellen could picture the Headless Horseman in a place like this. Lurking around the next corner. Waiting for an opportunity to strike . . .

Ellen's hand dropped to the knife strapped to her side.

"Why did you have to teach the Headless Horseman right before we came out here?" she complained.

A wolfish smile spread across Carter's face. "Are you scared?"

"You think it's funny?"

"I think it's charming you can be frightened by a folk tale that dates back to the Middle Ages. Especially these days."

"The sad voice of experience."

"And age," he added.

Ellen rolled her eyes. "Oh, please! You're not old," she replied. "You're still high on the chili list."

"On the what?"

Ellen stopped to look at him. "You don't know about the chili list?"

"Do I want to know?"

"Every year Miskatonic students vote on who the hottest teacher is."

"Oh Jesus," Carter groaned.

"Guess who's been number one several years in a row?"

He broke out into a fierce blush. "*Oh Jesus.*"

"According to voters, the touch of gray makes you look even sexier."

Carter waved his hands in the air. "Too much information. Way, way too much information!"

"Well, if you ever want to know more, the website is—"

"Not. Interested."

Ellen smiled, warmed by the exchange. The feeling didn't last long. The skeletal trees, the heavy slate sky . . . she already felt like they were in a twilight world. A world that was about to get darker.

"I keep thinking about the others," she murmured.

"Others?"

"You know that Spielberg film about aliens? The one that isn't *E.T.*?"

"*Close Encounters*," Carter offered.

"The character Richard Dreyfus played. Remember how obsessed he was with getting to Wyoming after the aliens contacted him? When the government arrested him, they said that a lot of other people got the same message, but only a few made it as far as he did."

Uneasiness crept into Carter's eyes. "What are you getting at?" he demanded.

"The creature's been hammering people with nightmares. Trying to broadcast to as many people as it can. Do you think we're the only ones who made it this far? I mean, beside the frat?"

His hand caressed the gun strapped to his side. "I sure fucking hope so."

They fell silent when they reached the clearing. Bentham Corners spread out before them—a dark, cheerless village clinging to the side of a hill.

Ellen visited many ghost towns. She enjoyed their quiet serenity—the whistle of the wind through gutted buildings, the weeds that invaded every nook and cranny, the cooing of the birds resting in the rafters. Even the voices of the dead were more subdued. There was none of the greediness, none of the desperate grasping she felt in other places. She could walk through a graveyard and not be assaulted by the demands of the dead.

Bentham Corners offered no such comfort. The town didn't fade away, the victim of a slow economic decline. The end came suddenly, in a spasm. As they walked into the village, they came across signs of lives violently interrupted. Suitcases lying on the street, their belongings long since scattered to the winds. Rusted out cars, keys dangling from dead ignitions. And toys. Lots and lots of toys. Porcelain dolls, metal trucks, a small arsenal of BB guns. Childhood possessions dropped in the rush to flee.

Ellen wrapped her arms around her body and shivered. "God, this place reminds me of Pripyat."

Carter looked up from a toy he was inspecting. "You've been to Pripyat?"

"I wasn't supposed to. Joshua forbade it, but we were living in Kiev at the time and I . . . well, I couldn't resist." Her face darkened as she remembered the abandoned city five miles from Chernobyl. "I wish I hadn't gone."

"Why?" he asked.

"I don't know how to explain it without sounding like a complete lunatic."

"Try."

"This place feels a lot like Pripyat. Sure, people died here, but the miners and the nuclear plant workers, they knew they were going to die. They resigned themselves to their fate. But the others, the ones who were forced to evacuate, they left more of themselves behind. They became ghosts, too."

"And you can feel them here?"

"They're like a fog." Her voice tightened around the words.

Ellen put her hand on the ground. A vibration crawled up her arm. *It's here. Waiting . . .*

Loud voices broke the stillness of Bentham Corners. Ellen and Carter looked at each other and scurried for the safety of a nearby house. Once inside, they dropped below a window and peeked over the broken glass.

Two men appeared on the empty street. *More members of Joey's frat*, she thought. *Jesus, how many of them are out here?*

Ellen held her breath as they walked by the window. There was no need. The men were in the middle of a heated exchange. Oblivious to anything except their argument.

As soon as they passed, she rose to her feet. Carter was gone. "What the—" Ellen whispered.

She wandered through the shadowy house, searching for him. There was nothing but dust and dried mouse droppings. She hissed her frustration. *Where could he have gone? Where could he have gone in the ten seconds I was concentrating on those men?*

When she reached the bedroom, she plopped down on a dusty mattress. She idly opened the drawer on the nightstand. Sitting almost dead center in the drawer was a stack of letters, bound together with string. The top letter was dated July 13, 1945. Ellen shivered. July 13. The day the mine collapsed. Even though she had never seen his writing before, she knew it was him.

Ivan. Ivan Leibowitz.

I have no idea who I'm writing to. I see you in my dreams, which is strange because you should be in my night-mares. You are Hitler's ideal woman. Blond-haired Aryan goddess. A cruel bitch. The she wolf who laughed as she beat us. The kind who spat in my face as they hauled us off to the camps. Strange, a girl like you would have a Jewish name . . . Jessica. Hebrew for "God beholds."

Ellen leapt off the bed. A cold cascade rushed down her spine. *He knows my real name. He died forty years before I was born and yet . . .*

"He knows me," she whispered.

"I can see you as well."

She spun around to face the man lurking in the corner. He was Andrew Carter, at least in the flesh. But the body language was wrong. It was tense. Hostile.

Ellen was suddenly aware of how large Carter was. *He could snap my neck*, she thought. *He could snap my neck before I even raised my hands. And then there was the gun . . .*

"You *should* be afraid," Ivan Liebowitz replied as he advanced on her. Carter's light-blue eyes burned with pure hatred. He walked around her in slow circles.

Inspecting me like they did at the camp, she thought with a shudder.

"I expected you to be bigger. But you're so small."

Ellen tried not to look at the gun strapped to Carter's side.

"I'm not a Nazi, Mr. Leibowitz. I wasn't even alive when you were in the camps. You've been here a long time. A very long time."

The man's face clouded. "Am I dead?" he whispered.

Ellen nodded.

His knees buckled.

Ellen grabbed his arm (*Carter's arm*, she corrected herself) and guided him to the bed.

He latched on to her wrist. "If I'm dead, how am I here?" he demanded. His grip was firm, but he had moved beyond the idea of hurting her. "How am I able to touch you? Are you dead, too?"

"You're in the body of someone else. Someone who's alive."

She pulled up Carter's shirtsleeves and exposed his arms. Ivan's eyes widened when he saw his camp tattoo was no longer there.

"Whose body am I in?"

"It belongs to my teacher."

He gazed at her for a long time. Then he closed his eyes, letting out a long, sensual sigh. He reminded Ellen of someone savoring a fine wine.

"Oh, he wants to be more than your teacher."

Carter leaned back on the bed, giving her an unmistakable come-hither stare.

What the hell is going on? Ellen wondered as she returned his gaze. *Is Ivan using Carter's body to express Carter's desire? Or am I seeing Ivan's desire reflected in Carter's eyes?*

"We don't have time for this," she blurted. "I need your help. People are in the mine. And I think they've reawakened the thing you buried."

He jerked, abandoning his seductive pose.

"But that's impossible. I—"

"What did you do?" she asked after a long silence.

He pursed his lips. "I did what I had to."

"You need to tell me what happened."

"There's no time. You need to *see* what happened."

He cupped her face in his hands and pulled her close. Ellen felt a rush of attraction. *It's not Carter,* she reminded herself.

Ivan Leibowitz pressed his forehead to hers. He took a deep shuddering breath.

Ellen's head spun.

She screamed as the world tore apart.

———————

Ellen struck her head on something hard. The blow revived her, but it failed to bring her to her senses. All she saw was darkness. She forced herself to blink, to open her eyes as wide as she could. Nothing changed. She was in a small space. She could feel it bearing down on her like a tomb.

A bubble of panic rose in her chest. *I'm in the mine. Oh God, I'm in the mine. Ivan grabbed me and dragged me into . . .*

Take it easy, her rational voice commanded. *Slow and steady. Keep your breath slow and steady.*

Ellen propped herself on her elbows. Something cold and heavy slid off her stomach. The object landed on the floor with a jangle and a thud. Now that she was awake her mind bombarded her with questions.

Where am I?

What happened?

Where did Carter go?

Is Ivan still with him?

In him?

She reached out, hoping to find him lying next to her. She was alone.

With shaking hands Ellen explored the dimensions of her enclosed space. The surface beneath her fingertips was smooth. It had a slightly grainy texture. After what seemed like an eternity of fumbling she found a small depression. She dug her fingers into it and pulled.

The surface yielded with an agonized squeal.

Ellen tumbled out of a closet. Three objects fell on the floor beside her: Carter's gun, his car keys, and a flashlight.

The moment she put her hands on the car keys, the images flowed like water. She watched Carter walk into the room and discover her passed out on the floor. In the distance she heard shouting. The frat boys, drawn to the sound of her scream. Carter dragged her into the closet just as they burst into the room. There was no violence. He surrendered with a matter-of-factness that stunned her. They pushed him out of the house and down the village road. To a place she knew too well.

The place she saw in her nightmares.

"He protected me. Jesus, he protected me," she whispered the words aloud.

Ellen put Ivan Leibowitz's letter on the floor, along with Carter's car keys. Then, with her hands bridging the two worlds, she closed her eyes.

"Help me find him. Help us stop what's happening. Help us get out of here."

The atmosphere in the room changed.

"Look at me," Ivan commanded in a low, hoarse voice.

The "real" Ivan Leibowitz stood before her. Short and slight, only a few inches taller than her, he had a pinched face and a thousand-mile stare that even death failed to erase.

"You told me what to do, but I don't understand," Ellen admitted.

Ivan shot her a cold, amused smile. "Oh, I'm sorry. Did *he* distract you?"

"That's not the way things are."

"He'd be a fool not to act on it," the ghost continued as if he hadn't heard. "If life taught me anything, it's to grab all the happy moments you can."

"Did you have many happy moments?" she asked.

"I don't remember. I thought I would when I crossed over, but—"

Ellen stiffened. "Wait a minute. You said you didn't know you crossed over."

He looked away. "I left you another note. In the church." He nodded out the window at the spire on a nearby hill. "If it's not there, you'll find something with my body. Take it."

"I don't want to disturb your remains."

"They're nothing. Just bones. The most important part of me survived."

"How do you know me?" she demanded. "Why was it me you contacted?"

The ghost reached out and brushed her cheek. "It's not for me to say," he replied, with what seemed like genuine sadness. "Goodbye."

<hr>

The church cast a long shadow over the street. Ellen lingered on the edge, like a diver afraid to jump. She didn't want to go inside. After everything she had seen, everything Ivan showed her, her head was spinning. She didn't know what to think. She didn't know what was real anymore.

And Ivan couldn't be trusted. That little slip about not being aware that he crossed over . . . *Hinky. Isn't that what the police call it when something didn't feel right? Ivan Leibowitz was hinky.*

He was also all she had.

She had to go inside. To find his note. To gather more information. Even if it was a setup.

Ellen's hand dropped to the gun at her side. The weight of the nine-millimeter gave her the courage to keep going.

The late afternoon light penetrated only as far as the entry-way. She pulled out the flashlight and moved deeper into the church. The place still hummed with energy. Ellen could see the ghosts of parishioners hunched in the pews, their presence burned into the room by a lifetime of ritual.

The spectral figures fascinated her. *Faith*, she thought with a twinge. *I wish I had faith. Maybe if I did . . .*

Her foot caught on a loose board. She tripped and landed hard on the floor. The flashlight skittered under one of the benches.

"Ow! Son of a—" She stifled the curse before it had a chance to bounce off the church walls. Cursing in the house of God seemed about as wise as smashing mirrors. *And I need all the help I can get*, she thought as she crawled under the pew.

Ignoring the dust and spiderwebs, she reached in and retrieved the flashlight. As Ellen checked to make sure it still functioned, she saw a book. A hymnal placed at eye level. At first she thought nothing of it. Hymnals were scattered all over the church, waiting for voices that would never return.

This one had an envelope stuffed in it.

Ellen pressed her head against the bench. A wave of dizziness washed over her. She closed her eyes and gripped the pew in front of her. After a few moments her head cleared enough to open the envelope.

> Jessica,
>
> I don't know how this death thing works so I'll spell a few things out, just in case. I took something from the camp when I escaped. A whistle. A small souvenir from those Nazi bastards. They thought I didn't know what it was, that I couldn't feel what it was. The master race? What a fucking joke! If anything happens to me, you will find it. Take it. Use it against anyone who tries to stop you. But be careful. It is a thing of great power.
>
> I hope it's enough.
>
> Ivan

The hiss of gravel cut into the words. Ellen looked up just in time to see a truck arrive. She snapped a cell phone picture of the letter and stuffed the paper in her coat pocket.

Richard Pierce was back. Ellen glanced at the glowing dials on her watch. A little over twenty-four hours had passed since his arrest. She watched as he hauled gas cans out of his pickup and marched toward the edge of town. She didn't need to get a good look at his face to know he was furious. His body language was as tense and hostile as Ivan's.

Ellen followed him. She was sure he would sense her. But Pierce was focused, so intent on making up for lost time he was oblivious to her. *No, that's not true*, Ellen thought. She was still in his head, along with the song she planted. She could hear him planning a gruesome revenge. Almost all his scenarios involved rape. Ellen wasn't surprised. Most of the men she crossed fantasized about humiliating her that way.

Not just those men, she thought. *Other men. Good men.*

Ellen didn't notice Pierce spin around until it was almost too late. She leapt behind an overturned hopper, nestling against the hill of rock that spilled out of the car. She pulled out Carter's gun and waited.

Pierce's energy bounced off the church, the house, then to the overturned car. He took a step in her direction. For a single breathtaking moment she was certain he found her.

She hummed the lyrics to "Never Gonna Give You Up" in her head. Pierce recoiled from the earworm, cursing.

"You know, I can feel you out there, but I'm not going to try to find you," he called out. "I have Carter. And I know you won't be able to resist coming to his rescue. You're like every other student of his. Every *dead* student."

Pierce scanned the town once again. Hoping his words would lure her out of her hiding place. Ellen kept her eyes fixed on the ground.

"I'll see you soon," he called out.

Ellen could hear the uneasiness in his voice. He wasn't quite sure what to make of her. *I'm not sure what to make of me,* she thought as she moved to her feet.

The landscape twisted as she headed closer to the mine. Anything natural—the trees, the gentle curve of the hill—had been cleared and flattened by human hands. Outside of the entrance to the mine was a generator and a pile of empty gas cans. One of them dripped its contents on the ground.

Ellen felt a swell of anger. She knelt and touched the earth. It writhed beneath her fingers.

You're in its territory now, her mind whispered, *close enough to touch.* She didn't know what side the creature was on. Or if it understood the concept of sides. All she knew was the only way to stop what was happening was to go underground. Deep underground.

She remembered the dream with Dante, a vision that now seemed like ancient history.

"The only way out is through," she whispered.

She took a deep breath and headed into the place that killed fifty-two men.

Chapter Twenty-One

The mine wasn't what she expected. Ellen pictured the kind of place she saw on television—a mine with a steep vertical drop, one that required the use of an elevator. But Bentham (as the historical society president was fond of pointing out) was a slope mine. To go inside, all you had to do was walk in. She just followed the set of stairs next to a conveyer belt. She didn't even need her flashlight. Pierce and his gang had rigged a string of lights along the walls. They looked like something you might find at a summer party. *Mood lighting.*

Ellen shook her head. The whole thing was surreal.

That wasn't the only thing. The walls around her sparkled. When she ventured underground, she thought she would be entering a world of deadness: a flat, featureless terrain. As she moved deeper into the mine she felt like she was walking through thick clusters of stars.

No wonder our ancestors lived in caves, she thought.

An image popped into her head. A slide from Carter's lecture about the Lascaux caves in France.

Carter. His name snapped her out of her daze.

After ten minutes in twilight the power cord from the generator curved, leading into a side space. Light blasted into the passage.

Ellen approached carefully, listening for any sound, any thought, any sign people were there.

Pierce's lair was unprotected. She didn't know what to think. Either it was an act of supreme arrogance or a sign that she was hopelessly outnumbered.

As she scurried across the opening, negative thoughts bombarded her. *What do you think you're doing? You have what? Carter's gun, your Bowie knife, and a mystery item. An item you have yet to find. Against how many people?*

Ellen stared into the darkness below—no more lighted path beyond this point—and bit her lip. She wanted to run.

You could do it, a voice encouraged her. *No one knows you're with Carter. Maybe Joshua, but he would keep your secret. You wouldn't have to bear the mantle of being the one who lost Carter. You wouldn't even be sure what happened to him . . .*

"No." Her voice was no louder than a whisper, but the word sunk into her, giving her strength. She drifted deeper into the mine.

Ellen smelled the passage before she saw it. Even though it had been more than sixty years since the collapse, a rotten smell lingered. Moisture dripped from the walls. Her flashlight landed on the dark, hulking forms of the mining equipment. Fallen beams crisscrossed the passage—all that remained of the scaffolding that protected the miners. A few feet away a rusting car lay on its side, half buried in the earth.

As Ellen wound her way through the tunnel, rocks crunched under her feet. *Iron pyrite*, she thought. *The load they were working on the day they died.*

There was no sign of the lost miners.

Ellen turned to go back to the entrance, to see whether the bodies were embedded in an outside wall. Ivan's voice bloomed in her head. *Down. Look down.*

She shone her flashlight on the floor. A rib cage. Stuck to her hiking boot. Ellen yelped and leapt off the body, a wave of nausea rising in her throat.

Skeletons littered the floor, their limbs scattered all over the ground. *More used machinery*, she thought numbly.

"I'm sorry. Oh my God, I'm so, so sorry."

It doesn't matter, Ivan replied. *Hurry. You must hurry.*

"All right!" she snapped. "You could have warned me about the dead bodies!"

Ivan had nothing to say.

She found his body at the foot of a twisted escape ladder. As Ellen inspected the remains she thought about what she read in the newspaper. Ivan Leibowitz was a hero. He stayed at his post, dying as he sounded the alarm. Sure, fifty-two men died. But eight survived, thanks to his bravery. His sacrifice. All this after he escaped from a concentration camp.

It hardly seems fair, she thought as she sifted through the pile of bones. *He barely had a chance to start his life again.*

Her eyes blurred. Ellen broke down, her tears spilling onto his remains. She held her breath. If a childhood of Disney movies taught her anything, it was that tears were enough to reverse a spell. Enough to bring people back from the dead.

Nothing happened. Even worse, she couldn't find the magical item she needed to defeat the monster.

She sat down and buried her face in her hands. *What now?* In sheer desperation she swept the flashlight over her surroundings one last time.

It didn't occur to her that Ivan's last memory was wrong—that the whistle was still on him when he died. Several feet from his body she saw something shiny.

Ellen scurried over to it. She pushed aside a rotting leather notebook and pawed the object out of the dirt.

A whistle. Attached to a necklace.

It was small, half silver and half ivory. An emblem was pressed into the metal—a sword wrapped around a coiled ribbon. The same ribbon people used for breast cancer or AIDS awareness.

She struggled to read the runic writing stamped into the ribbon. "Ahnenerbe," she whispered. The word popped into her head so suddenly she knew Ivan put it there.

She slipped the chain around her neck.

You have what you need. Get out.

"But—"

Get out! His rage shook the walls. Thunder roared in the distance as the ground beneath her lurched.

Is this even possible? Ellen wondered. *Can a ghost trigger a physical avalanche?* She didn't wait to find out. She ran for an emergency escape ladder and scrambled for higher ground. She was convinced Ivan would change his mind—that at any moment, a skeletal hand would reach out and pull her into the darkness.

When she saw a light above her, she allowed herself to relax a little. That's when it happened. Her muddy boot slipped on one of the rungs. Ellen grabbed onto the ladder. Metal screamed as it broke loose from its moorings.

For a breathless moment she hung in space. *Oh God, please*, she pleaded. *I don't want to die. I don't want to spend eternity here, rotting away with the others.*

A voice met her in the darkness. *Relax. Stay calm. Focus.*

The man talking to her was alive. His voice possessed a warmth, a vitality that Ivan didn't possess. Ellen closed her eyes. She let herself dangle another moment, long enough to take a deep breath.

She hooked her feet back onto the ladder and pulled herself to the section still attached to the wall. She scurried up the ladder to safety.

Thank you, whoever you are, thank you, she thought when she reached the next level.

Whoever I am? Who do you think this is?

Ellen's breath caught in her throat. Andrew Carter.

It can't be. It can't possibly be.

Then she remembered the first day of class, when she was convinced Carter tried to read her mind. How she recited a Lewis Carroll poem to keep him at bay.

"You're psychic. Oh my God, Carter, you're psychic," she panted.

Pathetic, isn't it? A psychic who hates psychics. Now would you hurry up and find me?

"Okay," Ellen whispered to her unseen companion. "Okay, okay."

Ellen surveyed her surroundings. Directly in front of her, roughly twenty feet away, another emergency ladder led to the level above. To the right the passage widened. She could hear the drone of men chanting. To the left, more mangled machinery.

Lights blinked in the distance. A generator.

Ellen headed toward the light, weaving between the rusted cars. Just as she was about to reach it, a pair of powerful hands grabbed her and pulled her back. *Oh God. It's all over. This is the end*, she thought.

Ellen knew better. Her troubles were only just beginning.

Chapter Twenty-Two

The frat boy dumped Ellen on the ground. She landed in a heap at Carter's feet.

"Look what I found crawling around the place."

Richard Pierce turned and sneered at her. "Did you search her?" he asked.

The assistant handed him the gun, knife, and flashlight. Pierce inspected the weapons as he placed them on a box behind him.

"My, my, aren't you prepared? Do you have cookies, too, little Girl Scout?"

"My Girl Scout days have been over for a long, long time," she replied.

Ellen climbed to her feet and glanced at Carter, tied to a chair. Except for another bloody nose and a black eye, he was okay. *For now*, a dark voice whispered.

Pierce's eyes locked on the necklace. "What's that?"

Ivan's words echoed in her head.

It is a thing of great power.

"A rape whistle," she lied.

He moved closer. "No one's going to hear it. Except for Carter. But he'll probably be dead by the time we get to you."

Richard Pierce touched her face, his hand drifting down her neck. Ellen covered the necklace with her hand. She could feel the energy throbbing beneath her fingers like a second heartbeat. *He'll feel it too, if you didn't think fast*, she thought.

"My mother gave it to me. On the day I left for college."

"Is that right? Boo fucking hoo."

The thought of Pierce having the whistle—*her only hope*—terrified her. Her mind raced, searching for a solution.

"Please. It's all I have left of her."

"The dead aren't going to help you."

Ellen looked at the ground and tried not to laugh.

Pierce dismissed her with a wave of the hand. "I don't have time for this. We have business to attend to. Matthew—"

Ellen's head jerked up. "Matt?"

Matt Chauncey. Another member of the frat. Whenever they had a barbecue, he was there, flipping the burgers with a big grin on his face. Now he was as vacant and dead-eyed as a shark.

Matt grabbed Ellen's hand and pinned it to the top of a crate. Another man stepped forward, wielding a hammer.

"Andrew's been very uncooperative. Let's see if you can persuade him to talk."

Ellen whimpered. She tried to curl her fingers, but Matt held them firmly in place. Pierce watched with a satisfied expression.

"This is the way it's going to work, Andrew. Every time you refuse to tell me the rest of the spell, I will break one of your girlfriend's fingers, and then—"

"She's not my girlfriend," Carter corrected him. His calm matter-of-factness cut Pierce short.

"Excuse me?"

"Oh, come on. You know how the girls flutter around me. She's just another groupie."

"A bimbo," Ellen offered as she bowed her head. She groped for the necklace, but her free hand was shaking too hard for her to get a good grip.

"You see? *She* gets it," Carter said.

"Well, let's see if you're telling the truth, shall we?" Pierce drawled.

Ellen put her head down. Out of the corner of her eye she saw Pierce motion to the man with the hammer. He raised the weapon.

"Ivan, help me. Please, please help me," she whispered. The words were barely out of her mouth when she heard a sickening whump. Ellen cringed, waiting for pain to shoot through her. When she heard a gasp, she looked up into the eyes of the man with the hammer.

Pierce had grabbed the man's arm midswing. And plunged a knife into his chest. The man wheezed and crumpled to the floor.

Matt jerked as if Pierce had struck him, too. "What are you doing?" he screamed as Pierce pulled the knife out of his friend. "What the fuck are you doing, old man?" He rushed Pierce.

This time Pierce went for the throat. Matt fell at his feet, his neck gushing blood. Pierce stared at the dying man with wide eyes, his face frozen in horror.

"I— I—" he stuttered, looking as helpless and lost as the men he just murdered.

Ellen almost felt sorry for him. Until Pierce lunged at her with the knife.

"*Ellen!*" Carter roared, straining against the ropes that bound him.

The blade stopped an inch from her throat, held back by a mysterious force. *Not mysterious*, she thought. *You know who it is.*

Ivan slid into her body like silk. He curled Ellen's mouth into a smile. "Oh, no, no, no. I'm not going to let you do that," Ivan said, slapping the knife out of Pierce's hand. "I'm not going to let you do *anything*, you miserable little man."

Carter stiffened. "Ellen?"

Ivan kept her eyes locked on Pierce. Ellen savored his fear. And the feeling dancing through her body, a sensation that cut through blood and muscle and brain. She never felt so much power in her life.

"They were just like you. Just like me. I thought I could control it. I know now what happens when people try to . . . tinker. Do you want to know why there are no ghosts in the mine?"

Pierce shook his head fiercely. Ellen tapped the whistle at her throat. "Because they're all . . . in . . . here."

"Ellen!" Carter yelled as she raised it to her mouth.

The next words came out in Ivan's raspy voice. "*Die Toten sind hungrig.*"

The whistle let out a high-pitched, agonizing scream. White blurs flew out of it, churning the air around them.

Ghosts, Ellen thought as the phantoms rose, buzzing around her like angry wasps. *All those men caught inside a—*

Ivan left to join them. Ellen howled in agony, her body lurching as his spirit departed. He joined the fifty-one men that swirled above her, gathering strength.

The shadowy figures were shifting, merging into a single entity. An entity focused on only one thing.

Her eyes settled on Pierce.

"The dead are hungry," she whispered, this time in English.

The spirits slammed into him.

Pierce's body began to twitch.

"Ellen, get away from him. *Now!*"

Carter's voice snapped her out of her trance. She grabbed the blood-stained knife and crawled over to Carter, carefully avoiding the cloud. As she sawed at the ropes that bound him Ellen could feel the energy building, pressing into her back.

She glanced over her shoulder. Pierce was curled up on the ground, mewling like a frightened kitten. The ghosts kept coming. They stabbed him again and again. Forcing him to relive the moment of their deaths.

Ellen had no sympathy for Richard Pierce. But to see him shredded by invisible spirits, to see him twist and jerk like a marionette—it sickened her.

A mob. Nothing but a mob.

Ivan's voice rose above the din. *You disapprove?*

The moment Carter was free, he grabbed her and dragged her away from the storm. "Don't look," he panted in her ear. "For the love of God, don't look."

Ivan *made* her look. The images danced across her eyelids like figures in a demented shadow play. The ghosts were inside Pierce now. His body crawled, boiling with their unseen presence.

Raped, she thought as she watched him slither. *Pierce wanted to rape me. Now he's the one being raped.*

Ivan stood beside the twitching man. Their eyes locked. He smiled at Ellen.

Carter shook her. Hard. "Beware the Jabberwock, my son! The jaws that bite, the claws that catch!"

"The Jabberwocky." The poem she recited the first day of class to keep Carter out of her head. It jolted her out of her stupor.

"Beware the Jubjub bird and shun the frumious Bandersnatch," she cried out.

"One, two! One, two! And through and through, the vorpal blade went snicker-snack," Carter shouted in her ear.

She could barely hear his voice above Pierce's screams.

"He left it dead, and with its head. He went galumphing back," she answered.

Pierce's cries rose to an impossibly high pitch. Then the noise stopped. It cut out so suddenly Ellen felt like she was falling.

She closed her eyes.

Waiting to shatter into a million pieces.

"Hey," a voice called out. "Hey!"

Ellen jerked.

Everything was silent. For a moment she wasn't sure where she was. Or who she was.

"Ellen? You okay?" Carter asked again.

Ellen sat up. Her mouth tasted like dirt. "I think so," she rasped. She flexed her fingers. *Not broken.*

Carter stared at her, his blue eyes black in the gloom.

"You came after me," he murmured.

"Of course I did."

"You shouldn't have done that," he said in a quiet voice. "You should have gotten out of here. Come back with some help."

"You would have been dead by then."

"And?"

"*And?*" Ellen scowled. "I was just supposed to leave you behind to—"

Richard Pierce whimpered, almost on cue. Ellen looked at the fallen man. She thought Pierce was dead. That the spirits tore out his soul, yanking it from his body like a weed.

He writhed on the ground a few feet away. Carter walked over to check on him. He turned Pierce over with his foot. The man's eyes were open, but he was gone.

An empty shell, Ellen thought as the last of the ghosts fled his body.

Carter raised his arm and shot the man in the head. The sudden blast made Ellen jump.

"*Jesus Christ!*"

"Relax," Carter commanded her.

He kept the gun pointed at Pierce. After what seemed like an eternity, he lowered it.

"What did you do? What did you just do?" Ellen whispered.

"Even your enemies deserve mercy," he insisted. "He was beyond hope. *Way* beyond hope."

"They won't know that," she protested. "When the police find the body they'll trace it back to you. They'll know about your past with him. I'll back you up, but I'm your student, and they'll think—"

"Ellen."

"Let me finish," she hissed.

"They won't find the gun because they won't find him. They won't find us either. Do you understand?"

She fell silent.

"We're beyond hope."

Ellen's eyes drifted to the gun. "Are you going to shoot me, too?"

Carter let out an exasperated sigh. He pushed the gun into her hands. "We still have work to do," he continued. "We have to stop what's happening. You saw what that thing did on the riverbank. Can you imagine it plowing through Boston? Or across New England?"

"I can," she murmured.

"I'm not saying this to be cruel."

"I know."

"And if I could do this on my own—"

"I wouldn't let you." Before she could stop herself, Ellen blurted. "I wish I'd gotten to know you better, Andrew Carter."

He looked at her, waiting for the punch line. When she said nothing, he filled the silence. "Tell you what. If we make it out of here, we'll have some tea and scones and have a nice chat."

"Vodka and scones," she replied.

"What?"

"I'm a vodka girl. Make it vodka and you have a date."

"It wouldn't be a *date*," he sniffed.

"Oh, for God's . . . relax, okay? I know you're not serious."

"Excuse me?"

"You have no intention of meeting me for tea or anything else. Even if we do get out of here, which seems, well . . ." She let the words drift off.

Get back to business.

"Before I got caught I heard some of the other frat brothers. They were chanting the same spell we heard at Mrs. Vargas's house."

Carter perked up. "Where?"

"I don't know. I was being dragged off by Pierce's thugs at the time. I kind of lost track of where I was."

"Do you think you can lead us in a general direction?"

Ellen led Carter back the way she came, weaving around a maze of mining equipment. Even though Pierce and his two assistants were dead, she felt vulnerable. Vulnerable and exposed. She already used the most powerful weapon in her arsenal. Now she had nothing.

As she navigated her way through the field of abandoned equipment, Ellen cursed herself. *You let Pierce push your buttons. You let him get so far under your skin that you went medieval on him. You used a nuclear bomb when a fly swatter would have worked. Stupid girl, stupid girl, stupid girl.*

"You're broadcasting," Carter called out.

Ellen gnawed on her lip. The word *broadcasting* made her think of Connie. How he forced his way into her head when she was making love to Stuart.

Carter stiffened beside her. "Connie did what?" Each word was slow and deliberate.

"I don't know. I'm not even sure it happened."

"If you think it happened, it did," he replied. His anger expanded until it felt like there was another person with them. "That bastard. He has no right. He has absolutely no—"

"It doesn't matter now, does it?" She gestured around them, at the mine that was likely their grave.

Carter fell silent.

"Can I ask you something?" she asked.

"Sure," he shrugged.

"Are you going to be in my head all the time now?"

"Until we either die or get out, yes. So keep your fantasies about me to yourself, okay?" he quipped.

Ellen smiled and shook her head. "I think I can just about manage."

Chapter Twenty-Three

"**N**iis Zamran Ciaof Caosga.
"*Zorge.*
"*Torsvi.*"

The words settled on Ellen like a clammy fog. They were the same words she heard at the frat. The chant sounded much worse down here, in the bowels of the earth. There was no sky or wind to carry it away. No buildings or trees to muffle the sound.

"*Niis Zamran Ciaof Caosga.*
"*Zorge.*
"*Torsvi.*"

The light got stronger as they neared the voices. Ellen tried to convince herself it was because there were more lamps. She knew better. The light was the color of hot lava. The color they saw when the fiery creature punched into their world.

Carter stopped where the passage widened and lifted his head. He looked like a deer sniffing the air.

"*Niis Zamran Ciaof Caosga.*
"*Zorge.*
"*Torsvi.*"

Carter pulled out a piece of paper. "Just what I thought. Fucking amateurs," he hissed after he consulted it.

"What?"

"They have a half spell," he explained. "A spell that attracts and binds. But they can't direct it."

"They've caught the chthonian, but they can't make it do anything."

"They can't even let it go. Not without being killed."

Ellen looked at the paper in Carter's hands. "Wait a minute," she frowned. "You have more of the spell."

"I hope I do."

"Where did you get it?" she demanded.

"Joshua helped me find the rest."

"Joshua?"

"We used his art dealer friends to find another copy of the book. Someone copied the missing page and sent it to us," Carter looked at her. "What did you think we were doing all that time in the study?"

One of the frat boys stumbled into the tunnel before Ellen could respond. They flattened themselves against the wall. Ellen was sure the man would spot them, but he had more pressing concerns. He unzipped his pants and rushed to the opposite wall.

Carter rolled his eyes as the man peed on the rock. Ellen clapped her hand over her mouth, trying not to laugh. *This isn't funny*, a voice scolded her.

Carter motioned her to pull out her gun. He cinched the belt of his coat between his hands, snuck up on the man, and stuffed the belt in his mouth. He hauled the man's head back.

The victim twisted and turned, letting out muffled cries. The man's eyes widened when he saw Ellen. She was just as surprised.

"Butch?" she called out. She barely recognized him. He no longer looked like the confident psychopath who took a shot at her. His eyes were glazed with desperation.

"Butch?" Carter echoed.

"This is the guy who tried to kill me, remember?"

"In *my* department," Carter growled in Butch's ear. "You listen to me. I'm going to tell you what to do. You're going to lead me to the others. And if you're lucky, I might find a way to get you out of here alive."

"Mmm, hmmphh," he nodded his head, his eyes darting to Ellen.

He's tired, she thought. *He's tired, and he just wants it to end.*

They followed Butch into an immense cavern, along a well-worn path carved into the earth. The trail led to a circle, which contained another circle with a large pentagram. Gaunt, hollow-eyed men knelt at the five stations of the star. They chanted the incomplete spell nonstop, their voices worn and cracked.

In the center of the circle was the chthonian. It hung in space, writhing and squirming like a worm on a hook.

For a moment all Ellen could do was stare. To see it, to finally be in the presence of the thing that had been in her. That had guided her steps to . . .

The creature blasted her with a white-hot wave of psychic energy. Ellen staggered backward, clutching her head. Her brain cramped. She could feel the creature's misery. Its confusion. And something else. Something that brought everything into agonizing focus.

She whipped out her gun and turned on Butch. "You bastard. You fucking bastard!"

"Ellen, what are you— stop—" Carter stammered. He sounded like he did just before she blew the whistle. When Ivan possessed her. *Possessed.*

Ellen lowered the gun. "It's a baby, Carter."

"What?"

"You want to know why I survived that night on the riverbank? Why that thing only knocked down a few trees and destroyed a single house? It's a baby."

"A baby?" he echoed.

"How else could I have survived such a long possession? I should be dead. We should both be dead," she added.

The color drained from Carter's face. He kicked Butch. The man plowed face-first into the ground. Carter stepped on his back and held him down.

"What were you thinking? What the hell were you thinking?"

"It wasn't my idea. Pierce thought— Pierce thought— that if we got a small one, we'd be able to—" he spluttered.

"To what? Make it into your little pet?" Carter's lips curled in contempt. "Did it ever occur to you that the baby has a mother? A mother that might have a little problem with that?"

"Oh God. Oh God, no. Oh God," Butch's voice was reed thin. On the verge of breaking. He squirmed under Carter's foot.

Carter stepped harder on the man's back. He looked like he wanted to grind Butch into the dirt.

"You started this. You're staying. Until the very end."

"Carter, stop!" Ellen called out. When he didn't respond, she marched up and snapped her fingers in his face. "Enough!"

He jumped, startled.

"Do we have a plan? Any sort of plan at all?" she demanded, her words tinged with panic.

Carter eased off Butch. He looked at her and rubbed his face. "We need to release it. We need to drop the magic circle and let it go."

"What? No. We can't—" Butch started to protest.

Carter gestured at the magic circle and the men struggling to hold it together. "How much longer do you expect this to last?"

Ellen turned to Butch. "How many people did you start out with?"

"Most of the frat. About fifty guys," he replied.

"And how many are left?"

"Me. And the five of them," Butch nodded at the men forming the points of the pentagram. "Oh, and Pierce. Pierce, Sam, and Matthew."

"They're dead," Ellen replied. "All of them. Gone."

Butch struggled to look up at her, but Carter's foot was still planted on his back.

"Carter, let him go."

Carter released Butch. The man stumbled to his feet, spitting dirt out of his mouth.

"They're dead? All of them?" he croaked.

"Pierce killed two of your brothers. Stabbed them to death. And when he came after me—"

"I shot him," Carter offered.

Butch absorbed the news in silence.

"We have to stop this," Ellen insisted. "If what Carter says is true, if the mother is coming to get her child and can't reach it—"

"We're talking disaster," Butch breathed.

She shook her head. "Not disaster. *Catastrophe.* A stars-falling-from-the-sky, end-of-days kind of thing."

All of this started when Butch Stillwell tried to kill me, she thought. *Now my life and the lives of countless others are in his hands.* Ellen waited, hoping the good in him would prevail.

Butch finally nodded. He looked tired. Resigned to his fate.

"We need to get inside the circle," Carter said. "We need to banish the creatures."

Butch led them deeper into the vast underground chamber, along the edge of the magic circle. Ellen could feel energy crackling in the air. She thought about the books at Mote It Be—all the endless New Age bullshit about ley lines, elemental energy, the thin places that separated this world from the next.

And now, here I am. Walking the line.

The creature twitched, almost in response. It sent out another surge of psychic energy. It bounced off the magical barrier. Light danced over their heads in a stunning aurora borealis.

Ellen's vision dimmed. Carter grabbed her by the arm. "Stay with me. You stay with me!" he hissed.

Ellen wasn't sure who spoke to her, Carter or the creature. She wrenched free of his grip and backed away. He grabbed her arm.

"Ellen, look at me. Hey, hey. Look at me," he said, his voice softer this time. "I can't do this alone. You have the connection. The only chance we have, the only way out—"

"Is through. I know. I know," she finished the thought.

The voice from her dream echoed in her head. *You will understand. In time, you will understand.*

Ellen and Carter took their places at the base of the pentagram, at the points of the star that were closest together. Two frat boys knelt in front of them. Their faces were red, sunburned by constant exposure to the fiery creature. As Ellen got closer to them she was overwhelmed by the smell of burning flesh.

How? She wondered. *How can they stand this?*

Butch knelt and muttered instructions into their ears. They nodded mindlessly as they swayed from side to side, their eyes rolling with each pass of the half spell.

They're already dead, Ellen thought. *Their minds are long gone. The fading pulses of a dead star.* And yet . . . Butch communicated with them. There was clearly some plan. *And I know only part of it.*

"That's the way it needs to be," Carter informed her. "You've had contact with the chthonian. It can't know what we're going to do. It might lash out at us."

Us? She thought. *Am I included in their calculations? Or is it already too late for me?* Ellen suddenly felt very lonely. She wished Ivan was with her.

"You ready?" Carter asked when Butch gave them the signal. She nodded her head.

Carter guided her hands to the man in front of her.

"Now," he prompted her.

"Niis Zamran Ciaof Caosga.
"Zorge.
"Torsvi."

Ellen heard the chant countless times before. This was the first time she spoke it. The spell tasted bitter in her mouth—bitter, oily, obscene. *Humans were never meant to speak these words,* she thought, *to control these things.*

The man in front of her moved to his feet. She kept in physical contact with him while they switched positions. Their voices rose in unison as they repeated the chant.

"Niis Zamran Ciaof Caosga.
"Zorge.
"Torsvi."

The man shoved her into the circle. Ellen tensed as she crossed over. She expected to feel a shock, a physical jolt.

The transition was smooth. She felt like she passed through a warm waterfall. Then she was in the middle of the magic circle. Looking up at a dome sparkling with light. She giggled, twirling like a child.

Carter appeared by her side. In the blink of an eye the world went black. Ellen stopped midspin. There were no more dancing lights. No sense of awe. She wondered if Carter was responsible for the sudden darkness.

"Get in touch with it, like you did at the river," he commanded her.

"Get in touch with it? I don't know—"

"Just do it!" he yelled.

Ellen stepped away from him. Her hand dropped to the empty whistle at her throat. *Nothing there anymore.*

She knew the rest of their lives would be measured in minutes. Maybe even seconds. *Make them count,* she told herself.

She walked toward the fiery creature, getting as close as she could. In the background the men continued their chant. Holding the world together one word at a time.

She closed her eyes, reaching out to the chthonian. It pushed her away.

Useless, she thought. *Not just useless. Insulting.*

"I don't know what I'm doing," she cried out to the creature. "I don't know what to do."

Intense light surged around her.

Ellen looked down. A human baby squirmed in her arms. It was red faced and howling, a bundle of helplessness and fear.

"A baby. I keep forgetting. You're a baby," she whispered. The thing squirmed in response.

With shaking hands Ellen reached out and touched it. The burns on her hand flared. The movement came easily, from a place deep inside her. Ellen lifted the baby up, toward the roof of the cavern.

"*Beranusaje a zizop!*" she cried.

The creature in her arms dissolved. It ran down her arms like molten wax. Ellen tilted her head back, trying to keep from drowning. From being completely engulfed by the creature.

Carter stepped in front of her. A strange, almost dreamy expression spread across his face. Like he was seeing her with different eyes.

Or maybe she was the one who . . .

He slammed his fist into her solar plexus. Ellen gasped. She tried to raise her hands, to defend herself, but she couldn't move.

Terrible, buzzing words rose around her.

"*Niis Zamran Ciaof Caosga.*
"*Zorge.*
"*Torsvi.*
"*Amayo De A Caosga.*
"*Conisa Ta Ol Alonusahi.*"

Carter's hand drifted across her stomach, pressing into her flesh. He continued the horrible chant. Something twitched under his fingers. He plunged his hand inside her.

"Oh, no. No, no, no, no," she twisted, adding her chant to his. *Exorcism. Oh God, I'm going through another exorcism.*

Relax, his voice broadcasted in her head.

"Carter," she wheezed.

Hold still, he commanded her. *Hold still and shut your mouth. Unless you want the damn thing to blast through your head.*

Carter yanked the creature out of her like he was unspooling rope.

It didn't hurt. Still, Ellen screamed. Her ears rang with the sound.

"Relax."

Carter rose with part of the baby in his hands. He marched toward the rest of the creature. This time, he bellowed the words.

"Niis Zamran Ciaof Caosga.

"Zorge.

"Torsvi.

"Amayo De A Caosga.

"Conisa Ta Ol Alonusahi."

Carter tossed the part he held high into the air. He moved his hands like he was conducting an orchestra.

The baby responded. It twirled and danced with the part he pulled from her body.

Ellen could only stare. *This isn't real. Carter— Carter can't—* her mind stuttered.

"Is the circle down?" he demanded as he continued to manipulate the creature.

"What?"

"The magic circle. I need it down. Now!"

The men holding the circle together were almost dead. As Ellen scrambled to the edge she could see why Butch went from person to person to explain Carter's plan. The men weren't just sunburned. The long exposure to the fiery creature blinded them. Their eyes were thick with cataracts.

"Butch! Butch!" she called out. She found him on the other side of the circle. He was on his knees—long, greasy hair hanging in his face.

"Down, down! We need to bring it down!" she shouted at him.

He lifted his arms and guided his brothers through one final chant. And when the last word of the spell was spoken, when the magic circled collapsed—

Nothing. Endless moments followed by . . . *nothing.*

They looked at each other, bewildered. "What did we did do wro—" Butch started. A powerful wave struck them. It clipped her, but it struck Butch full force. It lifted him off the ground and spun him like a top.

The same thing happened to all the men who formed the points of the pentagram. One by one an invisible force raised them into the air and twirled them.

Then it hurled their bodies into the wall.

Ellen shut her eyes as their bodies hit. She opened them only to look at Carter one last time. *Before the thing . . .*

He still held the baby in place, guiding it with gentle hands. Ellen frowned. *If Carter's still holding the thing in place, how could it attack . . .*

She was on her feet before she finished the thought.

"Carter. The mother! She's coming! *She's coming! Let it go! Let it go!*" she screamed as she ran toward him.

He glanced over his shoulder. At first he looked annoyed. Then the words registered.

He turned to the creature. The spell came out in a quick burst.

"Niis Zamran Ciaof Caosga.
"Zorge.
"Torsvi.
"Amayo De A Caosga.
"Conisa Ta Ol Alonusahi."

"Conisa Ta Ol Alonusahi! Conisa Ta Ol Alonusahi! Conisa Ta Ol Alonusahi!"

He lifted his arms and slammed his fist into the ground. The world erupted around them. The ground shook. A crack opened in front of Carter.

Ellen watched as the baby chthonian slithered into a crevasse. Back to its mother. *Maybe that will be enough,* she thought. *Oh God, please let that be enough.*

Ellen crawled over to Carter. He was on his knees, retching so hard his entire body shook. She wrapped her arm around him.

"Leave me," he gasped between dry heaves. "I've controlled them. Used them against their will. The mother will be coming for me, too."

"But you helped them," Ellen protested.

"It won't matter. Leave."

"No."

"*I said leave me!*"

"*And I said no!*" Ellen roared back. She ducked under him, lifting him to his feet. Debris rained down on them from the ceiling. It was only small rocks and little pucks of dirt, but Ellen knew it was only a matter of time before more dangerous projectiles came crashing down.

Then there were the lights.

Now that the creature was gone, all they had left were the feeble party lights. And they weren't going to last. Dread lodged in Ellen's throat. *Dark*, she thought, *it will be dark soon.*

The mother erupted out of the ground, riding a wave of deep, subsonic sound.

A curse escaped from Ellen's chattering teeth. "Oh fuck. *Fuck.*"

There was a sharp, whooshing sound, like the crack of a whip. Carter stiffened.

When she looked down she saw a tentacle wrapped around his foot. Carter locked eyes with her for a single, breathless moment. Then the creature yanked him toward an opening in the ground.

Ellen jumped across him, pinning him beneath her. Trying to keep him from being pulled into the abyss.

"He's not one of them! He's not one of them, you stupid bitch!" she shrieked as she groped for his foot, her fingers burning as she yanked at his shoelaces. "Let him go. Do you hear me? *Let. Him. Go. Now!*"

The thing tightened its grip.

Carter's body stretched.

He threw back his head and screamed in agony.

"Leave, Ellen. Just, just . . . let go," he gasped.

"Not a chance," Ellen snarled. "I'm not going to lose you. I'm not going to lose you to a fucking worm!"

The next time she reached down, his hiking boot popped off.

Carter scurried backward, trying to put as much distance between him and the creature as he could.

The air crackled around them, churning with energy.

"Run, Ellen. *Run!*"

Ellen couldn't move. She had nothing left. And the creature needed to take someone. It needed a sacrifice.

This is going to hurt, she thought as she waited for the chthonian to strike. *This is really, really going to hurt.*

She blacked out before the blow landed.

Chapter Twenty-Four

"Ellen."

I'm dead. That was her first thought as she swam out of the darkness.

All the elements were there. The bright light. An invisible presence calling her name. Ellen's eyelids fluttered. She slipped in and out of consciousness. After a few moments the invisible presence nudged her. Again. And again. And again.

Ellen groaned and turned on her side. "Leave me alone."

"You can sleep when we get out of here," a gruff voice replied.

Carter.

She opened her eyes. All she saw was darkness.

"I'm blind," she blurted.

"What?"

"I'm blind. I can't see you. Oh my God, the creature. It blinded me. I can't see! I can't see you!"

"Relax," he commanded her.

The emotions rose too quickly for her to stop them. "Oh God. *Oh God!*" she wailed.

"Ellen, calm down. Just wait a minute, okay?"

A beam of light pierced the darkness. He pointed a flashlight under his chin, like someone about to tell a scary story.

Carter's face was coated in black dust, his blue eyes glazed with shock. He reminded her of one of the doomed miners.

She threw her arms around him, pressing her face into his neck. "Carter," she breathed into his skin. "Oh, Carter."

His hands were instantly on her. "Don't touch me," he growled as he pushed her away.

"Sorry. I'm sorry. It's just . . . it's *so* good to see you." She looked around. "Where are we? What happened? Are we trapped?"

"I don't know." He turned the flashlight away from her to survey their surroundings. "I haven't had a chance to look around."

Ellen didn't want to lose the light. She grabbed his hand.

He hissed in pain. "Stop . . . touching . . . me."

When she looked down, she saw his bruised and swollen fingers. "You're hurt."

"I think I broke them when I punched the ground."

"Let me see."

"What?"

"Give me your hand. I want to take a look."

"No."

"Carter."

"*No!*"

"Oh, for God's sake, stop being such a pussy!" she shouted before she could stop herself. She clapped her hand over her mouth.

"Did you just call me a pussy?" he asked in a quiet voice.

Ellen groaned. "Yes. I did."

A smile spread across his face until he looked like the Cheshire cat. "You've got the balls of a bull, you know that?"

"Carter!"

His eyes danced in the dim light. "Oh yeah, that's *much* worse than calling me a pussy."

"Balls of a bull? I suppose I should take that as a compliment," Ellen replied.

"No. I really don't think you should."

That was all it took. It started as a giggle, then a chuckle. Before she knew it, she was in full-blown hysterics.

"Real dignified, Ellen," he observed as she rolled on the ground.

"Stop."

"I swear, if you pee your pants—"

"Stop, oh please, please stop," she begged him.

Carter finally fell silent, long enough for her to recover. Ellen wiped away the tears with the sleeve of her shirt. These tears felt good. They cleared her head.

"Okay. All right. Where were we?" she asked once she recovered.

"You were trying to get me to play doctor," he reminded her.

She tittered but managed to regain control.

"Please, Carter. There's not a lot I can do. Let me take care of you."

"Okay," he agreed.

Ellen took his hand and straightened his fingers on her lap. She could feel him watching her. Ready to pull away at a moment's notice.

"What's the last thing you remember?" he asked.

"I'm not sure."

"Do you remember the exorcism?"

She winced as she pulled a bandanna out of her jeans and tore the cloth into thin strips. "Now I know why you drug people first."

His injured hand flexed on her knee. "I wish I could have knocked you out."

"Me too," Ellen replied. "It wasn't as bad as the first time. I got the sense that . . . that it knew it was being pulled out by someone who didn't want to hurt it."

"That's crazy."

"I know. But here we are," she gestured vaguely at their surroundings. "Are we still in the place where the magic circle was?"

"We're inside what's left of it."

"What's left of it?"

"The mother lashed out as she left. Brought most of the cavern down around us."

"How did we survive that?"

"I don't know."

"So we're trapped?"

"I haven't looked around much but—" Ellen watched as he considered what to tell her. "I don't see any way out."

"Butch is dead," she said as she bound Carter's broken fingers to his uninjured ones. "I was standing right next to him when the chthonian threw him against the wall. It killed the others, too. Plucked them off one by one. I waited for my turn. I felt the thing turn to me. But it did nothing. It passed right over me."

"What exactly are you saying?"

"I'm not sure I'm *saying* anything, Carter. I'm just telling you what happened," Ellen paused to inspect her handiwork. "There, that's not bad, is it?"

"Is it true, what you told Pierce? Were you really a Girl Scout?"

"I was, but I never made it past Brownie."

"Why?"

"I refuse to speak without my lawyer present."

Carter smiled, his eyes lingering on her. "You saved my life. For what it's worth, I'm grateful."

"For what it's worth?" Ellen echoed.

"I don't think we have very long to live." He sat back, letting her absorb the news. "You know, you should be a wreck. A complete wreck," he observed. "I mean you freaked out a little, but most people would be curled up in a corner by now."

"Did you?" Ellen asked.

"Freak out?" He nodded. "I did it while you were asleep."

Silence descended between them, as thick as the darkness.

"I still have the gun. For when the time comes," he offered.

"When do you think that will be?"

"Dehydration will probably get us first. Three, maybe five days."

Ellen looked at her hands. They were red. Scorched from her latest encounter with the beast. "God, we've done a number on our hands, haven't we?" she said, desperate to change the subject.

"What?" Carter asked.

"You broke your fingers. I've burned mine, again."

"I suppose it's not too surprising. We're primates. We experience the world through our hands. And our eyes. If we were bats—" A strange expression drifted across his face. "No. It can't be," he whispered.

"What?"

He jumped to his feet and spun in a circle, the glare of his flashlight splashing the walls.

"What is it?"

His eyes blazed. "How did that thing communicate when it was with you?"

"Through images. Sometimes they were connected. Sometimes they weren't."

"When I dragged you away from the chthonian, I flashed on the Giant's Causeway," he said.

"The Giant's Causeway?"

"It's a place in Northern Ireland. A stone formation that looks like stairs coming out of the ocean. I went there as a child."

Carter stared into space. Ellen wondered if he was thinking about his father.

"When my life flashed before my eyes, I thought about that. Maybe the thing—"

"Tapped into that?"

"It's worth a look, don't you think?"

They had only one flashlight, so they searched the large space together. Carter lost a shoe during their struggle, which slowed them down even more.

As they made their way around the magic circle, she spotted the body of one of the frat boys. His foot poked out from the rubble. Ellen knelt and slipped off the man's boot.

"What are you doing?"

"You can't keep walking around in your socks." She compared Carter's foot to the dead man's shoe. "Give me your foot."

"I can manage."

She wiggled her fingers at him, reminding him of his broken bones. Carter let out a frustrated sigh.

"Is this something you learned in the Girl Scouts, too?" he asked her as she laced up the boot.

Ellen could feel him staring at her again. "What, grave robbing? First merit badge I got." The false cheer echoed off the walls of the cavern, mocking her.

After a few more minutes of searching, Carter directed the light at a curve of collapsed rock.

"I'm afraid you wasted your time finding me a shoe. We've come full circle."

"That's it?"

Carter sank onto the ground. He pulled out his gun and set it between them.

"Wait a minute!" she exclaimed. "You're going to give up? Just like that?"

"Ellen—"

She crouched beside him. "What about those guys in South America trapped in the mine? They got out."

"They were in an active mine. People knew they were trapped the moment the shaft collapsed. And their rescue . . ." Carter shook his head. "Their rescue was one in a million."

"Carter, please," she pleaded.

"We're buried under tons of rock. No one knows we're here. Do you understand? No one knows we're here!" he shouted. His next words were gentler but cut just as deep. "I don't want to die of dehydration. And neither do you. It's an excruciating way to go." He nodded at the gun. "This is the best way out."

Ellen joined him on the floor and reached for the weapon. *Well, if Carter doesn't think there's a way out . . .* The thought stopped her cold. *You're not thinking for yourself.*

She pushed the gun away. "Not yet," she blurted.

"What?"

"Not yet."

"Ellen—"

"Just— just— just— give me a minute, okay? Just give me a minute," she spluttered. "There has to be another way."

Turn off the light, a voice commanded.

"What?"

Turn off the light. The voice boomed in her head.

"Who was that?" Carter demanded.

Ellen looked at him. "You heard it, too?" When he nodded she sighed in relief.

Carter reached over and turned off the flashlight.

The cavern glowed. It shone with a strange bioluminescence. The radiant stuff was everywhere. On the ground. On the walls and what was left of the ceiling. There was even some splattered on them. Ellen thought of the old watches, the ones with clock hands painted with radioactive radium. She hoped this wasn't the same kind of thing.

"Carter?" she called out in a dazed voice. She didn't need the flashlight to see him. The light around them was bright enough.

"Yeah?"

"Do you see this?"

"Yeah."

"Why didn't we notice this earlier?"

"I don't know."

He grabbed her shoulders and turned her toward the magic circle. In the middle of the pentagram, in the spot they searched only moments before, was a cluster of rocks. Made of the glittering stone that surrounded them, it rose toward the ceiling. The steps were smooth, carved by a creature she knew she would never understand.

As Ellen approached the stairs she wondered how much of their world was shaped by chthonians.

Ellen laid her hand on the newly formed stone. It was warm to the touch. She stepped on the first stair, testing it.

Carter scowled at her. "Ellen."

"You don't trust it," she replied. "Well, neither do I. But it's better than putting a gun in your mouth, don't you think?"

"You have a point," he admitted after what seemed like a lifetime of hesitation. "But if we die, I get to say I told you so."

The journey to the surface took forever. Ellen didn't realize how deep they were until they had to climb out. And the stairs were steep, almost too much for her. She supposed that was the consequence of having something so massive create a way out. It could only see things in its own dimensions. She was thankful a smaller creature didn't engineer their escape route.

Every few minutes the earth below them shuddered. Sometimes they would pause and wait for the tremor to pass. Most of the time they kept climbing. They slogged along like two lost hikers determined to get back to the trailhead.

To a shower, warm food, and a soft bed. *And Joshua's lasagna.* Ellen's stomach rumbled to life. *God, I could eat a whole tray of Joshua's lasagna.* She quickened her pace, driven as much by her appetite as her will to live.

They emerged just as the sun rose over the mountains. It was an impossible moment, something that only happened in the movies. Ellen waited for the scene to dissolve. She expected to wake up and find herself still trapped in the endless darkness of the mine. She looked at Carter, his face warm in the glowing light.

He's here. I'm here. We're alive.

Ellen's knees buckled. She collapsed in a heap, like a marathoner crossing the finish line. "Thank you. Thankyouthankyouthankyou," she chanted.

Her hand fluttered to the necklace to thank Ivan. A cold flash shot through her. It wasn't there.

She yelped and scrambled to her feet.

"What's wrong?" Carter demanded as she clawed at the ground around her.

"I lost it. Oh my God, I lost it. It must have fallen off somewhere in the mine."

"You mean the whistle?"

"Yes."

Carter pegged her with a hard look. "The thing that made Pierce kill two of his men?"

"*You* have it."

"No. I don't," he insisted, but Ellen knew he was lying.

"You can't just take it! Ivan gave it to me!"

"Ivan? Ivan who?"

Ellen frowned. "You don't remember him? You don't re-member that he—" *Possessed you.* Ellen bit down on the words. "He meant for me to find it," she spluttered. "It might be dangerous in someone else's hands."

"Like it wasn't bad enough with you."

"It might hurt you."

Carter laughed. It was the coldest sound she ever heard. "Oh, please. Spare me the false concern. Even if I did have it, I wouldn't give it to you."

Ellen looked away, toward the ghost town. She stiffened. "Carter, where's Bentham Corners?"

"Don't change the subject," he snapped.

She ignored him. "We're standing right above the mine. The sun is rising in the east, so west is that way. Arkham is to the south. Bentham Corners should be right down—" Her hand froze.

There was no Bentham Corners. A dust cloud rose from the spot where it used to be. "Gone," she whispered. "Destroyed."

"Ellen?" Carter called out, from what sounded like a great distance.

"Yeah?"

"We need to get out of here. It's not safe."

"Yeah," Ellen agreed.

She took one last look, then turned and followed Carter into the sun.

Chapter Twenty-Five

The ride back to Arkham was tense.

Even though his fingers were broken, Carter insisted on driving. His mind churned the entire way, his thoughts muddy with misgiving. How he wished she didn't know his father was alive. Or that he was psychic. Or that, or that, or that . . .

It's only a matter of time, he thought as he stared out the dirty windshield. *It's only a matter of time before everyone knows. Before people start to invade me.*

Invade.

The word struck her as they approached the rings of suburbia. People were an invasion to him. Ellen suspected any kind of intimacy felt like an invasion to Carter.

She thought it odd he wasn't thinking about the mine.

A memory flared in her head. The sickening thump when Pierce plunged the knife into his men. She groaned and rubbed her face. *Maybe you should borrow a page from Andrew Carter's book.*

Ellen looked over at him. Bruises covered his face. He had a bloody lip. And his fingers . . . He gripped the steering wheel as gently as he could, but his face was tight with pain.

"You should let me drive," she suggested.

"No."

"You're in agony."

"I've had worse," he insisted.

"Is this just macho bullshit, or don't you trust me?" His silence filled the car. "I'm not going to tell anyone about what I know."

"Yeah, right. You know what Benjamin Franklin said about secrets?"

"No."

"He said three people can keep a secret if two of them are dead."

Nervous laughter escaped from her throat. "Oh, terrific, does that mean you're going to kill me?"

Much to her relief, Carter shook his head.

"Ben Franklin also wanted the turkey to be the national bird, so you can't always trust his judgment," she sighed. "Besides . . ."

"What?" he demanded when she hesitated.

"Even if I did say anything, who would believe me? Who would think someone like me could get close enough to learn your secrets? As you're so fond of pointing out, I'm a bimbo. A schoolgirl."

"Ellen—"

She pointed to one of the off-ramps to Arkham. "This is my exit."

"This isn't the way to your house."

"I'm not going to Joshua's."

They pulled up to the Victorian where she rented a room. It was the Tuesday before Thanksgiving break. The place was abandoned.

Thank God, she thought as she inspected herself in the mirror. Ellen looked as bad as Carter did. Her hair black with grime, her clothes torn and filthy. She couldn't see it, but she was sure she had blood on her. Whether it was *her* blood was an open question.

"Where are we?" Carter demanded.

"This is my safe space," she replied. "I come here when I need to hide."

"You do that a lot?"

"More than I'd like."

"I suppose you think we're even now," he said in a low voice.

"What?"

"I suppose you think we're even. Just because I know one of your secrets."

"That's not what I'm—" Ellen hesitated. *That's exactly what you're trying to do.* She slumped in her seat. "What do you want from me, Carter?"

"Another secret. A big secret."

Ellen smirked. "Is this your way of asking me if I have a crush on you?"

"That's not much of a secret."

She offered him her best poker face. "You're not my type," she insisted. "Let's just say my tastes lie elsewhere on the chili list."

He gave her a sideways look. "Women?"

Ellen shook her head. "Unbelievable," she murmured. She fell silent as snow began to fall outside.

"Joshua's not my uncle," she blurted.

Carter stiffened. "What?"

"You want a big secret? I don't think Joshua's my uncle. And I think the reason he adopted me—" Tears stung her eyes as she gave voice to her fear. "I don't think he did it out of kindness."

Ellen hugged her jacket tight to her body. She heard the crinkle of paper. Her breath caught in her throat. *The letter. Ivan's letter.* She dug it out of her pocket, half expecting it to fly away or disappear in a flash of flame.

She offered it to him. "And then there's this."

Carter scowled at the letter. "What's this?"

"A message from a dead man."

He grabbed it and started to read. "Your name's not Jessica."

"Actually, it is," she replied. "One of the few pieces of information I managed to pry out of Joshua."

"Jessica," he studied her as he tried the name on for size. "If that's your name, why don't you use it?"

"Because I don't know who it belongs to."

He pushed the paper back at her. "This is crazy!"

"Any stranger than what we just went through?"

"You're saying a man wrote to you. In 1945. Before you were born. Before Joshua was even born. A man who knows your true name. This. This . . ."

"What?"

"This feels like a desperate bid for attention."

"A desperate bid for—" Ellen spluttered. "Where the hell have you been, Carter? Were you actually with me in the mine? Did that feel like a desperate bid for attention to you?"

Carter said nothing.

"The world doesn't revolve around you. You do know that, right?"

"Not from where I'm sitting," he grunted.

"Then maybe you should get your ass out of your chair."

The silence that followed was deep. Deep and so still that Ellen was afraid of breathing. She knew she had gone too far. She didn't care.

Carter tossed his head back and laughed. It wasn't the slow build-up of her laughter in the mine. The outburst was sharp and violent, like the shifting of a seismic plate.

Pressure release, she thought.

He slammed his good hand on the steering wheel of the car. The horn blared, startling an old woman walking her dog. Ellen watched the woman scurry away.

"Real dignified, professor. Have you ever heard of a thing called Neighborhood Watch?"

He slid down in his seat, cackling. "Not a word. Not another fucking word out of you."

Ellen smiled, absorbing the sound of his laughter. *Such an ordinary sound. Such a wonderful, ordinary sound.*

She opened the car door, ready to face the world again. He pushed the letter across the car seat. "Don't forget this."

"You should keep it. It's part of a matched set."

"Matched set?"

"It goes with the whistle," she peered at him through the door. "I'll see you in class, Dr. Carter."

Chapter Twenty-Six

"Since Santa's busy this year, I figured I'd talk to one of his elves. Especially one that's psychic. Like my dad says, always get to the ones no one knows about."

I'm going to kill you, Norm, Ellen thought as she listened to the young boy babble.

The holidays were always a slow time at Mote It Be. When people thought Christmas presents, they didn't think spooky New Age bookstore. Especially a spooky New Age bookstore associated with Miskatonic. So her boss consulted his old business textbooks and had a brainstorm. Psychic elves.

Everyone knew the Santas at the mall were fake. Even a five-year-old understood Santa couldn't be everywhere at once. The real power behind the throne were the elves. They made sure Santa knew what each child wanted. But the ones that were psychic? They had a direct line to Old Saint Nick. And one of Santa's psychic assistants just happened to be in residence at Mote It Be. For a nominal fee . . .

That's how Ellen wound up dressed as an elf, with a ruth-less child perched on her lap. The boy's father was at the jewelry case with Norm, inspecting necklaces. She had to admit Norm's idea was a stroke of genius. She hated him for it.

The little executive jolted her from her thoughts. "Where are you on the org chart?"

"Excuse me?"

"Where are you on the organizational chart? Do you report directly to Santa?"

"I'm sorry. I can't tell you. That's proprietary information," Ellen parroted the words she remembered from a business class.

Her response seemed to satisfy the little executive. "Thank you for your time," he hopped off her lap and handed her a hand-scrawled business card. "This is where you can reach me."

As soon as they left Ellen drifted to the case that displayed tarot decks. Norm made a point of decorating this part of the store with blinking lights and colorful animals. He knew the spookier sections of the store needed a little extra cheer. Ellen took refuge there whenever she could.

In the week following Bentham Corners she fell into a deep depression. Even though she knew she was lucky, that she should be grateful she was alive, it was hard returning to reality. She found herself struggling through the gray everyday of papers, exams, and work schedules.

"That kid looked like a real shit," Norm said as he joined her at the counter.

"His father didn't look much better."

"Asked for our most expensive jewelry and then turned his nose up at it. Said it was too 'witchy.' That's like going into a bathroom and complaining about the smell."

Ellen bit off a laugh. She loved Norm's colorful sayings, but she knew he was self-conscious about his lack of education. She didn't want him to think she was laughing at him.

"To tell you the truth, I think I'm dropping the whole elf thing," Norm announced.

"Why? Business is better, right?"

"I don't know. It just sucks the heart and soul out of things, don't you think?"

She gave Norm a playful nudge. "My God, did you just say what I think you said, Mr. Grinch?"

At first Norm grunted. Then a grudging smile crossed his face. The phone rang before he could reply.

"Answer the phone, Logan. And don't screw it up this time," he commanded as he walked away.

Ellen rolled her eyes. The store didn't just have a psychic elf. It had a new greeting as well. "Your source for all good things, so Mote It Be," she chirped into the phone. The person on the other end chuckled. *Yeah,* she thought as she waited for someone to speak, *you try saying that twenty times a day.*

"Is Ellen Logan there?" a man asked.

"This is Ellen Logan."

"It's Andrew, Andrew Carter."

"Oh, hey. How are you?" Ellen breathed, with way too much enthusiasm. She couldn't help it. After half a day playing an elf she longed to talk to someone serious.

"Um . . . I'm all right," he replied. "Listen, do you have a few minutes? We need to talk."

"Sure. Let me give you my cell phone number. The boss doesn't like me talking on the store phone."

"I'm in the square."

"What?"

"I'm in the square," he said.

Ellen moved to the front window. The town square was right across the street, but she couldn't see him. Norm had painted holiday cheer all over the glass.

"Do you think you can take a break?" Carter asked.

"Yeah, sure. Just give me a sec, okay?"

She hung up the phone and nearly collided with Norm. Ellen was glad she didn't greet Carter by name. Norm was dying for a connection, any connection, to a Miskatonic celebrity.

"Go on. See your boyfriend."

"Boyfriend?"

"Oh, hey. How are you?" Norm batted his eyes and did a spot-on impression of her breathy greeting to Carter. Ellen blushed as she grabbed her coat. "Be back in ten, Logan," Norm called after her.

As she headed out into the cold afternoon, Ellen couldn't hide her excitement. This was the first time she'd seen Carter since Bentham Corners. Sure, she saw him every Monday, Wednesday, and Friday. But the man she saw in class, the man projected on a giant screen, wasn't the Carter she knew. He wasn't the man in the dim light of the mine, talking about suicide. Laying a gun between them so casually.

She supposed that was a good thing. It kept the experience from seeping into the other parts of her life. Still, every time she passed the stage after class, past the hordes of eager students begging for his attention, she felt a pang of sadness. She had been special. For one brief moment Miskatonic, Arkham, the entire Eastern Seaboard depended on her. And now . . .

Ellen stopped just shy of the square. It happened again. Her depression ambushed her. What started out as a reasonable train of thought spiraled into self-pity. She took a deep breath, focusing on the negative thoughts. Pushing them away.

Andrew Carter waited for her on one of the benches—dressed in a suit and a tie, legs splayed out. One of them bounced as he swiped at his phone. Carter may have been in his thirties, but he looked like an impatient teenager waiting for his mom to pick him up after school. She supposed that's what made him so irresistible.

Irresistible, the word echoed in her head. *Watch it, girl.*

Carter glanced up as she approached. He did a double take and burst into laughter. Ellen looked down. Even though her coat covered most of her outfit, there was no hiding the candy-cane stockings. Or her glittery green shoes.

"I swear to God, I'm going to kill Norm when I get back."

"Let me see."

"What?"

"Let me see Norm's latest creation."

"Not a chance."

"Please, Ellen. I've had a shitty day," he begged.

She threw open her coat with a sigh. It didn't occur to her that a passerby might think she was flashing him. Until it did. Her cheeks blazed white hot in the winter air.

"Not too bad," he decided. "Subdued, even. I'm surprised he didn't want you to show more cleavage."

She took a seat next to him, hugging her coat to her body. "Oh, he wanted me to show cleavage. I put my foot down," she replied. "Did I say foot? I mean my knee. In his groin."

Carter shook his head. "The man is a walking lawsuit."

"Better than some of the bosses I've had." She sighed as she crossed her legs, dangling her rhinestone shoe off her toe. "How've you been?"

"Do you really care?"

Ellen looked over at him, startled by the sudden hostility. "Yes, as a matter of fact I do."

"It's not going to be on the test."

"Ahh, you're having *that* kind of shitty day."

"I swear, there are times when I just want chuck it all," he admitted as he watched a boy stomp around in the snow.

The boy's mother sat nearby, watching them. Ellen nodded at the duo. "And do something like that?"

Carter chuckled. "I wouldn't go that far."

"What would you do?"

"I don't know. Open a New Age bookstore?"

"And deal with *our* customers? You wouldn't last a minute," she chuckled, amused by the thought of Carter selling therapeutic crystals.

He was quiet for a very long time. His leg started bouncing again. "I'm sorry," he blurted.

She glanced at him. "For what?"

"For being so mean to you when we first met, for bullying you in the mine, for accusing you of having a crush on me and then assuming you were gay when you said you weren't interested. Do you want me to keep going or is that enough?"

Ellen smiled and looked at her feet.

"You *are* a handful, that's for sure."

"I'm afraid I've made things worse." He took a deep breath and exhaled. "I showed Joshua the letter. From Ivan."

Ellen's breath caught in her throat. Anger tinted her cheeks. *He had no right showing Joshua something so personal. If I had known what he was going to do—*

You would have given him the letter anyway, a voice whispered. *Face it, girl. You need answers.*

"What happened?" Ellen asked.

Carter shook his head. "He freaked out. He turned white. Then red. He started yelling at me. I mean wrath-of-God yelling. He accused me of writing the letters. Of trying to gaslight him."

"Gaslight?"

"*Gaslight* is an old film about a husband who tries to control his wife by convincing her she's going mad."

"Why would he accuse you of that?"

"I have no idea."

Ellen gnawed on her lip. "What is going on?" she breathed.

"I don't know, but it was almost as if—"

"What?"

"You watch slasher films, right?"

Ellen stifled a smile. "I *am* a student of Miskatonic."

"You know, at the end, when they kill the maniac and everyone thinks he's dead. But when they go back to look for the body, it's gone? Joshua had that look. Like he thought things were over, but they weren't."

Ellen watched the boy play in the snow. She felt like she was on another planet.

"You might want to spend the night at your place," he suggested.

"That bad?"

Carter pursed his lips. "Look, I pushed Joshua's buttons when I was young. But I've never seen him like that. For a moment, for one crazy moment, I thought . . ." He shook his head. "I didn't know what to think. I didn't recognize him. He wasn't the man I knew."

Ellen shivered. She pulled her coat tighter, even though the chill had nothing to do with the cold.

Carter winced. "I'm sorry. I screwed up. Maybe if I did things differently, approached him another way. I mean, we've already established I'm not the world's most sensitive person."

"I'm not sure there *was* a right way to do it."

The mother marched up to the boy and grabbed his hand. *Play time is over*, Ellen thought as they retreated.

"Did you find out anything out about the letter?" she asked.

"I think Joshua might be onto something. About gaslighting."

"Why would someone want to gaslight him?" Ellen asked.

"I don't know, but it's more likely than a stranger writing to you before you were born."

"Well, there is one thing I do know. You didn't write them," Ellen insisted.

Carter raised his eyebrow. "What makes you so sure?"

"I took a picture of the letter before I gave it to you. I compared the writing to the comments on my tests. You still grade my papers, right?"

"Yes."

"It's not you."

"Nice work. I'm impressed," Carter said quietly.

Ellen looked away, pleased. "And I assume you compared my handwriting to the letter," she continued.

"It's not yours."

"Joshua?"

"Not a match," Carter replied.

"Pierce?"

A shadow drifted across his face. "I'm still trying to find a sample of his handwriting. Miskatonic has locked things down since he disappeared. No one can get into his office except the campus police."

"You did the right thing. You know that, right?" Even though no one was around, she dropped her voice. "It was a mercy killing."

"I wonder."

She looked him straight in the eye. "I don't."

Her cell phone alarm jingled. Ellen silenced it with a curse. They rose from the bench.

"I don't understand. Why do you even work there?" Carter asked, nodding in the direction of the store. "Joshua has money. You know that, right?"

"He's trying to keep me busy. So I stay out of trouble."

Carter chuckled. "That's working well."

"I suspect I'm paying for the mistakes he made with you," she shot him an appraising look. "You must have been quite the hell-raiser."

"I refuse to speak without my lawyer present."

"Good call."

Ellen glanced in the direction of Mote It Be. She didn't want to go back, but she knew if she lingered any longer Norm would come looking for her. She dug into her pocket and handed Carter a candy cane. "Merry Christmas."

"The same to you, little elf."

<hr>

Ellen waited a few days before she returned to Uncle Joshua's. She slipped in quietly, sniffing the air like a nervous deer. Ever since she was a child she could read the atmosphere of a house. It wasn't a psychic thing. She knew friends from emotionally charged households who had the same ability. It was second nature for them to feel the air when they walked in, to sample it for anger.

Ellen could tell right away Joshua wasn't there. With a sigh of relief, she put her backpack on the floor. The feeling didn't last long.

As she hung her coat on the rack, she noticed the door to his study was open. Joshua never left the door to his study open.

Ellen snatched the Maglite off the entryway table. "Uncle Joshua, I'm home," she called out in a false little singsong voice. Clinging to the wall, she moved toward the study, flashlight poised over her head, ready to strike. "Sorry, I'm late. My study group ran long. Are leftovers okay?"

The house swallowed her words.

The silence felt thick, expectant.

Easy, girl, she urged herself as she crept toward the open door. *Things are strange enough already. Don't gaslight yourself.*

She flicked on the light and burst into the room like a one-woman SWAT team.

Joshua's study looked the way it always did. Cluttered, chaotic, dusty. There were no signs of a struggle. *Struggle? How can you possibly tell in this disaster area?*

Ellen smiled. She thought about staying to see if she could coax any secrets out of the room. She forced herself to leave. Even though she was certain no one was in the house, she still needed to search the rest of the house.

A note waited for her in the kitchen. Joshua Logan was old school when it came to communication. He emailed and surfed the internet, but he refused to engage in anything else. He seemed to regard all other forms of social media as vulgar.

Ellen slid into the breakfast nook, plucking the creamy card off her pile of textbooks.

Sorry this is such short notice, but an opportunity came up that I couldn't refuse. I've flown to Japan to buy a statue of Enma. You remember Enma, the Japanese god of the underworld? They've found a statue from the seventeenth century and . . . well, you know

me. I just have to have it. Even if I do
end up selling it off.

I'll be gone about a week, but
rest assured, I'll be home in time for
Christmas. I know we haven't spent
much time together lately. We'll make
up for it over the holidays, okay?

She rested her head on the table.

Outside, trees swayed in the wind. Another powerful winter storm was coming, threatening to bury Arkham in a foot
of snow.

No anger, she thought as she stared the card. *No anger. No
fear. Not the slightest hint anything is wrong.*

Joshua did make periodic trips to buy art. Still, the timing
of his expedition troubled her.

What is going on? Those words were becoming Ellen's
mantra. Her own little ear worm.

Ellen swatted the card away like a pesky fly. "Enough."

There was nothing she could do. At least for now. It was
time to hit the books.

Chapter Twenty-Seven

The final in Carter's class was challenging. The exam itself wasn't the problem. Of all the classes Ellen took that semester, his was the easiest. It was the atmosphere. The test started out quietly enough, with everyone scribbling in their blue books. But as people turned in their finals, they stopped to have a moment with Andrew Carter. And he allowed it. Ellen didn't know whether the university demanded it or if he chose to be generous, but he posed for pictures. He autographed books. He even put up with some mild flirtation. By the time she turned in her exam, the place was a zoo.

Ellen didn't say goodbye. The crowd clustered around him made any meaningful conversation impossible. She handed her exam to the teaching assistant and headed for the door. Carter's eyes followed her as she left. She didn't look back. Another final waited for her across campus.

Three hours later she emerged from forensic anthropology a free woman. She let out a little war whoop, sharing her joy with the other emancipated students. A light snow fell as she headed home. Now that finals were over Ellen could finally think about Christmas. Her uncle was still in Japan, which gave her the perfect opportunity to buy his presents. She strategized as she walked, composing a list of things she needed to do.

A fresh carpet of broken glass greeted her when she got home. Ellen didn't mind. Even it seemed festive. Shards of green and red beer bottles glistened in the evening light. And someone was there, sweeping up the glass.

Ellen approached the Good Samaritan. "Look, I appreciate what you're doing, but I don't want you to get hurt."

The stranger waved his splinted fingers at her. "Too late."

"Oh, hey, Carter," she gushed before she could stop herself. "Joshua isn't here."

"I know." He dug into his pocket and handed her a card.

Andrew,

I'm sorry for the way I acted the other day. You came to me out of concern for Ellen, and I lashed out at you. I had no right. You obviously care for her as much as I do. I appreciate that. I really do.

I'll be out of the country for the next week or so. Will you do me a favor and check on her? Ellen has been preoccupied lately. Quiet. Please make sure she's okay. She means the world to me.

So do you, my boy

Merry Christmas

"I guess he really is in Japan," she said as she returned the letter. That small grain of truth made her feel better.

"Is that what he told you?"

"He said he was on the hunt. Chasing down a statue of Enma."

"Enma?"

"The Japanese god of the underworld," Ellen offered.

Carter rubbed at the stubble on his cheeks. The quarter ended only a few hours ago and he was already working on a beard.

"This statue he's after. Is it old?" he asked.

"He specializes in sacred art. He doesn't go running across the globe for cheap knockoffs," she replied.

Carter shook his head. "Crazy bastard."

A bolt of anxiety shot through Ellen. "What? What do you mean? Is he in trouble?"

"Relax. It's nothing. Just a difference of opinion," he reassured her. "Besides, he's not the reason I'm here. I thought this would be an excellent opportunity for us to have a little chat."

"Over tea?"

He opened the flap of his book bag and showed her a bottle of vodka. Good vodka.

Ellen smiled. "You remembered."

"I'm a man of my word."

She led Carter into the kitchen, to the only place in the house she considered hers. He slid into the breakfast nook and pulled the bottle out of his satchel. Ellen fetched some shot glasses.

"Let's get this out of the way first." He slapped her exam on the table facedown and pushed it toward her, like a player dealing cards

She pulled up a chair and eased herself into it. "You already graded my test?"

"It didn't take long."

Ellen hesitated. That was either very good or very bad.

"Aren't you going to look at it?" he asked.

"I'm afraid to," she admitted. "As Joshua said in the letter, I've been a little preoccupied lately. Unfocused."

She stared at the test so long that Carter finally flipped it over. Ellen yelped and clapped her hands. "I got an A!"

"You *earned* an A," he corrected her.

"Are you sure you didn't give me an A because I saved your life?" she teased him.

"I think I graded you harder *because* you saved my life," he grabbed a shot glass and twirled it on the table. "By the way, thanks. For stopping me from killing myself. And for keeping my secrets."

"Our secrets," she corrected him as she poured the vodka.

They raised their glasses and downed a shot. Ellen welcomed the silky warmth that spread through her body.

"Harold Graham died a few weeks ago," she announced after a moment of silence.

"Who?"

"The last survivor of Bentham Mine. The one we visited in the nursing home," she replied. "I went to his funeral. His widow told me he got worse right around the time we were in the mine."

Carter stared at her warily. "Uh-huh."

"Do you think—?"

"Don't go down that rabbit hole, Ellen," he warned her. "Harold Graham was an old man. He lived a hard life. Had an oxygen tank hooked to him. It's not surprising he died so soon after we visited him."

"You think it's a coincidence."

"Yes, just like I think it's a coincidence that Joshua left right after I showed him the letters."

"How did you—" she blurted before she remembered. "Oh yeah, you're psychic."

"I don't need to be psychic. It's in your eyes. It's all over your face." A blush swept through her like wildfire. "Don't be embarrassed, Ellen. Just don't do it."

"Do what?"

"Try to connect everything. You'll drive yourself crazy trying to find a pattern. And you'll probably be wrong. Even if you are right, well," his lips twisted into a grim smile, "it's a cold comfort."

"I'm not interested in comfort," Ellen insisted as she refilled their glasses.

"You still want answers?"

She nodded.

He reached into his pocket and pulled out Ivan's whistle. Ellen slapped the table. "I knew it! I knew you had it!"

The whistle was smaller than she remembered. Half of it was metal and half the antler of some unknown animal.

"Ahnenerbe," she whispered as she leaned forward.

Carter's face darkened. "Do you know what Ahnenerbe is?"

"I don't even know how to spell it."

"You don't know how to spell it but you—" He stopped himself. "Have you seen *Raiders of the Lost Ark*?" he asked her.

"Lots of times."

"You remember the Nazi that kept chasing Indiana Jones? The one who was after the Holy Grail? He was part of Ahnenerbe."

"Wait a minute. That group was real?"

Ellen remembered the climax of the movie, when the ghosts swarmed the Nazi, ripping him to shreds. She squirmed in her chair.

"Ahnenerbe means 'inherited from the forefathers,'" Carter continued. "They started out as a group of archaeologists who wanted to rewrite history. To prove that the Nordic people founded all the major civilizations."

"So they could cement their status as the master race."

Carter nodded. "They were harmless as first. I mean, for Nazis. They led expeditions to Italy, where they claimed to find Nordic runes in a cave. They went to Tibet to establish that the Gautama Buddha was an Aryan offshoot of the Nordic people. Then Himmler got involved."

"Himmler?"

He tapped the whistle. "Heinrich Himmler. The founder of Ahnenerbe. One of the architects of the Holocaust. A man obsessed with the occult." Carter paused to take a deep breath. "There were always rumors. That when Himmler got more involved the Ahnenerbe began to conduct experiments. Tests that involved black magic. I didn't believe it. I thought it was nothing but an urban legend."

"Until this," Ellen breathed.

"I had it tested." He pointed to the white section of the whistle. "Do you know what it's made of?"

"Ivory?"

"Bone. Human bone. Almost certainly from a victim of a concentration camp."

Ellen's stomach lurched. Only one thought filled her mind. *I put my mouth on that thing.*

"And the metal? What's that made from?" she squeaked.

"You don't want to know."

"Please," she whispered.

"It's mercury amalgam."

"Amalgam?"

"Fillings. Every piece of metal you see, even the necklace, was made from the fillings of teeth."

The entire world spun. Ellen stared at the chain. *How many? How many people are in this? There are thirty-two teeth in the head. Twelve of them molars. And how many fillings did the average concentration camp victim have in the 1940s? Not these people, they were probably chosen because they had more metal in their teeth. Harvested for . . .* Her mind gave out.

Ellen burst into tears. *Evil,* she thought. *In situations like this, even something as basic as math is evil.*

Carter pushed a glass of vodka at her. She downed another shot.

"I don't understand," she sniffed once she recovered enough to speak. "Why would the Nazis do this? Why make an object out of the remains of a group they despised?"

"For the same reason other tribes eat their enemies. Domination. Absolute and total domination. My guess is that the Ahnenerbe were trying to find another way to control their victims. To capture the energy of the souls they murdered. And they put it in an object so that they could carry that power. Summon it at will."

Ellen curled her hands into fists. *He knew. Ivan knew what it was made of. And he used it.*

Carter broke into her reflection. "How did you find this?"

"Ivan told me where to find it."

"But there was nothing in the letter about where—" He stopped abruptly. "There were more letters, weren't there?"

"No," Ellen insisted

"Then how did you find this?" he demanded.

"He possessed you."

"What?"

"Ivan Leibowitz possessed you."

"I don't get possessed," Carter sniffed.

"Well, you did a pretty good impression then," she insisted, plowing through the hard silence that followed. "We were in his bedroom. I found one of his letters and turned around to tell you and . . . you weren't you."

"How did you know?"

"Your body language was all wrong. And the look in your eyes." She shuddered. "I can be a pain in the ass sometimes. I know that. But what I saw was deep. Cold. Dark."

"Did I hurt you?"

"Ivan thought about it," she replied, remembering how he circled her, sizing her up. "Thankfully, I managed to convince him there was no way I was involved."

"And me? How did I get him out of me?" he asked.

She pursed her lips. Lying to him wasn't an option.

"Ivan didn't know he was dead, so I showed him your arm. When he saw there was no camp tattoo, the connection broke. He only had enough time to show me where to find the whistle, and then he was gone."

"And you went and got it?"

"I found it near his body."

He shook his head. His fury was as intense as Ivan's. "Do you realize how dangerous that was, Ellen?" he growled.

"We didn't have a lot of options at the time."

"And I suppose that's my fault."

"It isn't anyone's fault, Carter," she insisted as she looked across the table at him. He refused to return her gaze. Ellen sat back, letting out a long sigh. "So, I guess you won't be my mentor."

"Excuse me?"

"I was going to ask you to help me get into the advanced program at Miskatonic."

His lips curled into a sneer. "You? Are you fucking kidding me? No way."

His rejection stung. Ellen withdrew, reaching for another drink.

"Oh, for Christ's . . . Look, Ellen, you're talented. And you're brave. I won't deny that. But you're also incredibly irresponsible. You throw yourself into the deep end without knowing how to swim."

"And not teaching me to swim is going to help how?"

He crossed his arms and sat back. "I'm not doing it. I'm responsible for enough people as it is. And the last thing I need is Joshua on my back."

"You think he'd hold you responsible?"

"Oh, come on, Ellen! What would you do if you were in his position?"

Ellen fell silent. She knew he was right. It was never really an option in the first place. She downed another vodka.

Carter groaned. "Oh, don't do that. Don't get all pouty. I get enough of that in office hours."

"Don't tell me how to act!" she shot back, her anger rising in response to his. She quickly pushed it away. There was no point in making Carter an enemy. "I just . . . I sacrificed so much to get here, and I thought—"

"What? What did you think?"

"I always thought that when the pupil was ready, the teacher would appear."

"God, I'm so tired of that fake Buddhist saying."

"Joshua came along at the right time for you," she pointed out.

"What do you mean?" Carter demanded, his voice sharp with suspicion. "Did Joshua say he was my teacher?"

"No. I just assumed . . . Never mind," she dismissed the thought. "I guess that's it then."

"Guess so," he agreed as he gathered his things. He left the necklace on the table.

"Aren't you going to take that?"

"No. It was meant for you. Ivan guided you to it. He wanted you to have it. You're the one who needs to figure out what to do with it."

Chapter Twenty-Eight

Two weeks later, in the dead space between Christmas and New Year, Ellen stood outside the gates of a cemetery. She watched as a young rabbi and his assistant hovered over a small hole in the ground.

A stiff wind blew off the Miskatonic River. The air was heavy with the promise of more snow.

Joshua returned as promised, just in time for the holidays. He was a different man. *No, that's not true*, she corrected herself. *You're the one who's changed.*

Ellen noticed it the most on Christmas Day. They went through all their traditional rituals. He put on his Santa hat and handed out the presents. They sang Christmas carols. They had a huge midafternoon meal and spent the rest of the day in a food-induced stupor. Ellen enjoyed their time together, but it wasn't the same. The atmosphere felt forced.

"Hi."

Ellen looked up, relieved. She sent Carter an email and left a message on his office phone, but she wasn't sure if she reached him. "Thanks for coming."

He stared out at the graveyard. "Why are we standing outside a Jewish cemetery?"

"Because I didn't want to be the only one here. I thought it was important someone else witness this." She nodded at the men by the grave. "I went to Rabbi Goldman and told him what I could. About the letters. The whistle. He consulted with ZAKA and came up with this."

"ZAKA?"

"It's a volunteer group in Israel that specializes in retrieving body remnants. Mainly people who were the victims of terrorism. They did a lot of work after 9/11. Making sure both Jews and non-Jews got a proper burial." She huddled deeper into her coat. "They suggested the whistle be interred like any other body part."

"I see." He squinted at the small hole the rabbi hovered over. "Why aren't you at the gravesite?"

"Because I'm a *yidde'oni*."

"Excuse me?"

"A gainer of information from ghosts. Rabbi Goldman thinks I was in contact with a necromancer."

"Ivan?"

"Yeah." She leaned against the gate for support. "You can go in if you want to. Pay your respects."

"I'm staying with you."

Ellen glanced at him, touched by the small act of loyalty. "How many people do you think are in that . . . thing?" she asked.

He shifted in place. "No idea."

They fell silent and watched the ritual. The assistant produced a small box, cupping it gently in his hands. The rabbi closed his eyes and sang as it was lowered into the ground.

Ellen swore she wouldn't cry in front of Carter. The tears came anyway. "I hope they're at peace. Whoever they are," she said in a choked voice.

"You did the right thing."

"I hope so."

"You did," he repeated, more firmly this time.

Ellen kept her eyes fixed on the men by the graveside. The rabbi looked up and gave her a terse nod.

"Well, that's it then. The end of the journey." Another wave of sadness swept through her. "Can I ask you something?"

"Uh-huh," he agreed in a guarded voice.

"What happened to Ivan's letter? Is it being analyzed?"

Carter winced, scratching at his beard. "When I showed it to Joshua, he grabbed it and tore it up. I tried to stop him, but he was too fast."

The news didn't surprise her. All the rage Carter saw needed to go somewhere . . .

"It's all right. I still have a picture of it. Maybe we could—"

"Let it go, Ellen. You're not going to find anything about Ivan. I think he wanted it that way."

She stared at the anonymous grave. *How many people?* she wondered again.

"I have to go," he announced.

She latched on to his sleeve. "Wait." She dug into her coat and presented him with a set of keys.

"Another present?"

"The keys to the gate and the front door. I had a hell of a time getting them made—the locksmith almost had a heart attack when she saw them, but they work." The words came out in a jumbled rush. Ellen forced herself to slow down. "I don't know how you feel, but Joshua wants to see more of you. And I have my own life. I can't always be there to let you in."

He took them from her, dangling them in the sunlight. "My own set of keys. Gosh, does that mean I'm a grown-up now?"

"I wouldn't go that far."

Carter and Ellen shared one last smile.

She had no doubt she would see him again.

Introducing

If you enjoyed
Darkness Below,
look out for

Thin Places

Book Two of the Shadows of Miskatonic

by Barbara Cottrell

Available October 2023

Chapter One

If something lurked in the woods, Victor Ramsey would find it. He had no other choice. With only six months left in his senior year, he needed a thesis topic. Fast. His adviser was growing impatient.

That's what made the stranger's sudden arrival so remarkable. Just when he reached his lowest point, when Victor was about to abandon his dreams and pursue a more traditional major, his spiritual guide appeared. Sure, the guy was weird. Clad in a buckskin coat, threadbare shirt, and stained leather pants, he looked like a character out of *The Last of the Mohicans*.

Victor didn't care. He was desperate.

Even the darkness seeping into the Pine Barrens didn't bother him. He grew up in the backwoods of Maine, home to some of the densest wilderness in North America. Victor could navigate using only the trees as his guide. It took a lot more than a scraggly New Jersey forest to bother him. But the moment he stepped off the main road, his inner compass spun out of control. The Barrens confused him. It seemed like the Barrens *wanted* to confuse him.

Victor didn't like to give nature a human face. Nature deserved better, a lot better, but this place . . . A dark presence lived here. A dark presence determined to hurt him. Tree branches grabbed him as he passed. The stones wobbled beneath his feet. Birds chirped in the twilight, eagerly plotting his demise.

Against you, a voice whispered. *They're all against you.*

Victor stopped in his tracks. He dug into his jacket pocket and pulled out an EMF detector. Almost immediately the machine beeped. He stared in disbelief as the number registered. 206. A reading you'd expect from an electrical fault. A dangerous electrical fault.

"That would explain the paranoia," he muttered to himself.

His guide turned and looked at him.

"What?"

"My electromagnetic field reader. The readings are through the roof."

"That is to be expected. This place is full of iron. Machines do not do well here," the stranger explained.

Victor followed the man deeper into the woods. The light of the moon broke into patches, streaming into the narrow spaces between the trees. After a few feet it disappeared.

He stopped again. A voice screamed in his head. *Leave! Leave, leave!*

"Are you coming?" his guide demanded.

Victor knew this moment would forever define him. He could crawl away like a coward—his father's favorite name for him—or he could prove himself once and for all. He could prove he had what it took to graduate from Miskatonic

University. And if he didn't? Victor saw his life spread out before him, as flat and empty as his father's.

He dug into his backpack and put on a pair of night-vision goggles. It bathed the world in a sickly green hue.

"Yeah, coming," he called out.

Victor studied the man walking ahead of him. His guide was young, handsome in a rugged Daniel Craig sort of way, but his eyes held a darkness far beyond his years. Faint scars lined his skin. The patterns suggested some kind of tribal initiation. What bothered Victor the most was his face. It was rigid. The man held it like it was a mask about to fall off.

They hiked for most of the night. His wristwatch beeped every hour, reminding him of the world beyond the forest. The Garden State Parkway was only a few miles away. He read that you could see the lights of the Empire State Building from the top of one of the hills. He hoped they were headed there. He longed for a glimpse of civilization.

The EMF readings continued to climb. Victor's dread rose with it. Shadowy forms danced on the edge of his vision. Was his guide seeing the same things, too? He could hear the man muttering to himself. Victor tried to catch a few words, but the wind carried them away.

"Are we close?"

The man gestured to the top of the hill. "Do you see that ridge? That's Razorback Hill. It's where we're headed."

Victor gazed at the desolate, windswept peak. He knew he should be unpacking his equipment. He needed to take some measurements at the base of the hill. But excitement outweighed common sense. Victor scrambled up the summit, leaving his guide behind.

He gasped when he reached the top. Everywhere he looked there was wilderness—miles and miles of dark, unbroken forest. And sure enough, he could see New York City twinkling in the distance.

"Oh my God," Victor breathed.

"God does not live here, my friend," the man said as he pulled out a piece of chalk. He began to scribble on the granite slab where they stood.

A chill ran up Victor's spine. "What did you say?"

The man bowed his head and smiled. "God does not live everywhere in your world."

"My . . ."

Victor watched as the man filled the stone with figures and marks. The young student shuddered.

His guide stared at him with cold, appraising eyes. "Are you sure you want to go through with this?"

"Positive." Victor surprised himself with the firmness in his voice.

"Then you must prepare."

Victor took his time arranging his cameras. He hated the sloppiness of most paranormal investigations. Whenever something exciting happened, equipment always failed—it was out of focus or unsteady or worst of all, broken. He was determined to capture the evening's events from every conceivable angle.

His guide devoted the same care to his drawing. He scribbled on the rock, then like a mathematician pondering an equation, stood back to appraise it. Occasionally he made small adjustments. Victor was impressed by the man's ability. Even the most seasoned investigators at Miskatonic relied on books to write spells. That this man could do it from memory strengthened his resolve. Being on top of the hill helped, too. The air was clearer here. Less oppressive.

The man drew an open pentagram around his work. He straightened, finally satisfied.

"Are you ready?"

Victor moved in front of one camera and rattled off information. "This is Victor Ramsey on top of Razorback Hill in the Pine Barrens of New Jersey. With me is . . ." He gave the stranger a questioning look.

"My name is not important, friend. Like you, I am merely a seeker," the man insisted.

The guide kept his back to the camera. He motioned for his companion to enter the circle. Victor stepped through the opening. Once they were inside, his companion closed it.

Victor felt a rush of panic when he heard the rasp of chalk on stone. "Should I be doing anything?" he asked in a trembling voice.

The man looked up. His expression was a blend of pity and contempt. "Sit down in the center of the pentagram. And stay still," he instructed.

"Should I cover my eyes and count to three?" Vic knew it was a childish thing to say, but he couldn't help himself. It made him feel like he had some control.

The illusion shattered the moment the incantation started. Victor was familiar with the words. He studied the spell for countless hours in the Miskatonic Library. He wrestled with the words, trying to free them from a leather-bound book. This man had no trouble. They flowed out of him with cold, fluid grace. Victor closed his eyes, letting the words wash over him. They were hot and they were cold and they . . .

Tickled.

Victor giggled, even though it felt wrong.

The man's words came back to him. *God does not live everywhere in your world. Your world* . . . His eyes flew open. He struggled to focus on the guide he'd followed so blindly into the forest. The man whirled around the circle in a blur. Or was it the circle that moved? Victor looked at the ground, hoping to regain his balance.

The man stepped forward and struck him. Victor fell backward, smashing his head against stone. That's when he saw it.

A creature fell from the sky. Victor watched as it descended. Enormous wings. Pointed tail. Long arms and spindly legs. And claws. Outstretched. Razor sharp. Reaching out for him.

"No," he wailed. He flipped on his stomach and tried to scurry away. The thing pounced on him, sending a shock wave of pain through his body. Victor screamed as the monster dug its claws into his spine.

"Damn. You're not the one," the man announced sadly.

His spiritual guide said nothing more. He turned and walked away.

Chapter Two

"If there's anyone here, would you please give us a sign?"

Ellen Logan pointed her microphone into the darkness. Even though it was the dead of winter, the attic was warm and musty. But there was no oppressiveness, no feeling of being watched. Not a single sign the house was haunted.

She turned to her partner. "Are you getting anything?"

"I don't like the way Greg looks at you."

"What?"

"Greg." Phil Marcus was referring to the expedition's leader. "I think he's interested in you."

"Oh, for God's sake." Ellen tore off her night vision goggles and sat down on the couch. The cushions let out an exhausted *woof.* "You think everybody's interested in me."

"That's because they are," Phil insisted. He was Ellen's current boyfriend, a blond-haired, blue-eyed surfer from Redondo Beach. She thought a relationship with a guy like him would bring some much-needed light into her world. She was wrong.

"Are you getting any readings?"

"Nah. EMF is flat." Phil sat down beside her. "I don't get it, Ellen. Why do you still do this?"

"What do you mean?"

"The ghost hunting. You've put in the hours Miskatonic requires of students. Why do you still do it?"

Ellen shrugged. "Because I like it."

That was only half the truth. The real reason? It was all she had left. Already in the middle of her junior year, she hadn't been asked to join Miskatonic's advanced program. And without it she could never be a serious paranormal investigator. Her window of opportunity wasn't just closing. It was collapsing.

"Well, I don't think you should be doing this. Especially now," Phil insisted.

"What do you mean?"

"Jeez, Ellen, haven't you heard? There's a serial killer on the loose."

Ellen rolled her eyes. "There are always serial killers on the loose around here. I swear, there should be a major in serial killing at Miskatonic."

"I'm serious. They've found bodies scattered all over Arkham County."

"Ours is a dangerous profession."

"Profession?" Phil frowned at her.

"Yes. Profession," she shot back.

An awkward silence filled the room.

"Do you think this place is haunted?" he asked.

"Well, there's always the possibility we're here on an off night."

"Yeah, yeah." Phil motioned for her to get to the point.

"I don't think there's anything here. Even if it were an off night, I would feel something. Some residue or—"

A sudden impact rocked the house. The roof above their heads bulged and buckled. A fine layer of dust rained down from the rafters. Ellen looked at Phil. He stared back, his mouth hanging open.

She rose and grabbed her walkie-talkie. "Greg, this is Ellen," she barked into the receiver, calling down to the command post on the ground floor. "Is anyone on the roof?"

"I was just about to ask you the same thing. What the hell is going on up there?"

"Maybe a bird hit the house," Phil offered.

"Have to be a flying dinosaur to make that kind of racket," Ellen muttered. Flying dinosaur or not, she knew what she had to do. "I'm going to take a look."

"Are you fucking nuts?" Phil spluttered.

"We have to find out what it is."

"We don't have to do anything," he insisted.

Ellen stared at him until he crumbled.

"I can't stop you from going out there, can I?"

"No."

He hissed and shook his head. "Then for Christ's sake, be careful."

"I will."

The attic was in one of the towers, at the point where the strange angles of the house converged. Ellen crawled out of a window and up to the widow's walk. As she inched closer, she heard a wet, gurgling wheeze.

A man dangled from the railing of the widow's walk. His face was torn and bloody.

"Jesus Christ," Ellen pressed the button on the walkie talkie. "Greg, there's somebody up here. He's hurt. Call 911."

The battered man motioned for her to stay away. "No, please don't. It's a trap," he rasped, slurring his words. "Get away— it's watching— it's watching," the man spluttered.

"What's watching?" she asked.

She tried not to look at him. The sight of the man, impaled on that spike, made it hard to think. Every time he breathed his chest bubbled. And his hands—there were no fingers. They had been ripped off. Even the bones were gone.

Ellen closed her eyes and swayed. For a moment she thought she would lose her grip. "Will somebody *please* get help?" she screamed into the radio.

The man looked across the roof. Ellen followed his gaze. She saw nothing except a large stone gargoyle on the roof.

"Just hold on. Help is coming," she reassured the broken man. She listened for the sound of emergency vehicles. Only the wind rattled through the trees.

Phil stood in the street below, along with the rest of the ghost-hunting team. They gawked up at the house. Phil was filming her.

Impatiently she called down to her boyfriend, "Where the hell is the goddamn ambulance?"

"Ellen, move!" Phil shouted.

"What are you doing?" she yelled, feeling a surge of rage. "Don't just stand there! Call 911!"

"Ellen, move. *Now.*"

She heard a crisp, snapping sound, like the flapping of a sail. Except it sounded raspy. Leathery. Loud. She looked up.

A monstrous creature hovered over her, its huge bat-shaped wings unfurling in the winter air. Ellen's words came back to haunt her. *Have to be a flying dinosaur to make that kind of racket.* With its huge wingspan and long spiked tail, the creature filling the night sky reminded her of a dinosaur. But the shape of its body was all wrong. It was sleek. Humanoid. It had arms and legs. A torso. A head. Ellen paused. But no face. No eyes, no nose, no mouth. Nothing that connected it to the world as she knew it.

She was so transfixed she didn't see it swoop down on her. Only the cries of her friends snapped her out of her stupor. She rolled to the side as the creature punched through the roof. The sudden movement sent her sliding down the wood-shingled roof. *This isn't real,* she thought as her hands fluttered, searching for something, anything to stop her descent. *This can't be happening. I'm going to wake up. Any sec—*

Her feet caught on a storm drain. The old metal split from the house, rocking under her weight. The rain gutter held just long enough for her to swing her body through the attic window. She tumbled onto the floor, her breath hard, her heartbeat thundering in her ears.

She looked up at the roof. The creature was still there. It toyed with the broken man clenched in its talons. Ellen knew she should be running. She should be heading down the stairs to the safety of the group. But she couldn't move. She was trapped by it, by the mere fact of it, and by a single, terrible thought.

I've seen a thing like this before.

She closed her eyes and shook her head. "No. No, no, no, no," she chanted.

A moment later Phil burst through the door. The rest of the team followed, enveloping her in a cloud of noise.

When she looked back out the window, the creature was gone.

"Jesus, are you okay?" Phil rushed to her side. When he saw she was uninjured, he babbled like a hyperactive child. "Oh my God, I can't believe it! I can't believe what we— I got some incredible footage. It's a little out of focus, but I think we got it. *I think we got that thing!* We couldn't quite see what it was messing with, though."

"It was a man."

A shadow passed over Phil's face. His enthusiasm evaporated. "What?"

"The creature was 'messing around' with a man," she repeated, loud enough for the others to hear.

A hush fell over the group.

"The guy was hurt. Bad," Ellen whispered.

"Did you recognize him?" someone in the group asked.

She shook her head.

It was only then that the full significance of what happened hit her. She started to tremble. Pain shot through her body. She could feel bruises forming from her rough ride down the roof. *If it weren't for that storm drain, I'd be dead. Smashed on the driveway like a pumpkin.*

An ambulance wailed in the distance.

"We need to call our advisor and let him know what hap-pened," Ellen said.

"But he said only to call if it was an emergency," Phil protested.

"And you don't think this qualifies?"

He looked at her, stunned.

"Um. Yeah. I guess I should."

He unlocked his phone and called for help.

Acknowledgements

D*arkness Below* went through many incarnations before it assumed its final form. I would like to thank the people who helped me along the way.

My husband, Lance, who gave me the courage to give up an academic career to pursue my dream full time. He has been with me for the entire ride, and his enthusiasm and support have never wavered. I would not be the writer I am without him.

My early readers, Matt Pallamary and Jane Rogan Dwight, for helping me find the contours of the story. Without their guidance I would still be staring at a block of uncut stone.

I was fortunate to have three editors help me with the later versions. They each contributed in significant ways. Susan Gunter introduced me to Nathaniel Hawthorne's "Rappaccini's Daughter," which gave the garden scene added depth. Marianne Linder, who reminded me the story was about Ellen. I kept a three-by-five card with Marianne's mantra taped to my computer: "It's About Her." The words were essential to keeping the story on track. Robbi Sommers Bryant served as the master editor. An experienced horror writer, she guided the story through its final phases, including a last-minute edit when I added the voice of Ivan. She has always been there for me, not just as a great editor but also as one of my best friends.

Paul Carrick, who did the cover art for the book. Seeing the creature "in the flesh" brought the story to life for me in unexpected and powerful ways. I appreciate the visual insight he gave me. And Greg Chapman, who designed the cover that made this book look so professional.

Finally, I would like to thank the writers I consider my spiritual mentors: H. P. Lovecraft, who created the world at the center of my book. Rod Serling, who showed me how to explore Lovecraft's world from a different perspective. And Stephen King, the master of horror, who started this whole crazy journey with his short story "Crouch End."

I blame you all for my good fortune.

About the Author

Barbara Cottrell gave up her career as a professor to pursue her true passion: writing weird fiction. She is a lifetime member of the Horror Writers Association. She enjoys presenting her work in unusual venues like Mystery Writers in the Mausoleum. She also served as a judge and an editor on the Redwood Writer Anthologies *Redemption: Stories from the Edge, Endeavor: Stories of Struggle and Perseverance*, and *Remember When*. She lives in Sonoma County on a not-at-all-haunted vineyard. When she isn't exploring the dark side, she makes wine with her husband, Lance.

To find out more about her and the world of Miskatonic University, visit www.barbaracottrell.com.

www.ingramcontent.com/pod-product-compliance
Lightning Source LLC
Chambersburg PA
CBHW021136310726
48971CB00002B/343